THE OCEAN'S BOUNTY

The body lay spread-eagle over the rough rocks. A long thick rope of green seaweed was caught in the man's collar and strands splayed across his neck. There was more seaweed intertwined in the fingers of his left hand. His left arm was stretched almost straight out from his body, as if reaching toward the water. The right arm was bent close to the body, but there was no right hand. . . .

Father Mark Townsend had seen his share of dead bodies. But he had yet to encounter one sliced so brutally. Something struck him as strange.

"Is that the way you found him?" Mark asked. "Lying like that. You haven't moved him yet? I was wondering if there might be more cuts on his front."

The two officers bent and grabbed hold of the corpse. Both men had to strain to turn the dead weight over onto its back.

Immediately, Father Townsend's finger pointed to a small round hole in the dead man's canvas coat. . . .

Other Father Mark Townsend Mysteries by
Father Brad Reynolds, S.J.
from Avon Books

THE STORY KNIFE

A RITUAL DEATH

**FATHER
BRAD REYNOLDS, S.J.**

Brad Reynolds, S.J.

7/23/97

AVON BOOKS ◆ NEW YORK

AVON BOOKS
A division of
The Hearst Corporation
1350 Avenue of the Americas
New York, New York 10019

Copyright © 1997 by Brad Reynolds, S.J.
Published by arrangement with the author
Visit our website at **http://AvonBooks.com**
Library of Congress Catalog Card Number: 97-93007
ISBN: 0-380-78401-7

First Avon Books Printing: August 1997

AVON TRADEMARK REG. U.S. PAT. OFF. AND IN OTHER COUNTRIES, MARCA REGISTRADA, HECHO EN U.S.A.

Printed in the U.S.A.

WCD 10 9 8 7 6 5 4 3 2 1

A.M.D.G.

And for my parents,
Dick & Mona

(Happy 50th, Mom and Dad)

ACKNOWLEDGMENTS

Writing a novel is not always the isolated and solitary work some might think it is. There is often a talented and helpful support crew working with the author to make the story accurate and real. I am indebted to all of those who helped me bring this book to life.

I am particularly grateful to the Swinomish people, several of whom have generously shared their knowledge and experience with me: including the tribal chairman, Robert Joe, Senior; Jim Wilbur; and Ray and Dorraine Williams. My thanks also extend to Rick Balam, the Swinomish Director of Public Safety, and his assistant, Pam Bridgefield. These are people who patiently explained the inner workings of life on the reservation to me. I also drew upon the published wisdom of Chief Martin J. Sampson in his book, *Indians of Skagit County*. With such excellent resources, readers should know that any mistakes or errors in judgment about what is written concerning the Swinomish and the tribal police are mine alone.

I am also thankful for many others who generously gave me advice: Larry Wasserman; Cliff Anderson; Robert Parks; Dr. Mary Pellicer; Judy Painter, the research librarian at the Anacortes Museum; and Margaret Pederson at the Skagit County Historical Museum. A special note of thanks goes to Ron and Pien Ellis, intrepid island explorers and good friends.

And at Avon Books I want to thank my editor, Ann McKay Thoroman; Adriane Hirsch, my publicist; and

Lisa Eicher, the copy editor who catches so many of my mistakes. Thanks also to my always supportive agent, Ellen Geiger at Curtis Brown, Limited.

Nothing I write would see the light of day without the support and encouragement of my companions in the Society of Jesus, especially my Provincial, Father Robert Grimm, and the members of the Oregon Province. As always, some stepped forward to lend a hand. Father Pat Twohy at the Swinomish Spiritual Center has supported and assisted this project from its inception. Father Ted Fortier, with his recent Ph.D. in anthropology, was particularly helpful. And Father Roger Gillis provided support and useful advice.

None of the characters depicted as living at Shelter Bay or on the Swinomish Reservation are real. Puget Sound is and has been a waterway for smugglers, and the violent abuses against the Chinese, as described in the prologue, are accurate. But the smugglers' names are fictional. While many of the place names are real, descriptive details were often altered to better fit the story and frankly, to suit the author's whims.

Ambition, Avarice; the two demons these
Which goad through every slough our human herd.

—Edward Young
"Night Thoughts," 1742

PROLOGUE

Red skies at night, sailor's delight; horseshit!

Twenty minutes after casting off from the dock in Vancouver, Clarence O'Rourke was fumbling in the dark for his oilskins. Water was already dripping off of his hat's brim and his hair was growing damp. He could feel the wetness beneath his collar soaking into his shirt and his nose was starting to run. The rain was puddling onto the wooden plank seat underneath him.

Sailing through the dark with a wet butt was the worst of it. He tried to yank the dark slicker over his head without removing his hat but got hung up in the garment's opening. For a few moments only the crown of his hat was visible as the oilskin's dark drapes sloped down his body. He looked like a rain-slicked rock tumbled into the stern of the small sloop, the raindrops drumming in small patters against his sides.

O'Rourke jerked the slicker down with an oath, and in the process dumped more water down the inside of his shirt. *Sailor's delight, horseshit!*

The last of the yellow gas lamps on Vancouver's shore disappeared as he guided his narrow sloop out the wide bay. Once clear of the point he tacked south, toward home. Both the rain and the wind were now at his back, and his boat's canvas sail billowed from their combined force. With luck he would be home before dawn.

Clarence O'Rourke fumbled beneath the voluminous folds of his slicker with his right hand, guiding the tiller with his left until he found papers and tobacco in his coat pocket. Hunching over, away from the rain and wind, he deftly rolled a smoke, then struck a match against the dry underside of his boat's wooden seat. The match sputtered then caught and O'Rourke, cupping the flame in his hand, raised the match to the hand-rolled fag in his lips.

He had a thick and drooping mustache and tonight, a stubbly beard that looked about four days old. His full, oval face was pleasant looking enough, despite deep wrinkles pulling down across both cheeks. O'Rourke had thick, bushy eyebrows, and what hair that was left sat high up and behind a broad expanse of forehead. The skin beneath his jaw was beginning to sag and he had big, floppy ears. Clarence gazed at the world through soft brown eyes that seemed to linger on anything that caught his interest. The old man's general appearance was that of a kindly and slightly befuddled grandfather, who, on this particular night, was stealing across the Canadian border with three Chinamen and 160 pounds of opium.

The opium was divided into five packets, each wrapped in waxed cheesecloth. O'Rourke had stuffed the parcels into five flour sacks, then finished filling each bag with table salt before sewing it shut. The three Chinamen were tied up in larger gunnysacks and now lying in the soggy bottom of his boat.

He lightly touched one with the toe of his boot and the bag squirmed.

"How do you like your land of opportunity so far?" O'Rourke sucked one last draught from his cigarette before flipping it into the water. He looked around him at the darkness. "Rain's just part 'a the price of freedom," he drawled. "You and your friends had best get used to it if you're plannin' to stay in these parts."

There was no response from the sodden bag lying at his feet and Clarence had not expected one. They mostly spoke gibberish anyway. They knew enough to say Seattle, and that was all O'Rourke needed to hear. Then it was just a matter of negotiating the cost and arranging the rendezvous. Convincing them to let him tie them into gunny sacks was always a little tricky, but when he made like he would leave without them they always acquiesced. Most were so eager to find jobs with the railroads or in the mines that he could have made them ride standing on their heads and they would have agreed. He always made certain he had their gold before he cast off.

If he made it safely home with his cargo intact, Clarence O'Rourke stood to make a tidy sum. A hundred dollars apiece for the Chinamen and twelve bucks a pound for the opium would almost make the horseshit cold and dark worthwhile. But he had heard rumors that a fast, new revenue cutter, the *Oliver Wolcott*, was working Puget Sound. Two months earlier custom agents nailed Big Tom Franklin with three hundred tins of unstamped opium, and now he was a resident at Washington's state penitentiary on McNeill's Island, south of Tacoma. But Big Tom was a jackass and did not know half the tricks that Clarence O'Rourke knew.

After twenty years of sailing contraband across the watery border between Canada and the U.S., O'Rourke knew quite a lot. And such knowledge proved profitable. He and his wife, Isa, now owned a homestead on Sinclair Island plus a cabin on the south shore of Guemes Island. He ran two sloops, a ketch-rigged thirty-eight-footer he called the *Martha-Ann*, and this twenty-eight-footer, the *Sentinel*. Neither one showed her name though. There was no sense tipping off anyone watching the dark sloop slipping past that Clarence O'Rourke, King of the Smugglers, was sailing by.

Twenty years of running opium, Chinese wine, and coolies adds up to a tidy little sum. And Clarence O'Rourke always invested wisely. He never cached his stuff anywhere near his places on Sinclair and Guemes. There were plenty of other islands in Puget Sound where he could hide his contraband, with lots of hidey-holes far away from prying eyes. O'Rourke had gold and opium stashed in half a dozen places where no one would ever find them.

Someday, when he got tired of outwitting custom agents, he planned to move on; maybe down to San Francisco and the Gold Coast where he would live the life of a gentleman. Maybe find himself one of those dancehall cuties. He already knew he would be leaving Isa behind. She would never want to leave her tribe. And besides, a new life in Frisco deserved a new wife to go with it.

Something's wrong.

O'Rourke spun in his seat and searched the darkness around him. But in the blackness beyond his boat he could see nothing. He could sense the danger though, and instinctively his hand left the tiller and felt along the shelf just below it. The familiar shapes of three revolvers impressed themselves across his palm. Rain hitting against the billowing canvas sail was blocking all other sounds, but he knew he could not risk lowering the sail, however briefly. He adjusted the boom instead, trying to catch a little more wind, hoping for a broad reach. He knew it was important to keep in front of whatever was out there. Out in front and silent. That was how you stayed alive.

Clarence O'Rourke carried no charts and no compass on board his sloop. After sailing Puget Sound for so many years, he knew exactly where he was most of the time. The fact that he was running full sail through a rainstorm in night's darkness meant nothing. O'Rourke knew that Frustration's Rendezvous, on Patos Island, was already forty minutes behind him. One night, Old Man Harris had to dump his cargo off Rendezvous when a revenue cutter got too close. And the next morning five coolies washed up onto the beach, their hands and feet still tied together. Folks on the island dug one large grave for all five. Harris told O'Rourke he felt real bad about that. Especially since he had neglected to collect his fares ahead of time.

"Live and learn," Clarence O'Rourke muttered to himself.

He sensed the ship before he heard it. Cutting swiftly through the water straight towards him, she was moving up fast off his starboard side. A long sonofabitch, maybe seventy feet, coming on hard. Two masts: he could hear the wind whistling through their rigging. Too big to be the *Grant*, it had to be that new one, the *Oliver Wolcott*. Probably running out of Port Townsend. But how did they know he was out here?

O'Rourke tacked away from the oncoming boat, hoping to lose them in the dark. He searched for the horizon, trying to distinguish between land and sky, but all he saw was blackness. He leaned against the tiller, silently urging his sloop forward. If he could make Frenchie's Harbor he could hide until the coast was clear. Even as he thought it, O'Rourke knew his plan was hopeless.

Horseshit! Lunging from his seat, he swore into the night. Without pausing he bent over the first of the three gunnysacks, grabbing it at both ends. The man inside wiggled in surprise, but remained silent. In one fluid motion O'Rourke tossed him overboard. The gunnysack hit the waves with a flat splooshing sound. He threw the other two over in quick succession. The sacks floated on the water's surface for just a moment, the terrified men inside them struggling in vain before they sank beneath the waves. He returned to his seat and grabbed the tiller again. The *Sentinel* was four hundred pounds lighter now and he could feel the difference in how she slipped through the water. But he also heard the creaks of timbers behind him, and he knew his pursuers were still gaining.

O'Rourke heaved himself up once more and moved toward the bow, grabbing each flour sack and tossing it over the gunwale. The five bags of opium and salt sounded like small Chinese as they sank beneath the waves.

But unlike the drowned coolies, these packets would rise again. Puget Sound's cold waters were already at work dissolving the salt. And once it was melted, the buoyant blocks of opium would float to the water's surface, still shrouded in the white flour sacks, easy to spot against the gray waters of the sound. The trick was in knowing how far his packages would drift and in what direction. But after twenty years, Clarence O'Rourke knew the currents well enough, and he usually managed to find at least half of his jettisoned cargo.

The King of Smugglers had used this trick for years. When the revenue cutters finally pulled alongside his sloop and the custom agents insisted on boarding, they found nothing they could hold him for. They might wonder why O'Rourke was sailing with a leather poke filled with three hundred dollars in gold, but they could hardly arrest a man for that.

His cargo gone, the smuggler settled back into his seat, his left hand once again resting lightly on the tiller. The rain had stopped. Now, over his right shoulder, he could just discern the black mass of the ship behind him. He had time for one cigarette and reached beneath his slicker. His tobacco was still dry but the rain had soaked his papers. First no cargo and now no cigarette. O'Rourke angrily wadded the wet papers into a sodden ball and threw them at the cutter.

Sailor's delight, horseshit!

ONE

"At last year's Opening Day, Dutch Olsen knocked Art Manning right off the dock and into the drink."

GrandSam was talking directly into Father Mark Townsend's right ear while he was trying to drive. He had been talking nonstop for the last half hour and Mark was getting a headache.

"But the good news," Nan interrupted her husband, "is that Dutch helped fish him out. The year before he just walked away and left Art in the water."

GrandSam grunted.

Being the priest in the family carries certain obligations. Long ago Mark had accepted that fact and, for the most part, was faithful to his familial duties. Baptisms, funerals, weddings—all part of belonging to a family. He realized they were obligations he could not avoid. And with the exception of the weddings, he fulfilled his role in them with good humor and priestly grace. The blessing before meals was another duty unless GrandSam, patriarch of the Townsends, was present. Then his grandfather assumed the honor of intoning the ritual prayer.

For the last five years Mark had been given a new obligation: a midweek visit to his grandparents' home in LaConner in early April to view the tulip blooms. For

three days Father Mark Townsend chauffeured his grandparents, GrandSam and Nan Mary, up and down the country roads of Skagit Valley while they gazed out at field
after endless field of tulips.

For decades farmers had quietly planted and harvested
their tulip bulbs in the flatlands surrounding the Skagit
River. An occasional tourist would wander through, but
for the most part the quilted acres of bright reds, yellows,
greens, and pinks were viewed and enjoyed only by the
farmers and their families who were in the business of
raising tulips. *"Pretty"* was just a by-product. No one
thought twice about it until the chamber of commerce and
some of the local businesses in Mount Vernon put their
collective heads together and came up with the Skagit
Valley Tulip Festival. Now for three weeks every spring,
the narrow back roads of Skagit County were clogged with
buses, bicycles, campers, and cars of every description as
hundreds of thousands of tourists invaded the flatlands to
see the blooms. Roadside stands, hastily thrown up, reaped
the harvest, selling everything from homemade jam to
weather vanes, leather purses, birdhouses, and yes, tulips.
Even Kodak was there, peddling film and cardboard cam-
eras. Weekends were the worst. At times traffic got so
thick around the tulip fields that gridlock stalled every car
on the country roads for two miles in any direction.

Mark Townsend loved his grandparents dearly but
dreaded the tulips. Not just the inching down backroads
behind a diesel bus, but all the other little duties included
in his visit. There was the annual luncheon with Nan and
the five other ladies who cleaned the small Catholic
church in LaConner. There was the nightly chess game
with GrandSam, scheduled for the half hour between an
"I Love Jeannie" rerun and "Wheel of Fortune." And
there were the ritual breakfasts when they shared news
about all the other grandchildren: who is getting divorced,
who is pregnant, who is not, who calls, and who is unemployed. Every time Mark left the table he was convinced they ought to hire a family therapist for the
exclusive use of the Townsend family.

At last year's Fourth of July Townsend picnic he had

tried to suggest that perhaps the other grandkids could share in tulip duty. His own sister's reply was the unkindest cut of all: "We'd hate to disappoint GrandSam and Nan like that," she smirked. "Everyone knows how much they look forward to Father's visit." She looked around at the other grandchildren, nodding and grinning their agreement. "Besides, Mark, the rest of us have real jobs."

Pam liked to pretend that Mark's life as a Jesuit priest was nothing more than celebrating weekend Mass and sipping tea with lonely widows. But as a real estate agent in Seattle, she had enough opportunities to drop in to visit her brother in his parish office at St. Joseph's Church. Somehow she consistently managed to ignore the clamoring phone and brimming appointment calendar on his desk. As far as Pam was concerned, her brother the priest had it made. Mark loved his sister, but he knew he would never convince her to pull tulip duty.

"Oh drat! Turn around," Nan ordered from the back seat of the car.

"What the hell for?" barked GrandSam.

"I forgot milk," she replied. "If you want cereal tomorrow we have to turn around."

Mark was already signalling to turn the corner toward LaConner's market.

"I don't know why you can't think of these things earlier," his grandfather griped. "Father Mark has a lot better things to do than to be driving you all over hell for a carton of milk."

Mark winced. He hated being called Father Mark and hated the querulous tone in his grandfather's voice. This was another one of the tulip rituals he could do without—his grandparents' constant bickering.

"Forget it then," Nan pouted. "I'll just make a trip back later on. It's only three blocks out of our way, but if that's too much to ask."

"It's not a problem," Mark quickly answered, looking back at her in the rearview mirror. "I've got nothing to do up here except be with you two. Besides, it'll only take a minute.''

GrandSam looked over at Mark. ''That's what you think. She'll get in there and we won't see her again until Christmas.'' His grandmother shot her husband an icy look over the back seat as Mark pulled into the market's parking lot.

The two men waited in the car while Nan shopped. Although it was early in April, the day was sunny and mild and the air in the closed car was soft and warm. GrandSam was soon dozing, his eyes closed and his chin resting on his chest. His thick glasses had slipped down and were perched at the end of his nose. Mark's grandfather was a short man but with a powerful physique. He had worked for over forty years on Seattle's piers, first as a stevedore, then eventually moving into management. He had a barrel chest and hands that were scarred and beaten from his years on the docks. Except for some white fringe just over his ears, he was completely bald. Sam sported a small goatee which Nan hated. She claimed it felt to her just like a pig's hind end. GrandSam wanted to know when his wife ever petted a pig's butt.

Father Townsend's grandparents had moved to La-Conner when Sam retired. They owned a small, comfortable house in the development called Shelter Bay, located across the Swinomish Channel, opposite the town of LaConner. ''I worked on the water my whole life,'' GrandSam had proclaimed to his family, ''now I aim to play on it.'' He bought a thirty-two-foot Tolleycraft cabin cruiser and the two of them cruised down the channel that emptied into Padilla Bay, off the eastern point of Anacortes. From there they could sail out among the myriad islands dotting the northern end of Puget Sound. GrandSam talked continuously about taking their boat, which he insisted on naming the *Queen Mary*, up the Inside Passage to Alaska. Nan kept him closer to home by threatening mutiny. So far, the two of them had only made it to the southern end of Canada's Vancouver Island.

Nan was the perfect foil to GrandSam. She was as short as her husband, but was thin and delicate where he was bulky and bold. She kept her long white hair rolled into a tight bun, letting it down only at night before bed. She had a strong and determined-looking face, with a long, narrow nose and a sharp chin that jutted out, especially when she disagreed with her husband. Her eyes were dark brown, almost black. She had never worn glasses and claimed she did not believe in them. Mark's Nan Mary had polio as a young child and she walked with a brace on her right leg. But she had decided as a young girl not to let her infirmity ever get in her way. Although now in her early eighties, she remained spry and energetic. She maintained perfect posture and refused to lean against the back of a chair. Nan seemed always perched forward, ready to hurl herself at anything or anyone that got in her way.

Mark's grandmother came out of the market carrying a brown bag filled with a lot more than milk. He hurriedly got out of the car to help her, but she shook her head vigorously.

"I've got it. I've got it. Don't worry," she commanded.

"Let me at least get the door," he offered, opening the car's back door. Sam stayed dozing as both of them climbed into the car and Mark started the engine. As he started backing out of the parking space a loud siren suddenly began to shriek. Startled, Mark slammed on the brakes and GrandSam woke with a start.

"What the hell . . . !"

The LaConner Fire Department was located adjacent to the market, and any time there was an emergency the siren sounded to summon the volunteers. Cars and pickups would begin rolling up next to the teal blue building in quick order. Mark began pulling away.

"Let's wait around and see what's going on," his grandfather suggested eagerly.

Nan rolled her eyes. "Go on, Mark, let's get out of here. Your grandfather has got nothing better to do than chase fire engines."

"I was just thinking that someone might be in trouble and need a priest," Sam innocently protested.

"Oh, for heaven's sakes, Sam! If you want to see fires

sign up to be a volunteer. Quit trying to use Mark as your
excuse." GrandSam scowled but kept quiet. The rest of
the trip back to their house was made in silence.

The town of LaConner sits on the east bank of the
Swinomish Channel. To get to the other side you cross
the Rainbow Bridge, a high arching, orange bridge at the
south end of town. As Mark drove over it, he passed two
or three vehicles racing toward the fire house. The land
on the other side of the Rainbow Bridge belongs to the
Swinomish Indian tribe. Shelter Bay, where the Townsends lived, was developed on reservation land that is
leased from the tribe. To get to it, you have to turn at the
tribal cemetery and drive past a cluster of Indian prefab
housing. A guard's house, sitting in the middle of the road,
marks the beginning of Shelter Bay. Once you are waved
through you begin driving along winding roads past expensive wood homes nestled among stands of fir, pine,
and cedar trees. All of the utilities are buried underground
so there are no telephone or electricity poles to mar the
landscape. The streets are named after Northwest Indian
tribes: Quinalt, Tualip, Moclips.

The road Mark took dipped down and ran past a small
nine-hole golf course and a man-made yacht basin where
a couple of hundred boats, including the *Queen Mary,*
were moored against wooden docks. The Shelter Bay Club
House and the development's offices were located between the golf course and the water. On one side was a
swimming pool and on the other, tennis courts. Shelter
Bay was a pristine and peaceful place, filled with well-
appointed homes and expensive playthings for the people
who lived there. Many, like the Townsends, were retired.
But there were also quite a few summer homes, used only
on the weekends and during two or three months of the
year. Situated halfway between the Canadian border and
Seattle—a little more than hour's drive in either direction—Shelter Bay was an accessible spot for both popu-
lations.

Sam and Mary Townsend lived in one of the more modest homes, on a side street up on the hill overlooking the
golf course and yacht basin. Unlike many of their neigh-

bors, the Townsends did not have much of a view. But they were within walking distance of the club house and Nan got her morning exercise by hiking around the perimeter of the golf course.

Mark pulled up in front of his grandparents' house. Before he had time to turn off the engine his grandfather was already out of the car and barrelling towards the front door. In the back seat, Nan smiled apologetically.

"Weak bladder," she remarked as her husband scooted into the house.

Father Townsend helped her out of the car, lifting the groceries from her arms. Father Townsend was a tall man in his late thirties, with a head of thick, light brown hair, only slightly gray. He had a bristling brown mustache that Nan hated as much as her husband's goatee. Nevertheless, she doted on her grandson the priest.

Once inside the kitchen, she took the shopping bag back from Mark and began arranging food in the refrigerator. The sound of a flushing toilet was followed immediately by a loud ringing. On the second ring Nan poked her head from behind the refrigerator's door.

"Mark honey, would you mind answering that for me, please?"

Mark lifted the phone off the receiver. "Hello?"

"Sam!" a woman's voice was sobbing loudly. "I need you! Hurry!"

TWO

Jeanne Olsen was not a woman given to histrionics. Ordinarily she was quiet and shy, even mousey next to her husband, Dutch. But it took Sam several minutes on the phone before he could get her calmed enough to find out what was wrong.

What was wrong clouded his round face with worry and concern. When he finally hung up he continued staring at the phone while Nan and Mark waited. Finally he turned to face them.

"Jeanne wants me to go with her," he said softly, "to look at a body. She's heard they found one over by Sneeoosh and they think it might be Dutch."

"Oh no, Sam." Nan lay her hand on her husband's arm. Dutch Olsen was her husband's best friend. "What happened?"

Sam shook his head and looked at his wife. "I don't know. She got a call about half an hour ago from someone who heard they found a body on the beach. It might be Dutch. That's all she knows. She wants me to go with her to find out."

"Let me get my coat and I'll go with you."

"No, please stay here, Mother. I don't know what's going on, but I'd rather go alone. Unless . . ." he hesitated, looking at Mark. "Unless you'd go with me, Mark. Could you do you that?"

His grandfather looked so vulnerable. His eyes, blinking behind those thick glasses, were full of fear and doubt. "Of course I will, if that's what you want."

"I think I do," said Sam, holding onto his wife's arm. "Jeanne's waiting at their house for me, so we'd better get going."

They drove out of Shelter Bay and headed back across the Rainbow Bridge in silence. As they wound down the hill towards town, Sam began giving Mark directions to the Olsen's house. The couple owned a small place next to the channel, almost directly beneath the bridge. Both Jeanne and Dutch had grown up in the Skagit Valley. They were high school sweethearts and after Dutch finished his time in the military, they had married and settled down in the little house next to the channel to raise their family. LaConner was small and off the beaten track back then. The hordes of tourists and sightseers had not started arriving until the early seventies, and by then the Olsen children were grown and out on their own. Dutch and Jeanne continued living in their house, which was now probably worth twenty times what they had paid for it in the forties.

Dutch had built a short dock out into the water and kept his fishing boat tied there. He and Sam spent many afternoons trolling from that boat, or used it to scoot up the north fork of the Skagit River to an old river shack Dutch had built for duck hunting. If the truth were told, there was a lot more poker playing than actual hunting at the shack in recent years, but Dutch, Sam, and two or three other oldtimers continued telling their wives they were off to The Lodge for a little hunting. The same story was used even when hunting season was over, but no one bothered to try and find another excuse for the time they spent together playing cards and drinking Jim Beam.

Jeanne Olsen was waiting on the front porch when they arrived. She started towards the car and both men got out to meet her. Sam introduced her to his grandson.

"You're the priest, aren't you?" She gave Mark a weak

smile and shook his hand. It felt thin and fluttery in his. "It's nice of you to come along. I told Sam I didn't think I could do this alone." She appeared so much calmer than she had sounded on the phone that Mark wondered if she had taken a tranquilizer.

"You need to drive back over the bridge," GrandSam instructed him after they had helped Jeanne Olsen into the back seat of the car. Mark pulled out of the driveway. "We have to go up through the reservation."

There are two communities in LaConner. Whites live on the town side of the channel and the Swinomish Indians live across the water. The reservation opposite the town is actually on an island called Fidalgo. And the Swinomish tribe's reservation sits on ten square miles at the east end of the island. Their land includes the property leased to the Shelter Bay development. The center of the Indian community is on the banks of the Swinomish Channel, directly across from the town of LaConner.

A fish processing plant was built right at the water's edge, and the Indians tied their gillnetters and other boats to the docks out in front. Set further back from the channel, along with several rows of houses, were buildings for the health clinic, tribal offices, and the tribal court.

GrandSam directed Mark back across the bridge and down a wide street through the center of the Indian settlement. Jeanne sat silently in the middle of the back seat, watching out the window as they entered the reservation. A number of the small wood-framed houses had large piles of nylon fishing nets in their front yards with men making repairs at two or three of them. An empty fireworks stand stood in front of one house, awaiting next summer's July sales. Wooden carvings of eagles, bears, and totem poles stood in front of another. A small hand-painted sign announced that they were for sale. When they got to the baseball field, Mark turned left onto Sneeoosh Road as GrandSam directed.

His grandfather twisted in his seat and looked back at Jeanne. She turned from watching the passing scene and faced him expectantly.

"What happened, Jeanne?" he asked the woman quietly.

"I don't really know." She looked down at her hands which were tightly wringing a handkerchief in her lap. "Dutch left yesterday morning. I thought he was going up to that old shack of his, The Lodge. Anyway, he took his boat so that's where I thought he went. He didn't come home for dinner, so I guessed he was staying up there. You know how he is about that place." Her eyes began to tear over.

"What time did he leave?" Sam asked.

"I don't know. I did some housework and lay down for a little nap about eleven. When I got up for lunch he was gone." She shook her head. "I can't believe it's Dutch, Sam. This is the opposite direction from his shack. There'd be no reason for him to be over here. This is a mistake. I just know it is." Jeanne turned and stared out the window as tears began to roll down her face. "I just know it," she whispered to herself.

Sam turned back around and pointed to a turn in the road.

"That's where we want to go," he told his grandson. "That's Pull and Be Damned Road."

Mark flipped on his turn signal as he looked at GrandSam. "What's it called?"

Sam grinned at his grandson's reaction. "Pull and Be Damned. Don't ask me why, but that's the name." He turned his head towards the back seat. "Do you know where that name came from, Jeanne?"

"They used to do a lot of logging back in here," she answered. "I always thought it had something to do with the teams of mules they used to haul the logs."

The road was narrow and ran straight back through tall fir trees and thick undergrowth crowding both sides of the drive. Mark caught occasional glimpses of water through the trees off to their right. He had never been back into this area of the reservation and was surprised to find it so developed. More and more houses were beginning to appear as he drove further down the road. They were set well back from the road, almost hidden among the trees and thick growth of ferns and blackberry brambles. He saw smoke curling from stove pipes over a few of the roofs and realized they could not all be summer or week-end cabins. They passed one little cottage painted bright yellow, surrounded by tulip beds. In the driveway, a boat resting on a trailer was covered by a blue tarp. A stack of firewood leaned against the side of the house and a cocker spaniel lay sprawled across the back porch. He raised his head and gave a desultory bark as Mark drove past.

As near as Father Townsend could see there were no other signs of life along the road. There was no sign of a sheriff's car or emergency vehicles of any sort. GrandSam was leaning forward in his seat, apparently searching the road ahead for the same thing.

Jeanne's voice came from the back. "I think we're supposed to turn down Capet Lane."

Almost immediately the sign for Capet Lane appeared in front of them and Mark turned towards the water. The narrow drive sloped down the hill and at the bottom a tight knot of cars, including two with lights on their roofs, was parked in a vacant field just to their left. One was a Skagit County sheriff's car, and the insignia on the door of the other indicated it belonged to the Swinomish Tribal Police. LaConner's aid car was also parked nearby. Mark found a parking space a little ways beyond the ambulance. The three of them got out and started down a twisting path towards the beach. The faint murmur of men's voices came from below the bluff in front of them.

When they reached the edge they saw a knot of men standing on the beach below them. About a dozen men had formed a loose circle on the rocky beach. The tide was out, otherwise where they were standing would be covered under about two feet of water. At their feet, in the center of the circle, lay a bright yellow tarp, covering what Mark presumed was the body.

A young man wearing mechanic's coveralls and a base-ball cap spotted the three of them standing on the bluff and nudged an officer wearing a tan uniform and trooper's hat. The policeman gave them a startled look and started

scrambling over the rocks towards them as GrandSam began helping Jeanne onto the beach.

"Be careful, it's a little tricky getting down there," the
old man warned. "If you grab hold of that madronna tree
you can ease yourself down onto that little ledge and then
step down."

Mark held her left hand as she leaned forward and
caught the trunk of the tree with her right. At the bottom
of the bluff the officer hurried to help her the rest of the
way down, frowning up at Mark and his grandfather as
he did so. Next Mark helped GrandSam down the same
way, then followed behind him.

The officer waited until Mark was on the beach before
speaking. "Can I ask what you folks think you're doing?"
His badge identified him as a Skagit County deputy sheriff
and his name tag read "Hayes."

Both Mark and Jeanne Olsen began to answer, but
GrandSam beat them with, "We're here to see the body."

Hayes gave the old man a cold, hard stare.

"I'm Mrs. Olsen," Jeanne hurriedly introduced herself.
"I received a phone call from someone who heard men
talking over the police radio. They said there was a body
here and someone thinks it's my husband." Her voice
caught and she drew a deep breath. "His name is Dutch
. . . Alfred Olsen." She pointed to the yellow tarp. "I want
to know if that's him."

Deputy Sheriff Hayes told them to wait while he picked
his way back over to the group of men huddled around
the body. He leaned close to the other officer as he spoke,
both men casting glances back at the three figures standing
there.

Finally, Hayes shrugged and started picking his way
back across the rocky beach to them. "Follow me," he
said curtly.

The beach rocks were still wet from the receding tide
and they stepped carefully, trying not to slip. Small bar-
nacles coated the sides of the black rocks, and their shells
crunched beneath their shoes as they walked. The ripe,
rich smell of seaweed and salt hung heavy in the damp
air around them. When they neared the yellow tarp the

circle of men solemnly opened up, allowing them to step into the center. The other officer stepped forward and removed his hat.

"Mrs. Olsen?"

Jeanne nodded nervously.

"I'm Mike Jennings," he introduced himself, "from the tribal police. Thank you for coming here. I know this can't be too pleasant for you."

Jeanne leaned against Sam and clutched tightly onto his arm. Her voice was not much more than a whisper as she looked down at the tarp. "Is this Dutch?"

"To tell you the truth, ma'am, we're not sure. One of these fellows," Jennings paused long enough to nod towards one of the other men standing in the group, "thought he recognized your husband. There's no ID on him. Whoever called you must have heard some talking over our radio. I'm sorry you had to learn about it this way."

"Do you know what happened?" Sam interrupted.

Jennings looked at him with the guarded curiosity that comes naturally whenever a policeman finds himself talking to someone he does not recognize. "Some kind of boating accident, as near as we can tell, sir." He pulled a small writing tablet from his shirt pocket. "Could I get your names, please?"

"I'm Sampson Townsend from Shelter Bay. Mrs. Olsen asked me to bring her here."

"And you, sir?" The officer turned towards Mark.

"Mark Townsend. I'm his grandson."

"Father Mark Townsend," GrandSam informed the officer. "My grandson is a Catholic priest."

The officer gave Father Townsend another look before he continued writing. Mark interpreted it as a look of faint doubt. There were stares from some of the other men as well. The priest was wearing a gray Georgetown sweatshirt under a blue Goretex parka, blue jeans, and old running shoes. The closest thing tying him to the Catholic Church was the sweatshirt from the Jesuits' school in Washington, D.C., but Mark realized half the gangbangers in the world also wear sweatshirts from Georgetown University. When he had finished writing, Jennings politely asked the silent crowd of men to move down the beach away from them.

"Mrs. Olsen," he began formally, "if you will step around to this side, I will ask you to identify the body if you are able, please."

The three of them followed Jennings around to the other side of the tarp, nearest to the water. The officer squatted down and cautiously lifted one corner of the tarp, inching it back until a man's pale, wet face was exposed.

Jeanne Olsen sagged against Sam and he quickly had to wrap one arm around her waist to hold her up. A low sob came from deep inside her as she bit into her lip and began to cry.

"Oh, Dutch," Sam sighed.

"Is this your husband, ma'am?"

Jeanne nodded once. Jennings quickly pulled the tarp over the face and stood back up. The four of them stood in awkward silence, staring at the plastic tarp for a few moments before Jeanne managed to clear her throat enough to speak.

"I want to see him," she managed to say with a choked voice.

"Ma'am?" Jennings looked confused.

"I want to see all of him," she requested again, looking directly at the policeman.

The deputy sheriff stepped forward. "I don't think that's a good idea, Mrs. Olsen. Your husband sustained some wounds that aren't too pretty to look at."

Jeanne Olsen gave the deputy an angry look and this time her voice sounded loud and determined, "I want to see my husband's body. All of him." From further down the beach, a few heads snapped up at the sound of the woman's voice.

The two officers looked at each other, neither one anxious to remove the tarp. Finally Hayes gave a shrug, grabbed the tarp, and yanked it off, revealing the corpse.

"Oh, Christ!" GrandSam exclaimed as he turned his head away. Jeanne gasped and tightened her grip on his arm.

Dutch Olsen's body lay spreadeagled on his stomach over the rough rocks. His wet khaki trousers had slipped down to his thighs, exposing his green boxer shorts. He was wearing a brown canvas coat. A long thick rope of green seaweed was caught in the collar and strands splayed across his neck. There was more seaweed intertwined in the fingers of his left hand. His left arm was stretched almost straight out from his body, as if reaching out toward the water. The right arm was bent close to Dutch's body. But there was no right hand. Just below his coat sleeve jutted a sharp point of white bone and the jagged raw stump of what used to be his wrist. Across the broad expanse of Dutch's coat, eight deep slices cut across the man's back. The canvas material was pulled away from four of them and sliced raw flesh was exposed. The wounds looked about three to four inches deep and were anywhere from four to seven inches long. The man's back looked as if a machete or meat cleaver had hacked through the coat in deep, curving slices. Blood had stained the canvas a dark, reddish-brown, but there was no blood in the wounds themselves. The body had been washed clean by the seawater. The skin around the open gashes was puckered and white, but inside of the wounds the flesh had turned a pale and sickly gray.

Father Townsend had seen his share of dead bodies; had witnessed deaths in homes and hospitals, even a couple on highways. While in Alaska he had discovered the body of a murdered state trooper, and had once helped pull the bloated body of a drowned woman out of the water. But he had never seen anyone sliced so brutally, nor had he ever looked into the insides of someone who had been floating in the water. The officer was right—it was not a pretty sight.

Deputy Hayes unconsciously and indecorously touched the body with the toe of his boot. "We figure these cuts were made by a boat's propeller," he informed them, glancing at Mrs. Olsen, who continued staring in horror at her husband's body. "That's why there's that curve, like from a blade of the propeller hitting him."

Mike Jennings, the tribal policeman, stepped in front of

the deputy sheriff and held a hand out to Jeanne Olsen, who was growing very pale. "Do you need to sit down, Mrs. Olsen?"

"No, thank you, I'll be all right." She shook her head as if to clear it. "Have you found his boat?"

Hayes began to answer but Jennings beat him to it.

"One was sighted next to Strawberry Island, over near Deception Pass. They said it's a small Bayliner, but that's all we know at the moment. Someone is there now, and they're going to tow it over this way."

"Dutch had an old Bayliner," Sam volunteered, "an eighteen-footer."

Jennings nodded. "That's about the size of this one all right."

"But that's a good mile and a half away from here," Jeanne Olsen observed.

"More like two," corrected Sam.

Hayes jumped in to explain, "You gotta figure with the currents and the tide . . ."

"Depending on where the accident occurred," Jennings picked up where the deputy lamely had left off, "the boat may have headed off in a different direction. Especially if the motor was still running after it hit the victim . . . Mr. Olsen."

"Would you please cover my husband back up," Jeanne asked stiffly. Deputy Hayes casually lifted the tarp and snapped it above the body, letting the plastic settle back down over Dutch Olsen's remains. He acted like he was making a bed, and both Jennings and GrandSam gave him an exasperated look. Decorum was obviously not the deputy's long suit.

One of the other men farther down the beach called over to them. "Looks like they're bringing in that Bayliner."

In the distance, two boats were rounding the north end of Hope Island out in the bay and the people on the beach strained to get a better look. A gillnetter was in front, followed about twenty feet behind by a smaller white boat bobbing in its wake. Mike Jennings fished a small pair of binoculars from one of his jacket pockets and focused them on the two boats.

"That's a Bayliner," he confirmed, holding the glasses out to Jeanne. "Can you recognize it?"

"My eyes aren't that good," she offered, taking the glasses and handing them to Sam Townsend.

Mark's grandfather studied the boats as they drew closer and then nodded, handing the glasses back to Jennings. "That's her."

There was nothing more they could do on the beach. The tribal policeman explained that Dutch Olsen's body would be taken to the county coroner's office as soon as they finished photographing its position on the beach. Because Dutch was discovered on reservation land, the handling of the reports would be done both by the Skagit County sheriff's department and himself until jurisdiction of the case could be sorted out. Deputy Hayes was nodding his agreement with Jennings's observance of proper protocol. Mrs. Olsen could begin to make whatever arrangements she cared to, Jennings told her, and she would be informed once the coroner released the body. They would see to it that her husband's boat was returned to Olsen's dock once it had been inspected.

Mark Townsend was growing increasingly uneasy as the policeman continued explaining the procedures to Mrs. Olsen. He wandered a few feet away from the small cluster of people standing next to the covered body and turned to stare up into the trees lining the bluff. Something felt wrong to him, but he was at a loss as to what it might be. The Jesuit turned back and studied the tarp a moment, then shook his head and rejoined the group. Jeanne and GrandSam were thanking the two officers for their work.

"Well then," Sam said to Jeanne, "are you ready to go?"

She nodded and the three of them started back toward their car. The other men further down the beach began drifting back to the body as soon as they had turned away. Mark could hear their feet scrabbling over the rough rocks behind them and a bitter picture of crabs scuttling toward carrion came to his mind. He helped his grandfather and

Mrs. Olsen climb back up onto the bluff before saying anything.

"You go on to the car," he told them, "there's a question I want to ask the policeman. I'll be right behind you."

He hurried back across the rocks. They had already removed the yellow tarp and the circle of men watched as one of them began snapping photos with a Polaroid. Jennings looked up questioningly as Father Townsend reached the edge of the group.

"Is there something you wanted, Father?" The man stopped taking pictures and the others turned around to face the priest.

"Is that the way you found him?" Mark asked. "Lying like that? You haven't moved him yet?"

"You don't move anything until you've recorded the scene," Hayes explained to the Jesuit.

Mark continued approaching Dutch's body until he stood beside it. He was studying the wounds in the back. Mike Jennings was watching the priest's face.

"What is it?" the policeman finally asked him.

Mark glanced up at him, slightly embarrassed. "I was just wondering if you had turned him over yet."

"Not yet," Jennings confirmed. "Is there something wrong?"

The priest tugged at the end of his mustache and looked down at the body again.

"I was just trying to imagine what it would be like," he said hesitantly, "if you were run over by a boat." He knelt down next to the body and began tracing in the air above the gashes cross-hatched across the dead man's back. Then he pointed to the right arm. "I can see where you could lose a hand if you put it up to try and block the motor from hitting you." His fingers returned to tracing the air above the eight wounds. "And I think I can picture how the propeller might slice into you like this and this," he said, pointing to the two wounds nearest the shoulders. "But I'm surprised that there are eight cuts and that they're going in all different directions." He looked up into the faces peering down at him. "Either the boat or the body would have had to keep moving around, wouldn't it?''

Hayes was scratching his head, trying to make sense out of what the Jesuit was describing. But Jennings was listening attentively, nodding for the priest to continue.

"And so I was wondering," Mark carried on, "if there might be more cuts on his front. Maybe there was someway he got himself caught in the propeller?'' The priest's voice sounded doubtful.

A muffled ''No way in hell'' came from one of the men in the back.

"There's one way to find out," Jennings replied, turning to the photographer. ''Are you done, John?'' The photographer took two more pictures in rapid succession and then indicated he had enough. With Hayes at the feet and Jennings at the shoulders, the two officers bent and grabbed hold of the corpse. Both men had to strain to turn the dead weight over onto its back.

Dutch Olsen's eyes were wide open but staring sightlessly up at the circle of men leaning over his remains. The pupils were turned inward and only the whites of the eyes were showing. His canvas coat was zipped tight up to his collar. They could see no gashes on the front of the coat nor on the man's legs. But then Father Townsend's finger pointed to a small round hole in the canvas, halfway up the coat on the right side. It was ringed with a small, dark, reddish-brown stain.

The men were silent as they studied the wound, trying to absorb its significance. Finally Deputy Hayes's voice broke the silence.

"Looks like we've got us a little homicide, Mike." His tone of voice sounded more than a little possessive.

THREE

A bullet hole, coupled with eight random slashes and a missing hand, made Dutch Olsen's death look less like a boating accident and more like a murder. A lot more like murder. And suddenly the rocky beach off Pull and Be Damned Road began taking on the appearance of a crime scene. The Skagit County's deputy sheriff and the Swinomish tribal policeman worked quickly to move the bystanders out of the area and to secure the scene. Not that there was much of anything to secure. About all they had was a dead body on an empty beach, apparently washed there by the tide. When the gillnetter that was towing Olsen's boat drew close enough, Mike Jennings warned the fisherman to take the Bayliner directly to the Swinomish wharf and not to let anyone near it.

Father Townsend waited until he had driven the car back to the Olsen's house before he told his grandfather and Dutch's widow the bad news. Jeanne Olsen invited the two men into her house. She was upset and did not want to be alone. Mark waited until they were seated at the kitchen table before he told them why he had returned to the beach after leaving them at the bluff. He described what they had discovered when they rolled Dutch Olsen over. Officer Jennings would be by soon, he informed Jeanne, with more questions.

Both of their reactions surprised him. Jeanne Olsen sat quietly as she listened to Mark describe finding the bullet hole in her husband's side. She wondered if he could tell from the hole what kind of gun it might have been. She questioned him without any show of emotion. Mark replied that he could not tell what size of gun was used. Meanwhile, his grandfather's face was growing red with rage, his hands trembling.

"Do you mean to try and tell me that someone shot Dutch, then ran him over with his own boat? Animals!" he raged. "We're living with animals! What's happening to this world? Don't you worry, Jeanne," he bellowed, his hands pounding the table, "we'll catch the bastard who did this to Dutch!"

Jeanne grabbed GrandSam's hands in hers. "He considered you his best friend, Sam." Both of them began to cry.

By the time Mark and GrandSam left the Olsens' and returned home it was after dark. Nan was watching from her kitchen window for them and hurried out to accompany her husband into the house. Word of Dutch's death was already out, although she was stunned to hear her husband say it was probably murder.

Sam was tired and emotionally wrung out by the events of the day. So after a short whiskey and a cup of hot soup, Nan helped her husband into bed. He was asleep almost before his head touched the pillow. Mark was sitting at one end of the couch when his grandmother returned to the living room. She settled down next to him and took his hand in hers, rubbing it gently.

"Are you all right?" she asked him.

He smiled at her.

"Tell me what you're thinking about," Nan asked.

"I don't know," Father Townsend replied. "It's just that when you see something like that, you realize what a gift your life is. And how easily it can be taken away from you." Mark leaned his head back and stared at the ceiling.

"We always hear that God has a plan for each one of us, but I sometimes wonder," he mused. "Did He really plan for that man's body to end up on the beach like that?" He looked into his grandmother's face. "It's pretty hard to talk about a loving, merciful God when you see something like that."

Nan Townsend was intelligent enough not to reply. She realized her grandson was speaking from a place where reassuring words would not reach. As a Jesuit priest, he had dedicated his life to telling others about God. Whatever doubts he might be having now had to be resolved on his own.

She patted his hand. "You're supposed to go back to Seattle tomorrow." She said it as a statement, but Mark heard the question in her voice.

"Yes. Maybe I could call down and arrange a day or two more. I don't think there's anything too pressing at the parish, and Dan Morrow is there to cover any emergencies. Do you want me to stay?"

"I think it'd mean a lot to your grandfather," she replied. "He was very close to Dutch—like a brother."

"Tell me about him."

"Dutch? Oh, he's one of the local characters, I guess you'd say. He and Jeanne have lived in that old house for close to fifty years. Both of them grew up around here, married and raised a big family." Nan paused for a moment. "I suppose they'll be coming home now. Those poor children. And Jeanne." Her eyes pooled with tears. "I don't know what I would do if something like that happened to Sam." She clasped Mark's hand tightly in hers until she regained her composure.

"What'd he do for a living?" Mark had waited until she could resume.

"He worked at the Shell refinery over by Anacortes. You've seen those green smoke stacks and tanks when we've gone by there in the boat."

Mark knew where she was talking about. Both Texaco and Shell had large oil refineries on a point of land reaching into Padilla Bay. Huge tankers offloaded Alaskan crude from docks stretching out into the bay. Many of the pleasure boats heading into the San Juan Islands cruised through the Swinomish Channel and out past the refineries.

"Your grandfather and Dutch had so much in common. You already know about their poker games out at that shack on the river. For all the times Sam has told me he's going there to hunt, I've yet to see him with a duck. Not that I'd know what to do with it if I did," she admitted, smiling. "I think all us wives were happy to see them go out there for a few hours. When they retire, husbands can be a real pain around the house sometimes." Her eyes were clear again.

"And Dutch loved to fish. He knew these waters better than anyone, except for maybe some of the Indians. He grew up here, after all. Jeanne told me that when he worked at the refinery he'd drive his boat to work, trolling on the way there and on the way back home. That man did love to fish.

"I remember when that big court decision was made, giving the Indians all those fishing rights; Dutch was mad as anything. Oh, he was mad." She paused, searching her memory. "What was it called? Do you remember?"

Mark did. The Boldt Decision was still one of the most controversial court rulings ever made in the Pacific Northwest, and it had impacted fishing procedures throughout the United States. In 1974, a federal judge named George Boldt ruled that treaties signed in the 1800s gave fourteen Indian tribes the right to catch half of all the harvestable salmon and steelhead in Washington state. His decision spawned twenty-five years of lawsuits and appeals, not to mention protests by commercial fishermen and counter-demonstrations by Indian activists.

"Dutch was right in the middle of all of that," Nan told her grandson. "He was the local coordinator for a petition drive they got going against the judge. He'd harangue those poor fishermen on the reservation something awful. Once he even got in a fight outside the Channel Tavern with one of the Swinomish fishermen. Your grandfather was there when that happened. He could tell you about it. I learned a long time ago never to mention Indian fishing around Dutch Olsen. But whenever GrandSam wanted to get Dutch's goat, he'd bring up Judge Boldt."

The clock down the hallway began to chime and Nan stopped talking to listen.

"Mercy, it's ten o'clock," she announced when it was finished. "I don't want to keep you up."

"It's all right," Mark assured her. He could sense his grandmother's need to talk and he was only too happy to sit beside her while she worked through some of her own feelings around the death of a friend. He knew from experience it would help her and GrandSam to get through the next few days. "Tell me some more," he urged.

"Dutch was something of a history buff," she continued, "at least about local history. There isn't one part of this county he can't tell a story about. He could tell you anything you wanted to know about this whole area."

"I wish I could ask him about the name of this road we went on today," Mark interrupted. "It was a weird name—called Pull and Be Damned."

"I know where that is. Someone told me there used to be a tree out there where they once hung two Indians who had killed a white settler back in the old days. That's how it got its name. Too bad Dutch isn't here, he'd know." She fell quiet again and Mark wrapped his arm around her shoulder.

"Dutch was convinced there was some sort of buried treasure around here," she picked up her story. "He was always talking about his so-called research. I don't know what it was all about, but he was convinced there was gold hidden someplace near here. Your grandfather would know more about that. Every once in awhile Dutch and a man named Larry Robbins would drag Sam off to explore some secret place they needed to investigate. The three of them could be just like little boys sometimes."

Mark had a hard time imagining GrandSam acting like a little boy, scrambling through the woods in search of buried treasure. The mental picture failed to match any impressions he had of his grandfather.

"Dutch really thought there was buried treasure around here?" he asked, encouraging Nan to continue.

"Yes, he did," she assured him. "He was always heading over to Anacortes or into Mount Vernon to look up something at the library or in the museum. He told me there used to be pirates and smugglers all around here. There's a place called Ure Island not too far from La-Conner that was named after one of them. Dutch and GrandSam walked all over that island searching for lost gold. Though the only thing they found was a great spot for picking blackberries."

Nan opened her mouth in a wide yawn.

"Oh! Pardon me. It's past my bedtime." She slowly got to her feet and pecked Mark on the cheek. "Thank you for letting me talk, Mark," she said. "I know why you were doing it, and I think it helped. I should be able to sleep now. Don't stay up too late."

She turned away from him and began to limp out of the room.

"Nan?"

She failed to hear him and continued moving slowly down the hall. Mark was about to call after her, but decided against it. He had wanted to ask if she could think of anyone who might have wanted Dutch Olsen dead. But his question could wait. More than anything, his grandmother needed a peaceful night's sleep.

FOUR

Morning brought rain. During the night, thick clouds rolled in from the Pacific Ocean, covering the skies over Puget Sound, backing up against the distant Cascade mountains and darkening the skies over the Skagit Valley. Eventually the heavy clouds began to empty in a steady downpour of rain. Mark lay in bed until after seven, listening to the rain's patter on the roof, then got up to shave and shower. He had to call down to St. Joseph's to tell them he would be away a couple more days, and he knew Father Morrow would not be in the parish office until after he finished celebrating the six-thirty daily Mass. Then his associate would usually join with some of the parishioners for their ritual morning coffee at the Surrogate Hostess. So there was no sense trying to call this early.

Nan was already at work in the kitchen when he emerged. He kissed his grandmother as she stirred a mixing bowl and poured himself a cup of coffee.

"Where's GrandSam?" he asked.

"Oh, that man," Nan feigned exasperation. "He was up before dawn, banging around. I'm surprised he didn't wake you. He said he was going out to Dutch's shack with Larry Robbins."

"The Lodge?"

"That's what they call it," she snorted, leaving her cooking long enough to serve him cereal and toast. "But if you saw it, you'd call it a shack, too."

Nan returned to her mixing bowl. She was making brownies to take to Jeanne. The Olsen family would be arriving and the children and grandchildren would be hungry. In kitchens throughout Shelter Bay and LaConner, other women were baking or cooking dishes for the Olsens too, one of the comforting and helpful rituals that accompanies death. Nan asked her grandson if he would go with her when she went to deliver the brownies.

Sam had not returned before they left, so shortly before eleven Mark drove his grandmother to the Olsen home. There were already three other cars parked in front of the house. Two of the Olsen children had arrived with their families and another friend from Shelter Bay was there with her casserole. Although filling with people, the house was quiet inside as family and guests talked in low voices, expressing their shock and dismay over the murder of Dutch Olsen to one another.

Jeanne told Nan and Mark that she had already had a visit from the Swinomish Tribal Police earlier that morning. Mike Jennings had informed her that Dutch had been shot with a .22. The bullet had entered his right side, away from his heart, and lodged just beneath the ribs. The wound, said Jennings, would not have been fatal. The coroner's report was not back yet, so the exact cause of death was still to be determined, but the policeman wanted Mrs. Olsen to know that they were treating her husband's death as a homicide. Later, he informed her, he would be coming back to ask some questions.

"What kind of questions do you think he wants to ask?" Jeanne asked her friend.

Nan shook her head. "I'm not sure. Probably just some things about how Dutch was and who his friends were."

Jeanne's eyes moved back and forth between Nan and her grandson. "They wouldn't think I did it, would they?" Her voice was pleading. "I wouldn't be a suspect, would I?"

Nan hugged her friend tightly. "Of course not, Jeanne! For heaven's sakes, he was your husband. Everyone knows you loved him."

Jeanne Olsen's lower lip began to quiver and tears began to flow once more. She turned her head away from the two of them.

"Maybe you should sit down," Father Townsend gently suggested, helping her into a chair. "Is there something wrong?"

Jeanne pulled a well-used handkerchief out of her pocket and dabbed at her eyes and nose as Nan laid a reassuring hand on her shoulder.

"It's just that Dutch and I would sometimes argue," she whimpered.

"Everyone argues," Nan cut her off.

"Yes," Jeanne continued, "but we argued that morning, right before he left."

"Jeanne, that doesn't mean anything," Nan tried to reassure her. "All married couples argue sometimes, don't they, Mark?"

He knew that they did. But he also knew the police would pay attention if Jeanne told them she had fought with her husband just before he died.

"Yesterday you told GrandSam and me that Dutch took off in the morning for The Lodge," Mark reminded her.

"He was upset with me," she said, "and that's why I think he left. He used to go and stay out there when we had arguments." She looked up at the priest. "Sometimes he'd stay overnight."

"And you think that's what he did this time," Mark prompted her. She nodded her head.

"I think you just need to tell the police that," he urged Jeanne. "I doubt that would make you a suspect. Besides, you were here and he was out there. And he had the boat, right?"

Jeanne nodded again.

"Father Mark's right," Nan said firmly. "Just tell the police what happened."

*   *   *

More friends and neighbors began to arrive and the Olsen's small house was becoming crowded. Nan and her grandson stayed awhile longer, then said their goodbyes and left. Jeanne promised she would call when a time for the funeral was arranged. She wanted Sam to be a pallbearer, she said.

The two of them stayed in town for lunch, eating in one of the restaurants that overlooked the channel. Despite the inclement weather, the shops and restaurants were filled with tourists. The Tulip Festival was one of LaConner's busiest seasons. Rain or shine, the town was jammed with people and their cars. The Townsends were lucky enough to get a table by a window next to the water. Only a few boats were moving in the channel, but they enjoyed watching the water anyway, and staring across at the fishing boats tied up on the reservation side. Service was slow because of the crowds, and they took their time eating.

By the time they were back across the Rainbow Bridge, it was after two o'clock. The rain had continued falling throughout the day. They pulled into the driveway just as a very wet and muddy GrandSam was climbing out of his car.

"Look at you," Nan was loudly scolding her husband even before she was out of Mark's car. "Don't think you're going into my house in those wet clothes, mister. I won't have you tracking mud into the house."

GrandSam scowled at his wife and slammed his car door.

"What do you want me to do? Strip buck naked out here in the drive?" He began tugging at his belt buckle.

"Go on in the garage," she quickly ordered him, looking over her shoulder at their neighbor's house. "I'll send Mark out with a robe. You can leave your muddy clothes out there."

Mark helped his grandfather into his robe and slippers while the old man groused about his wife's insensitivity and constant abuse. Maybe he'd buy the lodge from Jeanne and just move out there, he threatened. Mark listened patiently as GrandSam continued his complaints on the way into the house. By the time the two men were inside, Nan had hot coffee ready and was putting aside her indignation, replacing it with concern.

"You'll catch pneumonia," she predicted, "and then you're going to want me to be nursemaid." She wrapped a blanket over GrandSam's shoulders while he sat and sullenly sipped his coffee. "That's all I need, is to have you sick."

GrandSam rolled his eyes and looked to his grandson for relief.

"How was your boat trip?" Mark asked him.

"It was okay," Sam said, appreciative of the opportunity to change the subject. "Larry Robbins and me went out to the lodge in his boat. We had some trouble getting back through the Hole in the Wall though. The tide was running out so we had to get in the water to pull his boat part of the way."

"That's how you got so muddy." Nan decided she was not finished with her scolding.

"Give it a rest, woman," her husband ordered sharply. His wife frowned and stormed out of the kitchen.

In the quiet that followed, Mark and his grandfather continued sipping at their coffee.

"We were looking for some things," GrandSam finally confided to him. "Dutch has some things hidden away that we thought we better find."

Mark waited and kept quiet. He knew that trying to urge his grandfather to say more than he was ready to would achieve nothing. GrandSam cocked his head and looked over at him.

"Dutch has been on the verge of finding some lost gold," he told Mark. "Years ago this area was used by pirates who were smuggling Chinese and opium out of Canada. Dutch is pretty sure that there is still some stuff hidden somewhere around here. He thinks one of them hid a lot of his money and then never came back for it."

"Did you find what you were looking for?"

"Not yet," the old man admitted. "Larry and I searched all through that shack but couldn't find anything."

"What were you looking for?" Mark's curiosity was aroused. Like everyone else, he was a sucker for stories about pirates and lost treasure.

"A stick," Sam said.

"What?"

"Yeah." He dropped the blanket from his shoulders and got up to pour more coffee. "There was a guy named O'Rourke," GrandSam began. "He supposedly lived over on Guemes Island with an Indian wife. Dutch said he was a longtime smuggler and made a lot of money bringing stuff across the border. According to Dutch, they caught him once down in Tacoma with 364 pounds of opium. There were Chinese working in the mines and building the railroads back then, and a lot of them were addicted to opium. The stuff was legal in Canada back then and smugglers used to bring it into this country and then trade them drugs for their wages. O'Rourke was one of the best. Or the worst, depending on how you look at it." The old man drank his coffee.

"But what about the stick?" Mark reminded him.

"Oh, yeah," Sam returned to the point of his story. "His wife was an Indian and she supposedly used to keep track of where O'Rourke hid his gold with some kind of stick that she'd carve on. Dutch said it was about two feet long and carved out of alder. Larry and I think he found it and had it hidden out at his lodge somewhere."

"What makes you think he had it?"

"One time he showed us a piece of paper with some markings," GrandSam explained, "and he thought he had them figured out. He wanted us to go over to Ure Island with him to see if we could find an old well."

"Nan said something about that when we were talking last night," Mark remembered.

Sam scowled at his grandson. He did not appreciate hearing that his wife had already infringed on his story. "Figures," he grumbled.

"Anyway, we looked all over and never found it. This Ben Ure was another smuggler. He had a saloon and dance hall on the island, and a lot of the bad guys used to meet there. At least according to Dutch. We found the remains of a place over on the side facing Cornet Bay. But no well.''

''And you think the gold might be hidden in the well?'' Mark was intrigued and found himself drawn into his grandfather's tale. The Townsends had a strong love for adventure coursing in their blood. Mark was no exception, which might help explain why he chose to become a Jesuit. Members of the Jesuit order are infamous for putting themselves in unusual and often risky situations.

''Who knows where the gold is?'' GrandSam replied. ''Or even if there is any? But Larry and I wanted to get out to The Lodge before the police did, just in case Dutch did have something hidden out there.''

Mark decided against raising any questions about the moral implications of what his grandfather had done. And he did not even want to consider the legal ones. Breaking into the cabin of a man who had been murdered would certainly be frowned on by the police. But GrandSam said they had found nothing, so no harm was done.

''We brought back half a case of whiskey Dutch had out there,'' GrandSam informed him, now adding theft to breaking and entering. ''And the guns.''

''Guns?'' Mark was suddenly alert. ''What kind? Was there a .22?''

GrandSam shook his head no. ''Only two shotguns,'' he said, setting down his coffee.

If there had been a .22 in the shack, it could very well have been the one used to shoot Dutch Olsen in the side. Father Townsend realized that was information for the police. Now he only had to figure out how to mention it without implicating his grandfather.

''Where are the shotguns now?'' he asked GrandSam.

''At Larry's. He'll give 'em to Jeanne once things quiet down.'' GrandSam stood and carried his empty cup to the sink. ''We didn't want to leave any booze or guns out there in case someone breaks in.''

Mark watched his grandfather's back as the old man rinsed out his cup. He knew what GrandSam really meant was anyone other than himself breaking into Olsen's river shack.

FIVE

Mark Townsend was not lazy. Hardly that. At the parish he was used to putting in a sixteen-hour day, often starting with the 6:30 A.M. Mass and ending with marriage counseling or a parish council meeting that ran until 10 P.M. The life of a parish priest was a lot more demanding than his sister (and many others) thought. So trips like this one, to visit his grandparents in LaConner, were occasions for sleeping in a little later than usual. Unfortunately, after years of waking up before six, Mark's internal alarm appeared permanently programmed. He very seldom was able to sleep past six. But even being able to lie quietly in bed, thinking his own thoughts, felt like a luxury.

He figured today would be his last day in LaConner. Tonight, after dinner, he would get back on I-5 and head south to Seattle. Or maybe wait until early in the morning before returning home. He rolled onto his left side, away from the light creeping into the window. With Dan Morrow at the parish to cover for him, there was really no need to return right away. No real need, but lots of compulsion. Like most priests, Father Townsend found it hard to be away from his parish family for very long.

He shifted back to face the window. There was not much for him to do here. The Olsens were not Catholic, so he would not need to offer his help with the funeral. And Jeanne Olsen had shown no inclination to call upon his skills as a counselor to assist with her own grieving. He turned his meditation to his grandparents. GrandSam seemed to be dealing with the death of his close friend in his typical blustery manner. He would make himself busy, finding projects to occupy his time, energy, and thoughts. Mark did not know for sure when and how his grandfather would deal with his own grief, but he strongly suspected that whenever that was, it would be done in private. He doubted if even Nan would be witness to her husband's emotions. His grandmother, on the other hand, would deal with their friend's death a little more directly. Baking brownies and visiting the widow was her way of acknowledging death's presence. Mark wondered what went on between the two of them in their private moments together; if they would talk about it at all, and what they might say to each other. After so many years of living together, he suspected that a great deal of what they were thinking and feeling was communicated between them without any need for words. That realization reawoke a very familiar ache deep inside the priest, and in the early morning silence of his grandparents' house he was once again faced with his own aloneness. He stirred restlessly. This was getting him nowhere. It was time to get up.

His meditations were conveniently interrupted by the sound of the phone ringing down the hall. It rang three times before he heard the gruff murmur of GrandSam's greeting. Mark glanced at the clock and was surprised to find it was a quarter past seven. He never stayed in bed later than here in LaConner.

Both GrandSam and Nan were at the table when Mark entered the kitchen. His grandfather had one of his wife's hands wrapped in his and he was speaking to her in soft, comforting tones. Nan was dabbing at her eyes with her free hand.

"Good morning," Mark greeted them. "What's wrong, Nan?"

She gave him a brief and troubled smile. "We just got some bad news, dear."

"They arrested Greg Patsy for Dutch's murder," GrandSam bluntly informed Mark. "He's a Swinomish."

"His wife is our housecleaner," explained Nan. "That was her on the phone. She was supposed to come to clean this morning, but she's in Anacortes at the jail, trying to see her husband." She dabbed at her tears with a crumpled handkerchief. "The poor woman, I feel so sorry for her."

"It doesn't surprise me in the least," GrandSam proclaimed. "Greg Patsy hated Dutch."

Mark poured himself a cup of coffee and joined them at the table.

"What for?" he asked his grandfather.

"Fishing. Ever since this Indian rights business, those two have been fighting each other."

His grandfather went on to describe Greg Patsy as one of the leading activists for Indian fishing rights on the Swinomish reservation. GrandSam claimed the man was rabid about enforcing their rights accorded the tribe by the Boldt Decision. As a board member on the tribe's fishing commission, Patsy used his influence to guarantee that Swinomish fishermen were given every advantage when the annual migrations of salmon began arriving in Puget Sound. He was a commercial fisherman himself and, in GrandSam's opinion, was determined to keep as many salmon out of the hands of white men as he could. Greg Patsy and Dutch Olsen had crossed swords over this issue on more than one occasion, he told Mark.

The most recent incident, he informed his grandson, was just four or five days ago. Patsy had set his net out for an early run of spring chinook and Dutch had supposedly run his boat through the middle of the Indian's net, tearing into it. The two men exchanged angry words across the open water, and later Greg Patsy filed a complaint against Dutch with the LaConner police. Dutch denied any wrongdoing, claiming it was an accident and that Patsy's buoys were floating too low in the water for him to see in time.

"Dutch told me he had to watch out for Patsy," GrandSam claimed. "He was scared for his life."

"Sam, that's a damn lie!" Nan angrily interrupted her

husband. "I was there that night. I heard what Dutch said."

"He said Greg Patsy told him he'd get him," Sam argued.

"That's right," his wife acknowledged. "But he never said he was afraid Greg was going to hurt him."

"I didn't say he did."

"You most certainly did! You told Mark he was scared for his life."

"Well, wouldn't you be! The Indian said he was going to get him. What the hell do you think that means, Mother?"

Both of them were madder than he had witnessed in a long time, and he knew their fight would only escalate if they were allowed to continue. Their tempers were being fueled by the raw emotions they were both feeling at the moment, Mark realized.

"Let's stop for a minute," he pleaded. "From what you're saying, it sounds like Greg Patsy and Dutch were anything but friends."

"Hardly!" his grandfather snorted. Mark held up a cautioning hand.

"But that doesn't necessarily mean he killed him."

"That's right!" his grandmother chimed.

"But," Mark reasoned, turning to Nan, "the police had to have had a pretty good reason for suspecting him. Otherwise they never would have arrested him."

Both GrandSam and Nan remained silent while they considered what Mark was saying.

"Until we know what evidence they have," Mark continued, "it's kind of hard to judge one way or the other. Don't you think?"

An uneasy truce was declared and breakfast was eaten in silence. As soon as he finished, Sam left the table, announcing he needed to see Larry Robbins. Mark and his grandmother were still when they heard his car drive away.

Nan waited until the sound faded into the distance before she spoke. "Your grandfather is really hurting. I'm worried for him. How he's going to get through this, I don't know.''

Mark said nothing in reply, waiting to see if there was more she wanted to say.

"When you get as old as we are, every time you lose a friend it feels like you lose a little piece of yourself. Then one day you wake up and realize that you know more dead people than you do living. That's when you start thinking about going to join them.'' She paused and looked quizzically at her grandson. "I think it's natural to want to be with your friends. Don't you?''

He nodded.

"You sort of expect it when you hear someone has died of a heart attack or cancer. I guess that's why they're called natural causes. Those are easier to accept. But when it's something unnatural . . . that's a little scary. Your grandfather is more scared than anything, Mark.''

He marveled again at how much his grandparents understood each other. And the familiar desire for that kind of knowledge of another arose inside him again.

"Will he be okay?'' he managed to ask.

"Eventually,'' Nan replied. "It'll take time.'' She reached across and patted his arm. "I'm glad you're able to be here. Now, if you'll help me clear the table, I think I'll bake something for the Patsys.'' She stood and started towards the sink, then slowly turned around. "That would be okay, wouldn't it? I mean, you don't think it would be presumptuous?''

"I think it would be a nice gesture,'' Mark said reassuringly.

He filled the dishwasher while Nan got out flour, sugar, chocolate, and mixing bowls, humming softly to herself as she worked. Mark poured himself the last of the coffee and perched on the edge of the kitchen counter, watching his grandmother.

"How long has Linda worked for you?''

Nan stopped stirring momentarily while she thought. "Oh, about a year and a half, I guess.'' She dipped her finger in the batter, tasting it. "A friend of mine recommended her. She cleans for several ladies in Shelter Bay.''

"Have you ever met her husband?"

"Greg? No, not personally. You see him around town a bit, but I've never been introduced." His grandmother's face took on the worried look she had whenever she was about to say something she considered critical of someone else. "I don't think he has a regular job," she said, "other than fishing."

Mark set out for a walk down to the yacht basin while his grandmother finished her baking. He promised to return in time for lunch. And afterwards he would drive her to the Patsy home to deliver her brownies.

By the time they were ready to go, it was two in the afternoon. GrandSam was still not back and Mark wondered if he and his friend had gone back to Dutch's shack. He hoped not. If the police found out they were poking around in Dutch's belongings they were likely to have questions.

The Patsy house was in a cul-de-sac three blocks off of Reservation Road, which was the main street running through the center of the Swinomish reservation. Their home was a one-story HUD prefab, painted a soft yellow, surrounded by a lawn that needed mowing two weeks ago. The driveway was blocked by a small wooden rowboat, tipped upside down and resting on saw horses. Someone— Mark guessed it had to be Greg—was sanding the paint off the hull down to the bare wood. A nylon fishing net was stretched out across the front yard and a mountain bike lay directly across the narrow walk leading to the front door. Nan and Mark negotiated their way past the net and around the bike.

Linda Patsy answered their knock. She cautiously opened the door just a crack, peering out to see who was standing on her porch. When she recognized Mary Townsend she pulled the door open all the way.

"Mrs. Townsend!"

"Hello, Linda." Nan offered the young woman her warmest smile.

Linda Patsy was a raven-haired beauty—one of those women whose age is impossible to guess. She could have been anywhere from her late twenties to her early forties. She was wearing Levi's and a flannel shirt and they looked good on her. Although her face was tense and drawn, it was still quite handsome. Her long straight hair was pulled back and tied into a ponytail. Mark found himself staring in awe, although he tried not to show it as his grandmother introduced them. Linda Patsy looked curiously at him.

"You're the priest, aren't you." She said it as a statement, not a question. "I see your picture hanging in the hallway when I clean. And your grandmother has told me lots about you."

"Only the good stuff, I hope," said Mark.

"She said you were coming up to see the tulips with them. That's nice that you do that."

An awkward silence fell over the three of them as they stood on the porch, no one quite sure what the next move was supposed to be. Finally Nan held out the plate of brownies.

"I brought you these, Linda," the old woman said, "although I imagine your friends have already loaded your kitchen with food."

The woman's face grew red as she accepted the plate.

"Not really. You're the first to come," she admitted, sounding embarrassed.

Mark felt awkward and turned to look around the cul-de-sac. He saw a curtain rustle in a window from the house across the way, but that was the only sign that anyone else was nearby.

"The house is a mess," Linda apologized, "but if you would like to come in . . ."

Nan glanced at her grandson to see if he objected before accepting Linda Patsy's offer. The Patsys' front curtains were closed and the small, cluttered living room was dark. The only light came from the television. A young child was sprawled on the couch, eyes glued to the set. Obviously embarrassed in front of her visitors, Linda was moving quickly through the room, gathering up clothing that was strewn across the furniture.

"Please sit down," she invited them, throwing the

clothes into a pile in the corner. "The couch potato there is Jesse."

Mark sat at the end of the couch. "Hello, Jess," he said cordially.

"My name is Jesse." The child jumped up from the couch and ran into the kitchen.

Blue jeans, black sweatshirt, bare feet, long, straight black hair, about ten or eleven years old and tough: Mark was guessing boy. Guessing wrong.

"She's upset about her dad," Linda Patsy said, apologizing for her daughter's rudeness.

"Poor thing," Nan murmured sympathetically, "it has to be horribly difficult for her. And you too, Linda."

The woman dipped her head in acknowledgement and looked around her darkened living room.

"They came for Greg early this morning." She was speaking so softly that Mark had to strain to hear. "None of us were even up yet. There were two tribal policeman and they came right into the house. They said they were arresting Greg for killing that white man they found on the beach. Jesse saw them handcuff her daddy." Her eyes were moving constantly, although she never looked directly at either Mark or his grandmother.

Mark followed her lead and looked down at the floor when he spoke to her. "Did they say why they think your husband did it?"

"They said someone told them. That's all they would say."

Father Townsend knew there had to be more than that. You do not arrest a man just because someone tells you he did it. Not unless they witnessed the murder or there was collaborating evidence. There had to be more.

"What happens next?" Nan wanted to know.

Linda Patsy was obviously distraught. For the first time since they sat down, she looked directly into Mrs. Townsend's face. Her own people had not yet decided how they should respond to this tribal crisis. Linda realized there was shame, embarrassment, and confusion about a member being arrested. And for the time being, for whatever reason, the people were deciding to let her be alone. Now this white woman whose house she cleaned and this priest were asking what no one else would. Linda Patsy had to decide how she wanted to answer.

"I don't know," she finally confessed, dropping her hands uselessly into her lap. "The tribe has an attorney, but they told me that Greg should get his own. Because this is on the reservation, they said the FBI might come. And Greg could be taken down to Seattle." She was trying hard not to cry in front of them. Her daughter was quietly standing in the kitchen doorway, scowling at her mother and the two white people in their living room.

"Linda dear," Nan's voice was soft and comforting, like an old familiar blanket, "what can I do to help?"

Linda looked at her daughter when she spoke.

"I have to know why they think he did it," she said. "I know that Greg was not friends with this man, but he would never kill someone. I have to find out why they arrested him."

"I'm sure Mark can do that for you."

Father Townsend stared at his grandmother with open dismay.

"Nan, I don't think I can find . . ."

"Of course you can, dear," she said, cutting him off. "You told me you met that policeman when you went to the beach with GrandSam. I'm sure he'll talk to you. After all, you're a priest."

Like many of her generation, Nan believed fully in the magical powers of a Roman collar. No matter what the circumstances the priest's collar could fix everything. Never mind that this was a murder investigation and that Mark was a total stranger to everyone involved. He was Father. And Father could do anything.

Linda Patsy was looking at him now with hope growing in her eyes.

"Now we can't make any promises." Nan was getting to her feet. "But Father Mark will see what he can find out. Meanwhile, I want you to take this." She reached into her purse and handed Linda a white envelope. "It's a little advance for housecleaning. It might be helpful for you."

Linda tried to hand the envelope back. "I can't accept this," she protested weakly.

"Of course you can, dear." Nan was already heading towards the door. "It's not that much, and you're going to have expenses helping your husband. It's just an advance."

Linda was profusely thanking both of them as they left the house and started toward the car. Nan wore a self-satisfied expression on her face as Mark helped her into the front seat.

"Nan, you shouldn't have told her I could help," he protested.

"Oh, I'm so sorry, dear." His grandmother did not sound sorry at all. "Have I put you in an awkward situation?" As if it was even a question. "It was just that poor Linda looked so helpless there by herself. I'm sorry if I spoke out of turn." She gave her grandson a generous smile. "Just do whatever you can, dear. I'm sure it'll be fine."

The Jesuits have an expression they use among themselves to cover just such scenarios: *Sometimes it's easier to ask forgiveness than it is to ask permission.* If women could be Jesuits, Nan Mary would have made a good one.

Just as they were pulling out of the cul-de-sac, a woman stepped in front of Mark's car, forcing him to brake to a stop. She stood directly in front of them, staring through the window at the two people inside. Whoever she was, she was not from the reservation. Her sandy brown hair hung down her back in two long braids. She wore a simple peasant blouse and a long denim skirt that went almost to her ankles. Gray woolen socks covered her feet, and she was wearing Birkenstock sandals over them. Her skin was white. The woman moved quickly around to Mark's side of the car as he began rolling down the window.

"May I help you?" she asked brusquely. She stood close to the car and kept a tight grasp on the door's handle with one of her hands as she peered in at the two occupants. It was an odd question to ask, Mark thought.

"Not really," he replied.

"I thought maybe you were lost. Sometimes folks come on the reservation and get turned around."

"No," said Mark. "We aren't lost. We were here to visit someone."

"Who?" She leaned closer to the window.

"A friend."

"A friend," she repeated doubtfully. She placed her other hand onto the lip of the car's window, as if she were going to try and push it down further. "And does your friend have a name?" she wondered rudely.

"Excuse me." Mark could hear the irritation in his voice. "Is this any of your business?"

Her green eyes narrowed as she stared hard at him. There was about half a minute of silence while she studied his face. Finally she spoke.

"You're on a reservation," she crisply informed him. "We have a lot of little children who play out in the streets, and whites aren't especially appreciated when they go racing through here. This isn't a place for tourists."

Mark was trying to keep his temper under control. "I already told you, we came to see a friend. We're not tourists." He offered her a tight smile. "Are you a member of the tribe?"

His question caught her by surprise and she took a step back from the car, releasing her grip from the window and the car's door handle.

"In a sense," she finally replied. "I'm an honorary member."

Nan leaned against Mark to look out the window at the strange woman. "I know who you are!" she suddenly announced in triumph. "You must be the sister who is working up here. I'm Mary Townsend, from over at Shelter Bay, and this is my grandson, Father Mark Townsend. A Jesuit priest."

Nan's introductions did little to break the tension. In fact, the woman's demeanor grew even colder.

"A Jesuit priest." She almost spat the words out. "What are you doing here?" she asked hostilely.

He did not know what this woman's problem was, but Mark was fed up with her third degree.

"Look," he answered, "I've already told you we were visiting someone. I don't know who you are, Sister, but why we're here has nothing to do with you."

A red pickup truck had slowed down and pulled over to the opposite curb. An older Indian couple looked out at the scene, watching as the nun stood in the street with her hands on her hips, facing off against the two whites in the car.

"I'm Teri Carter," she informed Mark. "Sister Teri Carter, and I live here. We've had an incident on the reservation and it involves a family in the cul-de-sac. They don't want to be bothered."

She was obviously trying to be protective of the Patsy family, but Mark was having a hard time understanding Sister Carter's confrontational manner and open hostility towards them. Hostility that only seemed to grow worse after she was told he was a priest. The tension between them was plainly evident. The two Indians in the pickup continued looking on with interest.

"Sister Carter," Mark began, trying to keep his voice calm and low, "my grandmother is a friend of Linda Patsy's. When we heard about her husband's arrest, we came over to see how she is doing and to ask if there was anything we could do to be of help. That's all." He tried to smile pleasantly. "We're done with our visit now, and so we're going back home. I realize this is an uncomfortable time for the people here, but we only came to offer Linda our support."

"That's very nice of you, Father Townsend." The tone of her voice dripped with condescension. "But this is a tribal matter. The Swinomish will handle it in their own way. Your intervening would be considered a real intrusion. I hope you understand."

An intrusion for whom, Mark wondered, although he had enough sense not to say it out loud. Sister Teri Carter obviously resented his presence, although he was unsure why; it was probably best to leave without disturbing her any more. He put the car back in gear and began inching forward.

"It was nice meeting you, Sister," Mark said as he drove away. Under his breath he muttered, "Have a nice day."

SIX

Mark was disturbed by his confrontation with Sister Carter, as was his grandmother. They had obviously upset her just by their presence on the reservation. The nun had appeared to grow even more incensed when she learned they had been visiting Linda Patsy. And while Mark did not try explaining it to his grandmother, he had a strong suspicion that his being a Jesuit priest only added to Sister Carter's animosity towards them.

Nan apologized twice more on their way back to the house for volunteering Mark to approach the police on Linda's behalf. But, she explained, Mrs. Patsy was alone, frightened, and concerned about her husband. Nan thought that her grandson could be of help. As always, Mark realized her good intentions and accepted her apologies. Trying, at the same time, to figure out how he could possibly find out anything that might prove helpful to the lovely Indian woman they had just left.

He stayed at the house only long enough to change into his clerics—black pants, black shirt, and white Roman collar. If he was going to get anywhere with the police, he figured it would be in his capacity as a priest. He did not like to admit it, but his grandmother had that pegged right. Although it had no magical powers, the Roman collar did open doors that otherwise would often remain closed. Father Townsend headed back to the reservation and the headquarters for the tribal police, hoping he would not bump into Sister Teri Carter along the way. Mark still had hopes to be packed and on his way to Seattle before the day's end, although he was beginning to have his doubts.

The police headquarters were housed at one end of the Swinomish Tribal Services Building. With antennas bristling from the roof and a huge satellite dish parked in front, Mark had no trouble finding the place. Officer Mike Jennings was off duty, he was told. But one of his assistants, Matthew Joseph, was available and could talk with Father Townsend. A young native woman led Mark down a narrow hallway to Joseph's office. Mike Jennings was a white policeman, but his assistant was Indian. He welcomed Father Townsend with a soft handshake although he looked directly into the priest's face as he greeted him, inviting him to sit down in a chair he hastily pulled next to his cluttered desk. Mark explained who he was to the young officer and that he had accompanied Dutch Olsen's wife when she identified the body. Joseph studied a file on the desk in front of him as Townsend continued his narration. He purposely left out his role in helping to discover that Dutch Olsen was, in fact, murdered. But the tribal policeman was on his toes.

"You're the one who found the bullet hole on Mr. Olsen's body," he noted, still studying the file. He looked up at the priest. "How'd you know he was shot, Father?"

"I didn't," Mark explained. "But I thought the cuts on his back looked like there were too many and in too many directions. It looked to me like a boat's propeller had hit him two or three times from different directions. That hardly seemed accidental. I wondered if there were cuts on his chest, and when they turned him over we found the bullet hole."

Joseph had pulled a photograph from the file and was studying it in silence. From across the desk Mark could see it was a photo of Olsen's corpse lying on the beach.

"When you explain it I can see what you mean," the

policeman admitted. "But I wouldn't have noticed it." He gave the priest an appreciative grin. "That's pretty good work, Father."

"Thanks," Mark acknowledged. "I understand you've arrested someone already."

"Early this morning," the policeman confirmed. "A tribal member, unfortunately."

"So I've heard." Joseph gave him a questioning look. "My grandmother knows Linda Patsy," Mark explained.

Officer Joseph bobbed his head. "A nice woman."

"Hmmm," Mark said. The two men studied each other in silence.

"How do you know it was Greg Patsy?" Father Townsend finally asked.

The policeman laid both hands on his desk and leaned back in his chair. "We got a tip."

"A witness?"

Officer Joseph tipped his head to one side, pursed his lips and let his eyes rest on the Roman collar. Mark did not think he was going to answer his question, but then the policeman surprised him.

"An anonymous phone call, Father. But you didn't hear that from me." Joseph leaned forward in his chair and whispered across the desk, "Someone tipped us to Greg Patsy," he confided, "and where we could find the gun."

"So you have the gun."

"It was in Greg's boat," the policeman told him. "Hidden."

Mark's grandmother would not be happy with this information. Neither would Greg Patsy's wife. Mark decided to continue fishing for a sliver of good news.

"Fingerprints?"

"Partials," the young policeman replied. "Patsy's. Those were the only ones we found. And," he raised his eyebrows dramatically, "Mike did his own little ballistics a little while ago. As near as he can tell, it's the same rifle that killed Mr. Olsen. Of course, the FBI will be able to tell us for sure."

Linda Patsy had said the FBI would probably become

involved because the reservation was under federal jurisdiction.

"Any guesses why Greg Patsy would have wanted to
kill him?"

Matthew Joseph shook his head. "I shouldn't say any
more, Father, I'm sorry. But there was enough to make
the arrest. I'm just sorry it's one of our own people."

"I've already heard about the problem with the net,"
Mark informed him, "how Dutch Olsen drove his boat
across Greg's net and cut it."

Joseph was surprised. "Well, if you know that, then
you know a lot of it. Patsy was pretty pissed about that.
But Olsen has been on him about the fishing rights for
years. I guess cutting his net pushed Greg over the edge."

What the policeman was saying made sense. Dutch Olsen pushed Greg Patsy too far one too many times, and
the Indian fisherman struck back. The ugly scene in Father
Townsend's mind played itself out: Olsen spotting the Indian in his boat with his nets and cruising close by to
harass him; Patsy threatening him with his rifle not to
come any nearer and Olsen ignoring him; the young man
firing, knocking Dutch into the water; then running him
over. Not a pretty scene to contemplate, especially when
Greg Patsy turns around and rams the body a second and
even third time. Funny he didn't dump the gun overboard
though. Funny, and dumb, the priest decided.

Mark thanked the policeman and they shook hands
again. Father Townsend found his own way out of the
building. He had just climbed into his car and was about
to start the engine when a furious streak of motion flew
past the hood of his parked car, spun sharply, and skidded
to a shrieking stop at his side, gravel spraying across the
bottom half of his car door. A small brown face under a
too-huge Redskins cap was staring angrily through the
glass at him. Mark rolled his window down.

"Hello, Jesse," he greeted the Patsy girl. "You'd better
be a little more careful on that bike. Especially without a
helmet."

"Are you gonna help my daddy?" Her voice was accusing.

Mark hesitated to answer. He never liked saying no to anyone. Nor did he want to admit to the young girl that it looked like the police probably had the right man.

"What do you think I could do to help him?" he asked instead.

Jesse scowled and looked perplexed. She kicked her front tire.

"He didn't do it, you know."

Father Townsend did not reply.

"I thought priests are supposed to help people." Jesse's eyes flashed angrily as she challenged him.

"When they can," Mark answered slowly. "But I think your daddy needs more help than I can give him."

The girl's face darkened. Her eyes held the threat of tears and her lip began to tremble. "God dammit!" she cursed. "Dammit! Dammit! Dammit!" She whipped her bicycle around and spun away, once again spraying Mark's car with gravel. He watched as she furiously pedaled up the road towards her house.

When St. Ignatius first laid down the rules for his fledgling order of Jesuits, he insisted that his priests and brothers give special attention and care to the needs of children. That provision was even included in the vow formula recited by the Jesuits. About most things, Father Ignatius was a very wise man—Mark had always felt that—but he now wondered how their Holy Founder would deal with a young Swinomish girl named Jesse Patsy.

GrandSam and Nan were having another fight. He could hear their voices from the driveway. Instead of quieting when he entered the kitchen, his grandfather turned his wrath on Mark.

"How could you?" he yelled at Mark as soon as he spotted him in the doorway. "It's bad enough that she butts in, but for you . . ." His grandfather stopped abruptly and shook his head in disgust.

"Dutch Olsen was my best friend," he continued in a quiet but flat voice. "We were as close as brothers. Like family." His cold look of betrayal moved between his wife and his grandson. "Now he's dead and you two are cozying up to the man who killed him. How could you do this to Dutch?'' He looked imploringly at Mark. ''How could you do this to me?''

Sam turned to his wife. ''I don't understand you either, Mary. We've been together fifty-four years and sometimes I think I don't even know you. You are some piece of work, woman.'' He picked up his hat and coat from the kitchen table. ''I'm not staying here tonight,'' he said, looking at both of them, ''not with you two.'' GrandSam brushed past his grandson.

Mark started out the door after him.

''Wait, Mark. Please.'' Nan held up a trembling hand. ''It's best to let him go.'' She passed her hand in front of her face. ''He needs to be alone.''

She fixed them a simple supper—soup and sand-wiches—and they ate mostly in silence. Mark felt awful. He knew his grandparents had their quarrels like all married couples, but he hated being a witness to them. And he deeply regretted being part of the reason for this one. Somehow he found himself caught between his grandfather's fierce loyalty and his grandmother's overwhelming compassion. They were both good people, but in this case their goodness was creating an awful rift between them. He could not help but wonder. After being married for fifty-four years, was it easier for them to bridge a rift like this or just let it fracture into a crevasse? And how many chasms could partners continue to leap over before one of them finally decided to give up? When he was young he had a board game called Chutes and Ladders, a game of avoiding the slides downward while managing to climb up the ladders to win. Sometimes Father Townsend considered marriage as one huge game of Chutes and Ladders. And right now, Nan and GrandSam were definitely in a chute.

There was certainly no way he could return to Seattle tonight. Not until some sort of peace was made between his grandfather, Nan, and himself. His grandmother went to bed soon after dinner. Mark stayed up and tried to read, but nothing held his attention. He finally gave up and turned off the reading lamp, leaning back in his chair. He tried some prayer but that was tough going, also. Too many distracting images kept crowding his thoughts. A tendril of green seaweed draped across Dutch Olsen's pale neck. Sister Carter's long braids. Light playing against the filaments of nylon net stretched across the Patsys' front yard. The nearly indiscernible rustle of curtains in the house across the cul-de-sac. His grandmother's hands dusted with flour and his grandfather's angry expression as he reached for his hat. The sight of little Jesse angrily pedalling away from him. *I thought priests were supposed to help people.*

Dammit! Dammit! Dammit!

SEVEN

True to his word, Sam Townsend did not come home. Father Townsend called St. Joseph's parish to inform them he was staying in LaConner a day or two longer.

"You're cutting into your vacation days," his co-pastor, Father Dan Morrow, jokingly warned him. "Either that, or I get Holy Week off."

"No way, Dan!" Mark protested. The days before Easter were the parish's busiest. "Besides, this isn't a vacation. Believe me."

He briefed his fellow Jesuit on his activities in La-Conner, starting with driving his grandparents around to the tulip fields, then describing the body on the beach off Pull and Be Damned Road.

"Pull and what?"

"You heard me," Mark said into the phone. "I haven't found anyone who can tell me what it means, but you'll have to admit it's a colorful name for a road."

"Sounds more than slightly off-color if you ask me," his colleague suggested.

"You would be the one to say that," Mark retorted. "So I won't ask you." He said good-bye to his friend and hung up the phone.

* * *

His grandmother had returned from her morning walk around the golf course, acting as if nothing was wrong. She was refusing to worry about her husband in front of Mark. "He'll come home when he gets hungry," she predicted. Meanwhile, she wanted the two of them to go back to Linda Patsy's so Mark could tell her what he had learned from Matthew Joseph. He had already briefed Nan, telling her that it looked like the police had a pretty good case against Greg Patsy. She frowned when he told her about the .22 rifle they found hidden on Patsy's boat.

"That doesn't sound very good," was all that she said.

The fishing net was no longer stretched across the yard, but Jesse's bicycle was dropped in practically the same place as yesterday. They could see the girl herself around to the side, throwing a hard ball against the house, catching it on the rebound. The rhythmic *thumpks* must be driving her mother nuts, Mark figured.

"You go on in," Mark told Nan. "I want to talk to Jesse for a minute." His grandmother proceeded up the walk while Mark skirted through the yard. Jesse saw the priest approaching but ignored his presence, continuing her throwing.

"You're pretty good with that," Father Townsend told her.

Silence. *Thumpk*!

"I know a lot of boys who can't catch that good."

Thumpk!

"Do you play on a team?"

Thumpk!

Mark's right arm suddenly shot out, brushing past the top of the young girl's head and intercepting the ball two inches before it reached her mitt. Startled, the girl jumped back from the priest.

"Jesse," he said, squatting down to be nearer her height. "I'd like to talk to you a minute." He tossed her the ball. She caught it and placed it in her mitt, solemnly waiting for what he had to say.

"You're old enough to know that your dad is in serious trouble," he began. "The police arrested him because they think he's killed another man. That's murder, and it's serious trouble. It's more trouble than I know how to handle.''

''Murder is a sin,'' Jesse told him.

''I know that,'' Mark said.

''My daddy didn't sin!'' she shouted at him before dropping the ball and mitt and running around behind the house.

Disgusted with himself, Mark rose to his full height. So much for being a pastoral presence and comforting the afflicted. He could feel Ignatius's frown of disapproval as he rounded the corner towards the front door. So much for his care of children.

''What is your problem, Father?''

Mark sighed heavily. ''Good morning, Sister.''

Teri Carter was standing on the porch, her arms crossed, waiting for him.

''I thought I made it clear yesterday that you should stay out of reservation business.''

''Yes, you did,'' Mark conceded. ''Very clear.''

''Then may I ask, what are you doing back here?''

Mark hesitated before answering her. There is a certain professional respect that members of religious orders are accustomed to giving one another. But for whatever reason, Sister Teri Carter was not cutting Father Mark Townsend any slack. Ordinarily he would feel absolved from the courtesies and respect he usually offered religious women. But he was unsure of himself on the reservation and did not know what claims this nun had here. He tried hard to swallow his anger.

''My grandmother lives in Shelter Bay,'' he explained, ''and Linda cleans for her. They're friends. Nan's concerned for her, so she's come over to visit. And she asked me to come with her. That's the only reason I'm here, I'm not trying to do anything else.''

But the nun was not buying. ''You've been talking with the tribal police.'' She made it sound like an accusation.

''Because Linda asked me if I'd talk to them. She wanted me to try and see what they had on Greg.''

Sister Carter uncrossed her arms and moved away from her position in front of the door.

"I realize you're trying to help, Father, but you're jeopardizing my own work here."

"I'm sorry," said Mark, "but in what way? What kind of work are you doing?"

She reacted to his questions as if they were challenges, taking a step backward, squaring her shoulders and raising her chin.

"I'm doing research on some of the tribal initiation rites of the Coastal Salish," she informed him. "Specifically, a critique of the conflictive values that postmodernism has placed on aboriginal tribal traditions. It's taken me a long time to establish a rapport with these people. Being white, as well as a woman and a religious, has put me at a disadvantage. But I finally have some stature in the community. Your presence can undo that. It's nothing personal, you understand."

In a pig's eye! Father Townsend knew enough about indigenous Northwest cultures to know that anyone with authentic stature in a tribal community would not be talking the way this woman was. Nor would they be as protective of their position as she was. Teri Carter was beginning to sound and look to Mark more and more like another Indian savior.

"Where are you doing your studies, Sister?"

His question caught her by surprise. Self-consciously, she began twisting one of her braids with her fingers.

"What makes you think I'm a student?"

"Your research is pretty esoteric," he told her. "And the way you described it made it sound like you might be doing anthropological studies."

"I'm a doctoral candidate at WSU," she admitted, blushing. "I'm doing research for my thesis."

"Washington State has a good anthropology department," Mark said, trying to establish some sort of rapport with the woman. "Is Dr. Eckstein still teaching there?"

"How do you know Eckstein?" she asked curiously.

"During our training in Spokane. Sam used to teach the Jesuits a summer course in anthropology. And a couple of years later I was assigned to work with the Yup'iks in

Alaska. Before I went I spent a semester studying with Sam Eckstein.''

He could tell from the look on her face that he had said too much. Not only was he intruding on her turf here on the reservation, but he now was also on a first-name basis with one of her professors back at her university. So much for establishing rapport.

"Just do me the favor of staying away from these people," Sister Carter ordered him stonily. "My position here on the reservation is delicate. I don't want you messing it up."

She stormed past him and headed down the walk. Mark watched her back as she headed across the cul-de-sac. Yesterday she had described herself as an adopted member of the tribe. Today she was describing her position as delicate. For some reason she found his presence intimidating, and she was obviously keeping tabs on where he went and who he was talking to. Mark wondered if it was just the fact that he was a priest, or if something more was bothering her. He watched the nun turn the corner at the end of the block before he went into the Patsy house.

Linda and Nan were drinking tea in the living room. The place looked a little tidier than it had yesterday. The TV was still on, but the volume was down and no one was paying it any attention. Mark accepted a cup of tea before he briefly described his visit with the tribal policeman. When he reached the part about finding the .22 hidden in the boat, Greg Patsy's wife began shaking her head furiously.

"That's not right," she insisted, interrupting him. "We don't own a .22." She pointed to a gun rack hanging on the wall down a narrow hallway. "We got two shotguns and a deer rifle, and that's it. Oh, and Jesse's BB gun. If they say they found a .22 on Greg's boat, they're lying."

Mark shrugged. He had no need nor desire to argue. All he was trying to do was tell the woman what the policeman had told him.

Nan set down her cup and moved to the edge of her seat, eager to say something.

"Linda, if you don't own a .22, and the police say they

found one, that means someone could have hidden it on Greg's boat to make him look like the murderer!'' The old woman's eyes were bright with excitement and her voice was filled with enthusiasm. ''That's proof that someone else did it, isn't it, dear?'' she asked her grandson.

Mark gave his grandmother a grin of appreciation. She was so full of energy and life and was trying so hard. He hated to disappoint her.

''Afraid not, Nan,'' he told her, still grinning. ''You see, we'd have to be able to prove that someone else put the gun there. And the problem is, they found Greg's fingerprints on the rifle.''

''He was framed!'' she insisted loudly, trying to rise out of her chair. Her brace slowed her though and she struggled against it. ''Everyone can see that!'' Suddenly she realized she was wrestling with her own chair. Nan meekly settled back down, still refusing to rest against the chair's back. ''At least I can see it,'' she murmured.

''I wish the police could,'' Linda said wistfully.

''Next time you see Greg, ask him about the gun,'' Mark instructed her. ''Ask him why his fingerprints are on it.'' Linda nodded. ''Maybe I could drop Nan off and then go take a look at the boat,'' he continued. ''Just out of curiosity.'' Linda nodded again, a little more vigorously this time.

''It's down at the channel,'' she told Mark, ''with the other fishing boats. The police have signs on it, but you can still stand on the dock to see it. I'd take you there myself, but I want to go to Anacortes to see Greg. I'll ask Jesse to show you where it is.''

They agreed to meet again later in the afternoon, before dinner. Linda would find out what her husband knew about the .22 and Mark would go to look at the boat with Jesse. The police were not allowing anyone to board the gillnetter, but maybe he could see something from the dock. Nan was beaming at Mark as he made plans with Linda Patsy, satisfied with his involvement. She knew she could count on her grandson the priest. Her husband wasn't going to be happy, but she could deal with him later. After fifty-four years with the old goat, Nan knew how to handle his temper tantrums and irascible moods.

Mark dropped his grandmother off back at her house. There was still no sign of GrandSam and Nan promised to call around to some of her husband's friends to try and find out where he was hiding. Mark turned his car around and headed back to the Patsy house to pick up Jesse. The child was waiting for him on the front porch and ran up to the car as soon as he stopped, yanking open the passenger's door and sliding into the front seat.

"Mom says it's okay for me to help you," she announced happily. "She says you're going to help get Daddy out of jail." Her earlier hostility seemed to be forgotten now that the priest was helping. Mark worried about how much her mother had actually said and how much the girl might be projecting. He did not want to disappoint the youngster any more than he already had. But realistically, he doubted there was much he could do to help Greg Patsy.

The Indian's running battle with Dutch Olsen was probably motive enough, and the discovery of the rifle on Greg's boat seemed to tie down the means. The fisherman had had his opportunity to commit the crime when he was setting nets in the cove in front of Pull and Be Damned Road, near where the body was discovered. Although Mark was not about to admit it to the child or her mother, getting Greg Patsy off would require something along the order of a miracle. And the priest already knew he was no miracle worker. Despite what his grandmother thought.

"I said I would go look at your dad's boat," Mark gently tried correcting the young girl. "But I'm not sure that's going to help your dad very much."

Jesse ignored his cautious qualification and directed him down to the waterfront. They parked in a gravel lot next to a fish processing plant. The pungent stink of drying fish slime hung heavy in the air. Scores of seagulls stood perched on roofs and pilings all around the plant, waiting for whatever scraps might eventually come their way. The dock was directly in front of them, with the tribe's fishing boats tied up and bobbing in the channel's swift current.

"You can tell the tide's going out, because the water is moving fast in that direction," Jesse informed the priest with pride, pointing toward the north end of the channel, out toward Padilla Bay. "It slows down before it comes back in." She led him down the sloping ramp towards the boats. The child pointed to a sky blue gillnetter in a slip near the shore. "That's my Uncle Trevor's boat. He can't fish now because he's in Seeowyn. But this summer he'll let me go out with him maybe."

"Where's Seeowyn?" Mark wanted to know.

She gave him a look of exasperation. "It's not a place," she said, rolling her eyes. "Seeowyn is up at the smoke house. It's when they tell you about the old ways. Uncle Trevor is right over there." Jesse pointed back up the hill behind them. The fish plant blocked the view, but Mark knew the Swinomish had a large lodge in a grove of trees back off of Reservation Road. Whatever she was talking about must be happening up there.

Figuring out which was Greg Patsy's boat was not difficult. There was a narrow continuous strip of yellow plastic tape stretched from bow to stern, marked CRIME SCENE. DO NOT CROSS. A hand-lettered cardboard sign was also taped to the boat's wooden side: KEEP OFF. There was very little for Mark to inspect from the dock. Patsy's boat was neatly painted a dark gray with green trim. Three eagle feathers and an orca were painted on the bow, near the boat's registration numbers. The thirty-foot boat was rigged for fishing as a stern picker, with the nylon fish net carefully wrapped around a huge reel anchored in the stern. A fish box was set into the floor between the reel and the small cabin. A door opened into the cabin from the stern end. The wheel and controls were located on the starboard side. Nothing was left on the deck that could impede quick movement or that could get in the way of a person moving back and forth between the boat's controls and the reel of nylon net as it was being dropped or rolled back on board. The boat was tidy and amazingly clean, considering the use it got.

Mark was trying to spot all the places where someone could hide a .22 rifle. He was leaning over the dock, looking into the stern when he heard Jesse scrambling over the boat's side.

"Jesse, you better get back off of there," he urged. "The police don't want anyone on board."

She gave him a defiant look. "It's our boat."

A loud voice cried out, "Hey, mister! Hey, you! What are you doing down there?" A young Indian man standing on the shore above the dock was glaring down at Mark. "That boat's off limits," he called down.

Mark nodded and waved, turning back to the girl climbing over the front of her dad's boat. "Come on, Jesse, get out of there!"

"Just a minute," she answered curtly.

"Get away from there!" the voice above them shouted. The man was running down the dock's ramp and two other men were now hurrying across the gravel from the processing plant.

"Jesse," implored Mark, "get out now!"

"Hold your horses." She was back in the stern now, looking behind the reel near the roller horns. Mark's attention was divided between her and the young man running rapidly along the dock towards them. The other two men were racing down the ramp in close pursuit. From the look of things, it appeared Father Townsend and the girl were caught red-handed.

"Good afternoon," Mark called back amiably, trying hard to sound innocent.

"Your kid's trespassing!" the young Indian said gruffly. "The police don't want no one on that boat." He was dressed in blue jeans so faded they were almost white and a gray sweatshirt with the sleeves cut off at the elbows. His long, glossy black hair was pulled back into a ponytail.

"Ah, bite me!" Jesse's high voice came from over the stern, where her small body was leaning over the boat's end. She looked like she was about to fall in.

"Jesse!"

The Indian's eyes left Mark Townsend and spotted the figure at the end of the boat.

"Is that Greg's kid?" he asked. He got his answer when

the girl's head popped back up above the stern and looked at him.

"Bug off, Eddie," she commanded the young man.

The two others who had hurried down the dock ran up behind the man called Eddie. One was a stocky white man with a thick red beard, wearing a flannel shirt stretched tight across a barrel chest and beer gut. The other was an Oriental with close-cropped gray hair, wearing slacks, a white shirt, and a pale green tie.

"What's going on?" the white man asked.

Mark began to reply, but the man Jesse called Eddie cut him off. "Not sure. That there's Greg Patsy's kid," he said, pointing to Jesse. "I don't know who this guy is."

"I'm Father Mark Townsend," he said, extending his hand. "We were just checking Greg's boat, seeing if everything is all right." Jesse scrambled back onto the dock, apparently finished with her inspection.

"Hey, Eddie," she greeted the Indian familiarly. "That's Eddie Walking Boy," she informed the priest.

"This is a private dock, Father." It was the white man's voice again. "And not a very safe place to be bringing a little boy."

"My daddy owns this boat," Jesse told the man defiantly. "Besides, I'm not a boy."

"Linda Patsy did ask me to check on the boat," Mark confirmed. "Jesse came along to show me which one it was."

"I think everything is okay," the Oriental assured his partner. He turned back to Mark and offered a slight bow with his handshake. "I am Li Kuhn Suu," he said, smiling, "with SinCan Fisheries. And this is my associate, Mr. Colin Petty. We heard Eddie yelling and thought there perhaps was trouble. You see, we help to manage the docks for the Swinomish tribe."

Mark offered a smile in return. "Perhaps I should have checked at the office before coming down here. I apologize."

Suu waved aside his apology. "Not necessary," he replied. "But because of Greg Patsy's unfortunate problems we are watching things a little closer."

"We get a lot of rubberneckers coming over from the town side," his partner added, "and the Indians don't want 'em climbing around their boats. We thought you were a tourist."

"That's right," Eddie Walking Boy chimed in. "Sorry, Father."

The two men from SinCan excused themselves and headed back to their fish plant. Eddie stayed with Mark and Jesse on the dock.

"I heard they might be taking Greg to Seattle," he said. "Is that true?"

Mark told him he had heard something similar.

"They should keep him up here," the young man asserted, "near his own people. That isn't right to take him away. Not until they prove he did it."

While Jesse explored the other boats along the dock, Eddie Walking Boy and Father Townsend strolled behind her. The Indian said he did not own a fishing boat himself, but he told Mark that he helped out when any of the other fishermen needed a hand. Greg hired him occasionally. And when the fish were running he worked for SinCan, offloading and weighing the fish as they pulled up to the dock. Eddie told the priest that he was saving his money to buy his own gillnetter. All he could afford right now was a rowboat. He was not around when they found the rifle, he said, but he heard it was discovered in Greg's storage box, wrapped in a plastic garbage sack.

"Come on, I'll show you."

Eddie walked Mark back to Greg's boat and pointed to a wooden box built beneath a narrow seat on the starboard side behind the wheel.

"There's no lock on that, is there?" Mark observed.

"We don't usually lock things," Eddied informed the priest. "Not on the rez."

"Linda told me that they don't own a .22," said Mark. "She thinks someone else put it on Greg's boat."

A look of doubt flashed across Eddie's face.

"Maybe," he cautiously allowed. "She would know, I

guess. But I heard that Greg's fingerprints were all over it.''

Jesse scowled at the young Indian. Mark expected her to let loose on him, but she held her tongue.

''That needs some explaining,'' Mark admitted. ''Linda's asking him about it right now.''

''If there's any way I could help him, I sure would. Patsys are good folk.''

Mark thanked the man for his help and, with Jesse at his side, started back up the dock. When they reached the car, Mark took one final look at the boats swaying gently in the Swinomish Channel's outgoing current. He also watched out of the corner of his eye as Eddie Walking Boy stepped carefully over the yellow police tape onto Greg Patsy's boat.

EIGHT

Mark was already back at his grandparents' when Linda Patsy returned from visiting her husband in the Anacortes jail. She called Mark as soon as she got home. Her voice was thick with worry and she asked him to come over for a visit. He was hesitant. Although Nan had managed to track down where he was, GrandSam was still not home. According to a friend of a friend, he was staying out at Dutch Olsen's hunting shack with Larry Robbins. The two men were going through Dutch's things, Nan was told, looking for clues.

"Old fool," his grandmother had snorted. She told her grandson to go visit Linda Patsy and not to worry about her.

Greg Patsy had admitted to his wife that he had wrapped the .22 in the plastic bag and hidden it in the tool box beneath the boat seat. He claimed that he had found the rifle lying in the bottom of his boat the morning after Olsen's body was discovered lying on the beach at Pull and Be Damned. The bad news: there was no way Greg could prove it.

"He didn't know whose gun it was," Linda tearfully recounted to Father Townsend. "So he was going to hold onto it and see if someone came looking for it. If no one claimed the rifle, he said he was going to keep it. That's why he wrapped it up and hid it in the seat.''

It sounded plausible, but was it truthful? The priest had no way of knowing. Greg Patsy's gillnetter was at the end of the dock. He supposed another boat could have glided by, close enough for someone to slip the rifle on board. But why bother? Why not just dump the .22 into the deep waters of Puget Sound where it would never be found?

"How many people knew Greg and Dutch Olsen didn't get along?" Father Townsend asked Linda.

"On which side of the channel?" she replied, sounding a little incredulous. "On the town side, I'd say everyone but the tourists. Over here, everyone and their dogs. They were always on each other about fishing rights," Linda added. "LaConner's pretty small. Everyone knew."

But she could think of no one, besides Dutch Olsen, who did not get along with her husband. Greg Patsy was a member of the Tribal Senate and respected by his people. He helped coach football at the LaConner High School, and was part of an active antidrug panel that regularly sponsored speakers and events at both the high school and grade school. Linda could think of no one who would want to frame her husband for a murder.

By the time they were finished talking it was after six and Jesse was impatiently hanging onto her mother's arm. They were due at the smoke house, Linda explained apologetically. Greg's brother, Trevor, was nearing the end of his initiation into Seeowyn, and tribal members were gathering for dances. Even though they could not speak to him it was important that the family be there for him. Mark indicated he understood and prepared to leave.

"Can't he come too?" Jesse begged her mother.

"Would you like to, Father? Have you seen our smoke house?"

Mark knew where it was, but he had never presumed to go near it.

"There's good food," Jesse promised. "You'd like it. Come with us."

Mark suddenly realized how hungry he was. His grandmother would have already eaten. He knew it would be a rare opportunity to experience one of the Salish cultural traditions.

"You're sure it'd be all right? I wouldn't be intruding?"

Linda reassured him. Guests of tribal members were welcome, she said, as long as the ceremonies did not include any of the secret activities of Seeowyn. She reminded him it would give him a chance to meet some other people from the reservation.

A steady rain was falling, so they drove the few short blocks from the cul-de-sac to the smoke house. As they turned off the pavement onto the muddy road leading to the lodge, they could see sparks rising in the darkness above the roof. A pale shaft of light lit the entranceway into the long cedar shake building. Mark parked his car at the end of a long line of cars and pickups stretched in front of the building and they hurried inside, past two tall totems on either side of the doorway. These were welcoming totems and, by the expansive spread of outstretched wings, Mark recognized the eagles that were carved at the tops of each one. The heavy wood doors leading inside the lodge also looked handcarved.

Three fires, crackling loudly, burned on the dirt floor in the center of the long hall. The room was hot and smokey, filled with the scent of burning wood. Staggered tiers of seating ran along both sides of the smoke house, separated by the fires burning in the middle . Four huge wooden support columns on either side supported the beams of the high ceiling. Each column was carved with a figure wrapped around the top half. The lodge looked nearly empty. Mark estimated there might be two or three hundred people inside the room that looked like it could hold nearly a thousand. Those present were arranged in small groups on the stepped platforms, with most gathered on the rows nearest to the floor. A few people glanced up when the three of them came in, but when they recognized Linda Patsy they quickly looked away. A young Swinomish man, his face painted black, approached Mark. He was carrying a short wooden staff. He was about to speak when Linda stepped in front of the priest.

"It's okay, Harold, he's with me. This is Father Town-send."

The Indian looked past Linda and studied Mark for a few more moments before he nodded and turned aside.

"Not too many whites come to these dances," Linda spoke quietly. "The floor manager was going to ask you to sit up near the top. But there's too much smoke up there. We'll stay down below."

She turned to the right of the doorway and began circling around to the other side of the fires. "There's LuAnn, Trevor's wife," said Linda, pointing to a woman sitting on the other side. "Let's sit over there."

Mark followed behind Greg Patsy's wife as she made her way around the perimeter of the dirt floor. The three fires crackled loudly in the middle of the room and he could feel the heat of their blaze against his side. He noticed people stopped speaking when they spotted Linda passing by them. A few turned their heads. Either she did not notice or was choosing to ignore the cool reception they were receiving, but in either case, Mark was seeing a brave new side of the attractive young woman. They reached the woman Linda had pointed out and climbed up four steps of seats to reach her.

LuAnn looked like she had her hands full trying to corral three young children; one at her breast and two at either side. She smiled up at Mark when Linda introduced him as Father Townsend, but made no effort to cover up her exposed breast.

"Where's Trevor?" Linda asked, looking around.

"He's not out yet," LuAnn answered. Her voice was high and soft.

Linda leaned towards Father Townsend and pointed at a figure across the room, beyond the third fire. "That's one of the initiates," she told him. "We call them the babies."

Mark peered through the smokey haze at a covered figure sitting in the midst of a group of people. The person—man or woman, he could not tell—was holding a long pole, decorated with dark colored scarves, shaking it slightly with both hands. Mark thought he could hear a small rattling sound. The figure's head was hidden beneath a thick hood made of braided rope. A cloak, made from the same material, was draped over the shoulders.

"What makes the rattling sound?" he asked Linda.

"Deer hooves," she told him. "They're tied near the top of the pole. He's dressed that way for protection. Babies are very vulnerable to the spirit world, so they cover themselves."

She turned back to the nursing mother and the two of them quietly began exchanging the day's news. Jesse had already scampered off to a group of her friends, leaving Mark with time to sit quietly and settle into the strange, new surroundings. His immediate impression was of sitting in a huge family room, and he realized that was probably the closest way of describing the space. Undoubtedly, in ages past, much of Swinomish family life took place in a smoke house similar to this one. The tiers rising up on each side would have defined the space for clans and individual families in the tribe. And he supposed the arena in the middle, with the three fires, would have been common ground for all. He did not understand the significance of the carvings on the eight upright pillars supporting the massive roof, but he guessed they had to be mythic figures relating to the history of the tribe.

As his eyes grew accustomed to the dim light of the smoke house, he began searching the faces in the crowd for anyone he might know. About a third of them had painted their faces. Most were black, although a few had applied a dark red. He thought he recognized the young tribal policeman, Matthew Joseph, in the middle of a knot of people across the room. And there was no mistaking one pale white face, sitting on the edge of a group of women, glaring across the room at him. Too late, Mark should have realized Sister Carter would be there, and that his own presence would be anything but welcome. He offered her a brief wave that was not returned. But if looks could kill. . . .

Her visiting done, Linda tapped Father Townsend's knee, drawing his attention away from Sister Carter's brooding face and threatening looks.

"You hungry, Father?"

Ravenous, he realized. They got up from their place and circled the fires to a doorway at the opposite end. They passed through a narrow hallway into another large room that served as the kitchen and dining area. Strong smells of cooking meat and frybread hung heavy in the air. A much larger crowd of people were in here, hanging around the food. Linda led him quickly to a buffet line, where they began heaping paper plates with salmon, potatoes, salad, and frybread.

Voices were louder in this room as the people competed with the noisy scrapes and clatters of cooking pots and water splashing into wash tubs. The mood felt less formal in here too, as friends and family members laughed out loud and called greetings to one another. Those in the immediate vicinity around Mark and Linda fell quiet as the two of them made their way down the food line. Linda acted as if nothing was wrong as she introduced him to tribal members. They nodded or spoke a brief greeting, but there was none of the familiar banter taking place in other parts of the room. Greg Patsy's arrest shamed the tribe, and members of his family were being forced to take the brunt of the people's embarrassment.

"How many days does this initiation go on?" asked Mark, trying to distract Linda from the ostracizing silence and looks.

"Days?" Linda popped a piece of frybread into her mouth, "try months. Seeowyn starts in October and goes until April." She pointed to a smaller doorway across the room. "Back there is where the babies live. Trevor moved in there six weeks ago."

Those who are learning the old ways have to isolate themselves from the influences and distractions of the modern world, she explained to Mark. If they have jobs they have to take time off, find someone else to work for them or quit. They arrange for others to pay their bills and to do any other chores that would involve contact with the outside world. Once they enter Seeowyn, they return to life as it was lived before the whites showed up with all their supposed improvements. Each baby is assisted by a babysitter who lives with him. Or her, explained Linda. Women participate in Seeowyn, too. They are each assigned to a small curtained cubicle where they sleep and store the few possessions they bring with them. At night, the babysitters stretch out and sleep at their initiate's feet, partially to be there in case they need anything, and partially to protect them from spirits. Every precaution is taken to protect not only them but those who come in contact with them. For that reason, no one but the babysitters and those conducting the ceremonies are allowed to speak with them. And whenever the babies are in the presence of others, they cover their faces.

"You'll see when they come out later," Linda predicted.

By the time they returned to the main room in the lodge, another two hundred or more people had arrived. The room was quickly filling up. Some were still moving around, trying to visit, but most had already found places to sit on the tiers where they watched the fires and waited expectantly. As they were making their way back to their seats, Mark spotted Matthew Joseph as the policeman moved through a crowd, and he was about to try to catch up with him when he felt a hand grab his left elbow. The grip was strong and firm. He turned to find Eddie Walking Boy grinning at him.

"I keep seeing you everywhere, Father. What are you doing here?" he asked amiably enough.

"Linda Patsy brought me," Mark replied. "She's teaching me a little about Seeowyn."

Eddie nodded appreciatively. "Not too long back," he said, "the Catholic Church wasn't too keen on Seeowyn. I remember when I was a kid, a sister told us this was devil worship. Scared the hell out of me."

"Hopefully we're all a little more enlightened these days," the priest replied, smiling.

"Yeah," Eddie agreed. "Our ways are different, but that doesn't make them wrong, does it?"

"Walking Boy sounds more Plains than Coastal Salish," Father Townsend observed. "Are you from here originally?"

"Yep! Born and bred. But you're right about the name being Plains. My daddy was Blackfeet. Mom's Swinomish."

"And you're a Catholic?"

"Every day but Sunday, Father." The fire's twinkle was reflected in the young man's eye. "That's my day of rest."

Mark smiled. It was a slightly new twist on an old joke. "Are there a lot of Catholics on the reservation?"

"Yeah, I guess so," Eddie told the priest. "We got a little mission church not too far from here, and a priest who comes to do Mass for us. There's maybe a hundred, a hundred and fifty on the rez."

"I met Sister Carter," Mark informed him. "Does she work over at the church, too?"

"Sister Wannabe?" Eddie snorted. "Not hardly. She's just here to study us. I didn't even know she was a nun until someone told me. About all she does is go around and ask people a lot of questions."

"She told me she's studying anthropology over at Washington State," Mark said.

"I heard," replied Eddie. "But she's beginning to hose a few people off. I heard she told a couple of high school kids that they should quit going to school because they were being ruined by white man's knowledge. What kind of nun would tell kids stuff like that?"

Mark did not know.

"People are saying you're trying to help Greg Patsy," said Eddie, studying the Jesuit's face. "Is that true?"

Mark gave a shrug. "I guess so. It's more like I'm trying to help Linda get a handle on what's happening."

Eddie turned and watched the people as they continued milling throughout the smoke house. "When they arrested Greg, a lot of us were pretty sure he did it. He never liked that white guy, Dutch. But something like this affects the whole tribe. So that means if Greg done something bad, then the tribe shares in it. That's a hard thing for us to accept." He turned back towards Father Townsend, but kept his eyes averted from looking into the priest's face. "I think if you could do something, most everyone would be willing to help. If there was something I could do to help, I would.''

''Thank you, Eddie, I appreciate hearing that. I'm not sure what more I can do, but I'll keep your offer in mind.''

There was a sudden shrill and loud cry from the other end of the hall. A young Indian woman was crying out from her seat near the floor of the smoke house. Her face was painted black and her hair was covered by a red scarf tied tightly in back of her head. Half a dozen men holding drums moved in a circle around the young woman and began pounding a steady beat.

''The warm-ups are starting,'' Eddie explained to the priest. ''I'd better go find my place.''

The two men separated, each heading in a different direction. Mark was still trying to spot Matthew Joseph, but the policeman had disappeared. The smoke house was nearly filled with Indians and the priest decided he had better rejoin Linda Patsy. As he began threading his way back towards her, the young woman who was keening stood up from her seat and began singing. The sound of the drums rose louder as the men accompanied the singer. She extended her arms in front of her and was jumping in short hops on the dirt floor. The smoke house was filled with sounds of her voice and the drums. Mark ordinarily felt quite comfortable moving through large crowds of people, but in this place he realized his presence was attracting a lot of questioning looks as tribal members tried to figure out who the white stranger was. As he made his way back around the dirt floor, he recognized that those who already knew him were briefing those who did not. And before the night was through, most of the tribe would know there was a priest in the area, and that he was there for the Patsy family. What he did not know was if most of the people would approve or not. Without the tribe's approval, Mark's presence would be unwelcome and his efforts to help, ineffective.

Father Townsend found Linda and her sister-in-law just about where he had left them, although they had shifted to a level about three rows higher, allowing some of the elders to have their places lower to the ground. The

woman's song ended as Mark settled next to his host, but
in another part of the room a young man was beginning
to keen, and eight or nine drummers encircled him, picking up a new rhythm with their drums. He stood and began
his song in a manner similar to the woman's. The drums
sounded like rolling thunder in the lodge. Three more of
the cloaked babies entered the room from the far door.
Each was being led by someone holding onto them as they
made their way around the floor to join family groups.
One of the figures made his way towards them, and
LuAnn moved closer to Linda as her husband and the man
who served as his babysitter climbed the steps to join
them. He carried a staff, like the others, and Mark could
hear the rattle. Tied near the top were about two dozen
small black hooves. The rattle was actually from the clicking of the hoofs as Trevor shook his staff. No one attempted to speak to the man, and he kept his head bent
down, withdrawn into his own world. But his presence in
their midst was a corporeal witness to the mystery and
sacredness of the rituals taking place in front of them.

As a priest, Mark Townsend was accustomed to litur-
gical ceremonies that incoporated similar objects and actions, including fire, music and movement, prayer, and
vested celebrants. The ceremonies in the Swinomish
smoke house, although unfamiliar to him, were strangely
comforting in their sacredness. And as the drumming,
singing, and dancing continued into the night, the Jesuit
found himself drawn into praying with and for the participants.

The dances ended shortly after eleven, and the people
quickly began filing out of the smoke house. By then,
Father Townsend's eyes were watering from the thick
smoke, but he noticed he was not the only one. His clothes
were thick with the smell, too. Nan was sure to notice the
odor in her house, Mark had no doubt. LuAnn's three
small children were sleeping, and he waited patiently as
Linda helped the woman awaken her children and gather
up their belongings.

Outside, the rain had diminished to a cold drizzle and
people were wasting no time getting to their cars and

trucks. As Mark led Linda and Jesse out the carved wooden doors of the smoke house and towards his car, a short figure burst towards them from behind one of the totems at the entrance. Sister Teri Carter was wrapped in an Indian shawl, with a deep scowl etched across her face.

As she was about to confront them, there was a slight tug on Mark's sleeve. Turning away from the nun for the moment, he found one of the young Indian men drummers who had led off the warmups. He was assisting an old woman, stooped and frail looking. Her steel-gray hair hung down in two long braids and she held a well-worn walking staff in her right hand. Her brown, wrinkled face turned upwards until she was looking at Mark's chest. With her left hand still on his sleeve, she murmured something that was lost in the night's sounds.

"Grandmother thanks you for coming tonight," the young man said earnestly.

Sister Carter had braked abruptly and taken a respectful step backwards, giving the priest room to turn towards the old woman.

"It was an honor to come," Mark replied.

The old woman dipped her head in acknowledgement and spoke again. Mark listened carefully, trying to understand her words. The young man also bent his head towards her, listening as she murmured.

"She remembers when the priests used to scold us for having Seeowyn. Her heart is very glad to have you here with us."

Father Townsend smiled an acknowledgement. The grandmother was already speaking again and he had no time for a reply.

The young man listened respectfully as she spoke. Her words were still indistinguishable and Mark realized she was speaking in her own tongue. She spoke for some time while Mark, Linda, Jesse, Sister Carter, and a few others stood quietly and patiently. When she was finally done, the old woman took a deep breath and looked back down at the ground while her grandson translated.

"Our people are sad for what has happened on our land," the young man began. "The death of the man from town is not a thing our people would have wanted. We are taught to be respectful of everything God gives us: the land, the salmon, and each other. Whoever killed that man does not honor our Salish ways."

The young man paused to take a breath. He appeared, for the first time, to be aware of the small knot of people who had gathered around them and he looked embarrassed. "Grandmother says that she knows that priests need prayers, too. Tonight, she will say hers for you."

"Please thank her . . ." Mark began. But the young man was shaking his head.

"There's more. She also wants you to know that the water that flows past here comes from places far away. Like the salmon, it moves wherever it wants to. Grandmother says, 'What the water brings us, it also takes away in time.' You should know that." He paused a moment to think, then concluded, "That's all."

"Thank you," Mark quietly said to the old woman.

She lifted her head and stared determinedly into the priest's face, then turned and started hobbling back into the smoke house, her grandson at her side. The people parted to let her pass. Mark watched until she was inside the building, then turned to face Sister Carter. The nun was nowhere in sight. Only Linda and Jesse Patsy were standing beside him, waiting.

"You're getting wet," Father Townsend told the two of them. "Let's get you home."

NINE

He was drowning. The Rainbow Bridge was breaking apart and Father Townsend tumbled helplessly into the swift water of the channel while wearing his vestments for Mass; a long, white alb, a heavy purple chasuble, and an inexplicably long green silk stole. The stole must have been thirty feet long; and it kept swirling through the water, twining itself around his body, pulling him down. Wrapping itself tightly around his neck, the stole was cutting off his breath, while just above him, thousands of bright red salmon kept swimming past, turning at the last moment to dart perilously close to his head. They were purposely dodging and trying to hit him. Mark attempted to raise his arms to ward them off, but the green stole pulled his arms tight against his body. As he sank deeper through murky depths he could the hear the blood pounding in his ears until he was afraid his eardrums were going to burst with the pressure. His feet hit something solid and slowly he moved his head through the thick water to look down. He was standing on the back of a body that was slowly sinking with him. The long green stole began winding down and around, binding his feet tightly to the body. Mark tried reaching down to free himself. It was imperative that he roll the body over to see who it was.

But the stole prevented him. A salmon bumped him hard in the small of his back, and then another. He felt a small, tight pain and realized he was being bitten by the fish. Looking back up, he saw a thin red tendril of blood swirling through the water above his head. More and more salmon began hitting against him, taking small bites as the pounding in his ears grew louder. Desperate for air, Mark began thrashing in his vestments, trying to unwrap himself from their heaviness and the stole that was choking him.

The bedsheet was tangled around his body and he was face down into his pillow. His room was filled with bright sunlight and his grandmother was knocking on the door.

"Mark! Mark, dear! Wake up! You have a phone call."

He sputtered that he was awake and began extricating himself from the sheets.

The kitchen phone was lying on the counter. His grandmother gave him a smile as he stumbled towards it, silently offering him a cup of coffee. He shook his head.

"Hello?" he mumbled. He was having trouble focusing his eyes, but the clock on the stove looked suspiciously like nine-thirty.

"Mark? Is that you?"

"Yes. Hello?"

"Mark, it's Ray. Ray Phillips. I didn't wake you up, did I?"

Father Ray Phillips was chancellor for the archdiocese of Seattle. At one time he had wanted to be a Jesuit, but left the novitiate to begin studies for the diocesan priesthood. Although Father Townsend's parish, St. Joseph's, was Jesuit-run, the priests who worked there were still answerable to the archdiocese. The two of them were friends, but Mark knew instinctively this was not a social call.

"Of course not," he lied.

"Right." Phillips was not buying. "I'm sorry to bother you. Your secretary gave me this number."

"I'm visiting my grandparents for a few days," Mark explained.

"I see." There was a long silence.

"Is there something wrong?"

"Have you bumped into a Sister Carter up there?"

Mark groaned out loud and signalled to his grandmother that he would take that cup of coffee now.

"She called the archbishop bright and early this morning and he routed the call to me. She's complaining that you're intruding in tribal business and upsetting the people. She wants us to order you back to Seattle." Father Phillips paused to let the weight of what he was saying sink in with his friend. "What's going on?"

Mark briefly tried to explain to the chancellor about the murder and the arrest of Greg Patsy.

"Yeah, but what does that have to do with you?" wondered Father Phillips.

The dead man was a friend of his grandfather's and the accused was the husband of his grandmother's cleaning woman. Mark was still feeling the effects of his dream; it felt like the stole was wrapping itself even tighter around his legs. He checked his feet just to be sure. He was trying to provide the chancellor with a clear explanation but it sounded too confused, even to himself.

"Things are just kind of a mess right now," he finished lamely.

"Sister Carter is assigned as a pastoral assistant to St. Paul's Mission there." Father Phillips's tone sounded slightly accusing.

"Honestly, Ray, I'm trying not to do anything to get in her way."

The chancellor pressed on. "She says that your involvement with the Patsy family is undermining her own position on the reservation."

"Oh, for Christ's sake!" Mark slammed his cup down on the counter, startling his grandmother. She gave him a look of alarm before hurrying out of the room.

"Listen, Ray. Teri Carter has been in my face ever since she found out I was up here. I haven't done anything connected with the mission or her work. Besides, from what I hear, she doesn't do that much anyway."

It was a cheap shot and Mark regretted it as soon as the words left his mouth. On the other end of the line, Ray Phillips remained silent.

"I'm about ready to leave," Mark told him, trying to sound conciliatory. "There's just some unfinished business with my grandparents, then I'm out of here."

The chancellor cleared his throat. "Don't get me wrong, Mark. I'm not calling because I think you're doing anything bad. It's just that Sister Carter is making a big deal about you being up there and the archbishop asked me to check it out. You're not in any type of trouble or anything—not with us. But you do have a nun who considers you one of her least favorite priests."

"I can live with that," Mark said wryly. "She's not on my list for canonization, either."

"We just don't want any Holy Wars started in La-Conner, that's all."

The chancellor's phone call was actually pretty reasonable, Father Townsend decided. A complaint had been made and it was Phillips's responsibility to check it out. He wasn't scolding or threatening Mark, he was merely trying to get his side of the story. No doubt, to report back to the archbishop.

"I think everything's going to work out," Mark tried to assure him. "I'll head back to the parish tomorrow."

"Give me a call next week," Ray Phillips said. "Let's get together for dinner or something."

"That'd be great," Mark agreed. He thanked him for the call and hung up the phone.

His grandmother was sitting on the living room couch with a magazine upside down in her lap. She looked nervously up at her grandson.

"You're not in trouble, are you?" Her dear old face was wrinkled with concern.

Mark dropped down next to her. "No, Nan. They just wanted to know what's going on up here."

"Because the last thing your grandfather and I would want is to get you in trouble." The stress of the last three days was showing in her face.

"I'm not in trouble," he told her again. "Don't worry."

His reassurances appeared to do the trick.

"How was your visit with Linda?" she asked.

Mark told her about going to the smoke house and watching the dances. He described the ceremonies he'd witnessed, purposely neglecting to mention what Linda had told him about the rifle. He did tell her about meeting the old Indian woman afterwards, and what she said about the water. As he repeated her strange message, *What the water brings us, it also takes away,* he remembered his nightmare and suspected the two were somehow related. An uncomfortable feeling came over him. He wanted to change the subject,

"What about GrandSam, any sign of him?"

Nan shook her head. "No. I thought he would have come home by now. But the funeral for Dutch is tomorrow, so I'm sure Sam will be back for that." Her voice sounded anything but sure, and the look on her face was less than confident.

"Maybe I should go get him," Mark suggested.

Hope sparked in her eyes. "Would you? I know Larry Robbins is out there with him, but that man doesn't have any more sense than your grandfather."

Mark felt he was partially responsible for his grandfather's departure. He knew GrandSam was angry because they had gone to visit Linda Patsy. Comfort to the enemy, he would call it. Never mind that Greg Patsy was innocent until proven guilty. Never mind that his wife had nothing to do with the murder anyway. And Mark knew his grandfather's prejudices well enough to realize Greg Patsy's Indian heritage already counted as two strikes against him. As far as GrandSam was concerned, his wife and grandson were consorting with his friend's murderer.

He patted his grandmother's arm and promised he would go after he cleaned up. Not until he was in the shower did Mark begin to question how he would get to Dutch Olsen's shack without a boat.

After a quick breakfast he called Eddie Walking Boy, hoping the young Indian would know someone who might have a boat small enough to get through Hole in the Wall and into the Skagit River. He was in luck. Eddie was at home and not only did he know of such a boat, but he was able to borrow it anytime he wanted. They agreed to meet at the dock in half an hour.

Nan insisted on packing what she kept calling a light snack: ham sandwiches, potato chips, cookies, apples, six candy bars, and a Thermos of coffee. By the time she was finished and Mark made it to the dock, he was fifteen minutes late. But there was no sign of Eddie yet. Although the sky was overcast, there were breaks in the clouds and shafts of thin sunlight were breaking through. A lone seal was bobbing in the middle of the channel and seagulls were diving and swooping overhead. Mark walked to the end of the dock and found an overturned wooden crate to sit on. A light breeze blew down the channel and wildly colored wind socks hanging off piers on the town side fluttered and danced. LaConner was decked out for the Tulip Festival and everywhere you looked there were bright colors to draw the tourists closer. The festivities on the town side made the reservation look all the more drab.

Breathing in deep draughts of the salty air, Father Townsend listened to the raucous cries of the gulls. He realized this was one of the few moments on this trip when he felt at peace. And he started reexamining the last couple of days—double-checking his memory—which confirmed what he was feeling; there was very little to any of the events that felt good or right. Alarms were tripping inside him. His Jesuit training taught him to monitor for movements of good and evil in his life, testing to discover which had the upper hand. As he contemplated the last two days, Mark was overcome with a strong sense of the evil around him. There were too many relationships that felt out of whack. His grandparents' bickering, Grand-Sam's anger and his willingness to condemn Greg Patsy for the death of his friend, Sister Carter's animosity towards him, and the tribe's silent treatment of Linda Patsy. The strain was causing a lot of people a lot of pain and sorrow. What this community needs is a spiritual chiropractor, Mark decided as he got to his feet. Or a good exorcism.

A long, sleek cabin cruiser was plowing slowly up the channel, its wide wake spreading across the water toward both shores. Mark could hear the waves breaking under the pilings beneath the shops built out over the water on the other side of the channel. As it drew nearer, the boat slowed perceptibly and began turning toward Mark's dock. The bridge was empty, so whoever was steering was doing so from inside the cabin. When it drew closer, Mark spotted the boat's name painted in dark green high up on the bow: *SinCan V.* At just about the same time, the port-side door slid back and the burly red-bearded man he had met on the dock the day before stepped out. He hurried to the bow and quickly secured a rope to one of the chrome cleats on the deck. Looping it under the railing, he leaned forward and waved to Mark.

"Give a hand, will you?" The man's voice was just able to rise above the sound of the boat's engine. Mark nodded back and moved closer to the end of the dock.

The boat's skipper continued throttling back until the *SinCan* was barely edging forward. When they were close enough, the man on the forward deck tossed his line to Mark. The priest grabbed for it but missed and the bright yellow coils splashed into the channel. He gave Father Townsend a look of disgust as he hauled the line up, coiled it around his arms, and tossed it again. Mark caught it this time and pulled against the huge weight of the boat.

"Don't try pulling it," the man warned, "just hold on and we'll drift into you."

With that the engine sounds changed as the skipper shifted gears. Slowly the stern of the boat began drifting inward, toward the dock. The priest started taking up the rope's slack in the process. Meanwhile, the man on board had hurried to the stern and stood waiting with another line in hand. When the boat was close enough, he jumped down and quickly began wrapping his line around one of the dock's cleats. As soon as he was finished he hurried forward and grabbed the line Mark was limply holding.

"Thanks," he said curtly.

"Good morning, Father!" A voice called from the boat's deck, now about four feet directly above Mark's head. He looked up and recognized the Asian who had also confronted him in front of Patsy's boat. "How fortunate that you were here to help us."

Mark smiled up at him. "I'm afraid I wasn't all that helpful." He gestured back at the man busily securing the *SinCan* to the dock.

"Don't worry about it," the Asian assured him. "Colin is a perfectionist when it comes to docking boats. No one does it right, according to him. I used to try and help, but he only untied everything I did and started over. So now I just let him do it."

"You have a beautiful boat," Mark told him.

"Thank you," the skipper replied. "But unfortunately it does not belong to me. The company, SinCan Fisheries, is the owner. Would you like to come aboard and look around?" Colin Petty shot his partner a dirty look, but kept on tying his knots, saying nothing. "We have some time, if you would like to look around, Father."

"I'd like to. Thanks."

"Colin," the skipper said, "help Father on board."

Petty grabbed a hold of the stern line and yanked hard, pulling the boat closer to the dock. "Get on," he gruffly ordered Mark.

The priest scrambled from the dock onto the boat's swim deck, then up the stairs to the main deck. His host stood waiting for him.

"Let me reintroduce myself," he said to Father Townsend, extending a hand. "Li Kuhn Suu." He gave the priest a slight bow, which Mark self-consciously returned.

"Do you live around here, Mr. Suu?"

"Please, it's Li. No, not in LaConner. I'm originally from Myanmar, although I presently live in Hong Kong."

"Myanmar?"

"You would probably know it by the old name, Burma." With a polite wave of his hand he invited the priest to move into the cabin. "But very soon I'm afraid I will have to move once more—probably to Vancouver."

"Now that Hong Kong is reverting to mainland China," Mark guessed. China's annexation of Hong Kong was causing a large exodus of Hong Kong residents to Vancouver, British Columbia.

"Precisely," his host replied. "So many citizens and industries are leaving there. It's tragic."

They were inside an expansive room with teak walls and plush white carpet. A tan leather couch stretched along one side of the cabin, with three brown swivel chairs arranged around it. In the center, a mahogany coffee table held a bowl of fresh-cut tulips. A silver bowl of mints sat on one side and on the other, a crystal ashtray and a book of matches. The book's silver cover was embossed with the boat's name, *SinCan V*. At the end of the room were two sets of steps, the ones heading up led to a galley and dining area. His host led the way forward of the galley and stopped behind a high cushioned chair. In front of them was a console with the boat's wheel and controls. Li Kuhn Suu spread his arms expansively over the chrome dials and gadgets.

"We have radar and a GPS-LORAN," he said. "That's the depth finder over there. And of course, VHF and CB."

Father Townsend understood very little of what the man was saying, but he was impressed. He politely looked at everything being shown him, then turned his attention to a set of stairs leading down toward the bow.

"Staterooms and another head," Kuhn Suu said, turning him back toward the stern.

"Are SinCan's headquarters in Hong Kong?" asked Mark, following his host.

"At the moment they still are, yes," replied Li Kuhn Suu. "But we also have offices in Vancouver, where we are relocating."

"Perhaps you'll change your name to CanSin then," suggested Mark with a smile.

Li Kuhn Suu laughed broadly. "That could suggest an unfortunate juxtaposition, wouldn't you say, Father? Come, let me show you the rest of the boat."

The *SinCan V* was fifty-five feet long and every foot was luxuriously appointed. There were two large staterooms below, one with a private bath. The hand towels were inscribed with the ship's name in silver thread. A smaller double bunk room was arranged in the far end of the ship's bow. Li Kuhn Suu opened doors, showing Mark into all the rooms, including the engine room, located beneath the back half of the main cabin.

"We have twin Chrysler diesel engines," he proudly informed the priest. "With two screws, the *SinCan* can almost turn on a dime. Very easy to navigate." He escorted his guest above, to the bridge. They could see Colin Petty on the bow's deck below them, scrubbing industriously along the boat's railing.

"There is so much expense in maintaining a boat like this," said Mr. Suu, watching the man below them. "Sometime I question whether it is worth it. Just to fill the fuel tanks is over a thousand dollars."

Mark gave an appreciative whistle. "A little too rich for my blood."

"Mine, too," smiled Suu. "God bless SinCan Fisheries. They purchased it to entertain clients. Most of our buyers come from Asia, and Colin and I are expected to show them a good time when they visit. We also use it when we visit our local suppliers."

"Like the Swinomish."

"We have bought a lot of their fish. Unfortunately though, the salmon runs in this area have seriously depleted." He raised his arms in an empty gesture. "I feel sorry for these people," he said, "their commercial fishing is almost through."

Mark heard the drone of an outboard. Scanning the channel, he spotted Eddie Walking Boy in a small skiff, heading into the dock. Walking Boy's tiny craft looked like a bathtub compared to the massive *SinCan V*. Eddie had not yet spotted Mark on the bridge, but was intently searching the dock, presumably for him. He waved, but the Indian did not notice.

"Do you know Eddie?" Li Kuhn Suu asked the priest.

"Just from the other day," Mark replied. "But we're going out in that boat together. Although after seeing this . . ."

Mr. Suu laughed delightedly. "I know what you mean, Father. Boats like this are easy to get used to." The two men started down toward the stern, Li Kuhn Suu leading the way. "I'll tell you what. Every year we arrange to take a group from LaConner out on a day cruise into the San Juans. We invite a few people from town and some from the reservation—the tribal chairman, the police chief, the president of the fish co-op. Next time I'll see that you get an invitation. You would be welcome to come along.''

"That's very kind of you," Mark told him.

Walking Boy was tying up at the end of the dock. He glanced up when he heard the two men's footsteps, and his mouth opened in surprise when he saw Mark walking with Li Kuhn Suu. He quickly tried to mask the expression on his face.

"Hey, guys," he said too quickly. "Sorry I'm late."

"No problem," Mark assured him. "I had a chance to tour the *SinCan*. Too bad we can't go in it."

"But another time, yes Father?" Mr. Suu greeted Eddie and then excused himself, heading up the gangway toward SinCan's office.

"Sorry for being late," Eddied apologized again, staring after Li Kuhn Suu. "My friend was baiting his crab traps and I had to wait until he got back."

"It's okay," Mark told him. He looked into Eddie's small boat and was surprised to find Jesse grinning up at him. "What're you doing here?"

"Going with you."

Mark handed Eddie the paper sack with Nan's sandwiches and the Thermos. "Are you sure that's a good idea? I appreciate your willingness to take me out to the shack, but maybe Jesse should stay here."

"No way!" the child protested, her face tightening into a scowl.

Eddie shrugged, raised his hands and gave the priest a look of hopeless resignation.

"Her mom said it was okay to go. I don't care if you don't."

Still uneasy with the idea but reluctant to confront the young girl, Mark clambered into the small boat and settled himself in the center of a narrow seat. Eddie pointed out the life vests in the bow as he quickly untied the boat and started the small outboard engine. It sputtered to life, and with a quick turn Eddie had them heading out into the middle of the channel. The gunwale was riding just a few inches above the water and Mark worried that if they passed a boat of any size, the other vessel's wake would very likely swamp them. But he kept his thoughts to himself and tried to focus on the scenery. Neither of the Indians seemed too concerned. Eddie was heading out the east end of the channel, under the Rainbow Bridge. Mark stared up at the supporting trestles as they passed beneath it, recalling his vivid dream from that morning. He recognized the Olsen home as they passed it. They were soon next to the entrance through the rocky dike built around Shelter Bay. Eddie's voice rose above the noise of the engine.

"Us kids used to skinny dip over there," he told Mark, pointing in the general vicinity of the dredged-out boat basin inside the development. Mark could see the tall masts of sailboats poking above the house tops built around the docks. "There were water holes when the tide went out, and when the sun was shining they got pretty warm. Lots of fun. Of course that was before they dredged it for the pukers."

"Pukers?" Mark was puzzled. "What are they?"

The Indian blushed. "Oh," he said, obviously embarrassed. "That's what some of us call the white men's boats."

Mark diverted his attention back to the shore. They were rounding a bend in the channel where the houses were out of sight.

"It's nice back here," he told Eddie, "without all the houses."

The Indian grimaced and pointed up. Father Townsend followed his arm and spotted the row of glass-fronted estates hugging the hillside two hundred feet above them. The view up there would extend from LaConner across the Skagit Valley to the Cascade Mountains.

Eddie swung the boat toward the left and pointed to a spot in front of them. "Hole in the Wall," he said. Mark spotted a break in the long dark line of rocks in front of them. "We go into the Skagit through there," Eddie informed him, steering the boat away from the opening. "But it's better to go in when the tide's a little higher, otherwise we could go aground. While we're waiting I'll take you out to the end of the channel."

Mark remembered his grandfather standing in his muddy wet clothes while Nan scolded him about walking into her clean house. GrandSam and Larry Robbins had gone aground at the Hole in the Wall just a few days earlier. He could picture the two old men clamoring out of their boat, sinking into thick brown mud up to their knees as they strained to slide Larry's boat into deeper water. Father Townsend was happy to wait awhile if it meant avoiding a similar scene. He relaxed, content to enjoy the ride. Jesse was in the boat's bow, trailing one hand in the current.

Eddie Walking Boy throttled up and the small outboard gained momentum, planing across the waves as it lifted higher. The youngster pulled her hand in and hunched her back against the wind.

"How low does the tide get through here?" Mark called above the noise of the engine.

"Depends," Eddie replied. "I've seen minus tides so low that you could almost walk across the channel in places. But other times it hardly drops at all. It depends on the season, the moon, and the weather."

The land flattened out on both sides of the channel. To their left, rafts of logs were lynched around pilings, awaiting their trip to a sawmill. Beyond the logs was a rocky jetty. To the right, a narrow spit of wet sand stretched for several hundred yards. At high tide it would be completely covered over. Eddie was pointing to an island covered by a thick forest in front of them.

"That's Goat Island," he said loudly. "And straight ahead, Whidbey Island."

A row of tall wooden pilings marked the end of the channel and Walking Boy ran his boat beyond them before turning to the right. Mark looked back over his shoulder, down the channel they had just left. The crest of the waves from their boat's wake were still visible far behind them. To his right he could see houses nestled among the trees—

more of the Shelter Bay development. Eddie was steering a wide arc past a shallow bay which ran right up to a narrow sandy cove Mark recognized as Martha's Beach. He had walked there from his grandparents' house several times.

Beyond the bend, a small promontory of land poked out from the shore, a couple of houses perched at the end.

"That's at the end of Pull and Be Damned Road," Eddie informed him. He cut back on the throttle and the boat slowed, settling back down into the water. They would not have to yell over the motor's drone now. "And out in front of us is Hope Island," he continued in a normal voice. "Good fishing right around here."

Mark was busy searching the shoreline, trying to spot the place where Dutch Olsen's body had washed up. When he and GrandSam had driven Jeanne Olsen to the site, the distance had seemed much greater. But to get there by road meant snaking through part of the reservation. Coming in by water, Mark suddenly was aware of how close it was to the channel they had just left.

"Go a little further into shore, can you?"

Eddie started to swing the boat starboard.

"Do you know where the name Pull and Be Damned came from, Eddie?"

The young Indian was about to reply when Jesse excitedly pointed out into the middle of the sound.

"Look!" she shouted.

Both Mark and Eddie turned to see what the child was pointing at, but all they could see was the gray water and, in the distance, the hazy shoreline of Whidbey Island.

"What was it, Jesse?" Eddie asked.

"A whale," she replied, her voice still filled with excitement. "Right over there. A big one!"

Both men looked with renewed interest. Sure enough, the black fin and humped back of a killer whale broke the water's surface about seventy-five yards away from them. The animal disappeared beneath the waves as suddenly as it had appeared.

"A big one, all right," observed Walking Boy, turning his attention back to the boat. He corrected their course toward the shore. "You want to look for where they found the body?" Mark nodded, returning his own eyes back towards the shoreline. The whale's presence nearby did not seem nearly as important at the moment.

With the tide several feet higher and covering most of the beach, it was difficult to find anything that looked familiar, especially when they were approaching from the opposite direction. Father Townsend was looking for a break in the houses that lined the shore, remembering how they had parked their car and wandered down through an empty lot before coming to the beach. There had been a small bluff, he recalled, and a madronna tree leaning out over it.

"There!" he said suddenly, pointing. "That's it!"

The rocky beach was all but completely covered, the water nearly lapping against the base of the low bluff. But he recognized the tree they had grabbed onto when they climbed down to the beach. This was the place. Eddie Walking Boy cut the engine and there was sudden quiet. The boat rocked as its wake slowly dispersed. The three of them sat in silence, watching the shoreline.

Eddie finally broke the stillness. "I heard his hand was gone."

"Gross!" Jesse exclaimed.

"What?" Mark was not paying attention.

"I heard his hand was cut off."

"Yes."

Eddie grunted and fell silent again. He shifted in his seat and looked out over the water as Mark continued studying the beach. But there was nothing to see except water lazily edging into the rocks. Overhead a seagull dipped down, tipping its head to study the small boat below, searching for morsels. Jesse waved an empty hand. Disappointed, the bird flew on. Mark tried to remember how the body had looked lying on the rocks. The head was turned toward the water. Dutch was lying on his stomach. The right arm was closer to the body than the left. He imagined the dead man's body as it drifted into shore. Had it floated on top of the water or below it? Did it rock like this boat or sag heavily, like soggy clothing? In his mind he watched as the tide slowly crept back out, depositing its terrible booty onto the beach. Mark was suddenly aware of how cold and damp the salt air was. He felt chilled and turned back toward Eddie and the girl. The Indians were sitting patiently, quietly watching the Jesuit priest. They had spent no time trying to imagine what had taken place here. There was too much in the present time to hold their attention. What was in the past was dead.

Mark pointed across the water, away from the beach. "Somewhere over there is where they found Olsen's boat."

Eddie nodded. "That's the way to Deception Pass," he said. "The tide would have taken it out. And from there the currents would have carried it right out to sea." He grinned as he turned back to restart the engine. Jokingly he added, "If it kept going, that old man's boat could have ended up in China."

TEN

By the time they got back to the Hole in the Wall it was high tide and Eddie Walking Boy guided their small craft through the rocky break leading into the Skagit River without hesitation. The Skagit was wide and slow-moving and the Indian turned upriver toward Dutch Olsen's shack. They did not have far to go. The shack was no more than half a mile up, around a sharp curve angling from the east.

The Lodge was not much to look at.

Built on top of a log boom, the weathered gray shack had a noticeable tilt at one end where the old logs, heavy with water, lay half-submerged. The building was larger than Mark had imagined. While it was hardly a hunting lodge, it did look like there was plenty of room inside for Dutch plus three or four of his old cronies. Small windows, set up high on the sides, appeared to be the only source for light. There were no electrical wires running out from the shore. Thin sheets of warped plywood were nailed to the top of the log boom, creating an uneven walkway in front of the shack. A small motorboat was tied to the boom and a thin wisp of dark smoke rose from the stovepipe sticking up above the building's roof.

Eddie cut back his engine, letting the current push the

boat in toward the boom. Jesse leaned out over the bow's gunwale to grab onto a scraggly piece of rope attached to one of the logs. Mark's impulse was to throw his arms around her tiny waist to make sure she didn't tumble into the river, but he managed to resist that impulse. This kid had no fear.

"Mark?" GrandSam's voice was loud with surprise.

His grandfather was standing in the door of the shack, looking out at them with a shotgun cradled in his right arm. From his grizzled appearance, he had not shaved in a couple of days. Father Townsend suspected there probably was no running water inside the shack either, which meant the old man would not have showered since getting there.

"So this is where you hide out." Mark tried to keep his voice light and nonchalant.

"What are you doing here?" his grandfather wondered.

Eddie Walking Boy had not turned off the boat's motor, and Mark realized both he and Jesse were holding the skiff next to the boom but making no effort to tie up. He tried picturing the scene from outside the boat, detaching himself and looking on from the other end of the boom: he saw a cranky old white man guarding the door with a gun while two Indians nervously watched him from the boat, anxious to cast off and get out of range of the .12 gauge. Mark could feel his own irritation boiling up inside of him and at the same time, a certain amount of shame for his grandfather.

"What's with the gun?" he asked.

GrandSam lifted his chin at the boat. "We heard you coming. Didn't know who it was. Are you staying or going back with them?"

"Nan was wondering when you're coming home."

"Today," the old man replied. "In a little while."

Father Townsend turned back to Eddie who had not taken his eyes off the gun. "Maybe I ought to stay here and catch a ride back with them," he quietly suggested. Eddie nodded but said nothing.

"I'll see you later on, Jesse," he told the girl. She watched him with solemn eyes as he awkwardly clambered out of the bobbing boat. "Tell your mom I'll call her."

As soon as he was clear, the Indians let go of the boom and the boat began drifting away on the river's current. Eddie shifted gears and the motor churned, moving them even further away from Mark and GrandSam. Both the man and the girl kept their faces facing the boat's front, turned away from the Townsends. Mark was already questioning his decision to stay.

"You always greet people with a gun?" he asked, turning to face GrandSam.

"We didn't know who you were," his grandfather explained again. "Besides," he said, lifting the gun up and pulling the trigger, "it isn't loaded."

GrandSam turned away from the door and as he did, Mark caught a quick glimpse of a man he supposed was Larry Robbins inside, hurriedly putting another rifle out of sight. He followed his grandfather into the shack.

Inside was brighter than he had expected. Windows in all four walls allowed light to spill onto a long wood table in the center of the room. There were candles and a Coleman lamp on the table. Dirty plates were piled at one end while the other was covered with papers. Old army cots were arranged in each corner of the room. A wood-burning stove—too large for the size of the place—was set against the back wall, its sooty pipe rising through the ceiling. A coffee pot and cast iron skillet balanced on its flat top. Both could have used a good scrubbing. Most of the wall space seemed to be covered with gun racks and old clothes hanging from hooks—heavy coats and pants, flannel shirts and raingear. The place was thick with the smells of wet clothes, fried bacon, stale tobacco, old whiskey, and older men.

Larry Robbins stepped out of the shadows, back into the center of the room, rubbing his hands on his pants. "Hi, Padre. Welcome."

He was a lean and shadowy-looking man. His skin had an unpleasant and sickly gray cast to it and his eyes were hooded and shifted constantly. Robbins was younger than his grandfather and Dutch, probably in his mid-sixties. His breath had a sour stench and his handshake felt greasy.

He was pumping the priest's hand a little too heartily and a little too long and Mark found himself instinctively backing away from the man.

GrandSam replaced his shotgun onto a gunrack. He and Larry had apparently returned with the same guns they had removed from the shack just a couple of days earlier.

"So, you guys having fun?" Mark dropped into a kitchen chair next to the table. "This is quite a hideout."

His grandfather poured him coffee from the pot on the stove, placed it next to him and moved to the other end of the table to sit. Larry remained standing. The coffee was scalding and as bitter as gossip.

"How's Mary doing?" GrandSam wanted to know.

"Fine," Mark replied, "but a little worried about you." His grandfather grunted.

"Larry and me have been going through Dutch's things. This seemed like a good time to do it."

Implying that it was a good time if Mark and Nan were going to associate themselves with Dutch Olsen's murderer. At some point Father Townsend knew they were going to have to face that issue head on. Now did not feel like the time.

"Are you finding anything?" asked Mark, looking at the papers scattered at Larry's end of the table. Robbins tried to casually place a protective hand over the top of them and he gave Sam a look of warning.

"Not much really," GrandSam said, a little too quickly. "Just a bunch of old stuff. Dutch was quite a packrat."

Mark was curious. "There's a lot of paper there," he observed. "Did you find any maps?"

Larry Robbins's hand flinched. Bingo!

"Sam found a couple," the man admitted, realizing the priest was watching his reaction. "But they probably don't mean anything."

"They're mostly just some old charts," GrandSam told him. "Copies of stuff Dutch found in the museum at Anacortes, it looks like."

"And newspaper clippings," Larry volunteered. "Old newspaper clippings."

"About smugglers?"

"About a lot of stuff," GrandSam answered. "But nothing important."

Old men were supposed to be as wise and crafty as serpents, Mark recalled. These two were as transparent as cellophane.

"Oh well, maybe you'll find something eventually."

The two of them gave simultaneous shrugs. "Maybe," GrandSam admitted, trying to sound doubtful.

Mark helped them clean up. Which meant next to nothing. Larry Robbins carried a frying pan outside to rinse off in the river while GrandSam gathered up Dutch Olsen's papers, stuffing them into a brown canvas fishing creel. Mark busied himself by shuffling furniture around, picking up discarded clothes and finding hooks on the wall for them. Robbins returned for the rest of the dirty dishes, which GrandSam helped carry outside. In the few minutes he had to himself, Mark made a quick tour of the room. But without knowing what he might be looking for, his search was next to futile. He did find a box of .22 shells on a shelf next to a gun rack. The box was half empty, but there was no .22 rifle on the rack. He checked the other two gun racks, but there was no sign of a .22 anywhere in the shack.

The two men were sleeping on cots located at diagonal corners from each other, affording as much space as possible between them. An untidy pile of clothes near each cot indicated which was Dutch's and which was Larry's. The other two cots were empty, except for a yellowed pillow at the head of each and woolen army blankets folded at the foot. A blanket was on the floor under one of the empty cots and when Mark bent to pick it up he felt the weight of something solid folded inside. Quickly, while listening for footsteps, he peeled back the blanket. Inside were two slightly oblong wooden plaques, a little larger than a man's head. One side was convex, like the outside of a platter, and rubbed smooth; the other was flat and rough. They were about two inches thick and four square but uneven holes were carved into both of them. The wood was old but still held the slight scent of cedar.

They could have been masks, except the holes looked too large. Mystified, Mark hurriedly rewrapped the blanket and put it back in place on the floor. He heard the two old men reentering the cabin and casually wandered back toward the table.

"Just about ready," his grandfather informed him, stacking wet dishes on the table. Both men headed toward their cots and started packing. Mark wandered outside to wait for them.

The shack was on an isolated bend in the river, there was no sign of any other building. He could hear a boat's motor in the distance, but it was impossible to tell if it was coming from up or downriver. Mark was startled by a loud squawk from the opposite shore as a slate gray crane leapt into the air. He could hear the beating of its long wings from across the river and he watched as the gangly bird flapped awkwardly out of sight.

Father Townsend suddenly felt weak and sick to his stomach. He stumbled to the edge of the deck, afraid he was about to vomit. His forehead turned sweaty and cold. Nothing felt right in Dutch Olsen's dank and smokey shack. The carved boards he had uncovered felt particularly disturbing to the priest. He shook his head, trying to clear it. Mark found himself dreading the boat ride back to Shelter Bay.

ELEVEN

The sky was clear and light and a thin strip of moon filtered into Father Townsend's bedroom. Long after midnight the priest lay awake, reviewing the day, counting blessings and regretting lost chances. He knew sleep was still an hour or two away. Mark hated sleeping in queen-sized beds. The vast emptiness beside him felt like an emotional and sexual morass that he was in danger of falling into with just the slightest movement. So instead of sprawling out in the bed, he found himself clinging to his edge of the wide mattress, trying to focus his attention on other, less challenging subjects.

Nan Mary had greeted her husband's return with a gentle casualness, as if GrandSam had only been away hours instead of days; as if he might have run to the store on an errand, or to a friend's for an afternoon game of poker. She gave him a peck on the cheek when Mark led him through the back door into the kitchen and made no comment about his matted goatee, the rough stubble on his cheeks, or his soiled clothes. As reconciliations went, Mark could not have hoped for one any more harmonious. Dinner was eaten mostly in silence, but it was a comfortable silence and no one seemed anxious to spoil it. He played the customary half hour game of chess with

GrandSam between *"I Love Jeannie"* and *"Wheel of Fortune,"* and an hour or so later both grandparents tottered off to bed, leaving Mark wide awake in the silent house, alone with his thoughts.

For the most part they were disturbing ones. And Mark tried putting them out of his mind as he moved quietly through the house, turning out lights and checking doors. Finally he found his way to his own room, but lay in his too-big bed, still wide awake and troubled in a room filled with the eerie glow of a pale moon.

In Seattle, on nights when sleep would not come, Mark often would dress and steal away for a drive. He found the sleeping city was strangely comforting as he moved through nearly deserted streets. He liked crossing over into west Seattle, following Harbor Avenue until he reached a narrow strip of grassy parkway next to the water. You could look back over at downtown Seattle from there, the night lights shining brightly in the city's tall office buildings. On more than one occasion, Mark had stayed long enough to watch sunlight break over the tops of the Cascade Mountains and edge down into the city as it stirred itself awake.

Quietly he lifted the bed covers off and dressed in his blue jeans and sweatshirt. Pulling on his jacket, Mark left his grandparents' house. His car's engine sounded like a jet plane in the night's stillness and Mark quickly backed away from the house, hoping his grandparents were not awakened by the noise. He turned down the hill, toward the golf course and boat basin.

Several things disturbed him. He could not shake the image of his own grandfather standing in the door of that shack, shotgun in hand. Or the darker image of Larry Robbins in the shadows behind him, also cradling a rifle. The nervous looks on Eddie's and Jesse's faces were painful to see, especially as he recognized the threat they experienced in the presence of his own grandfather. Staying at the shack with GrandSam instead of returning with them was probably a mistake. But choosing the two Indians over his grandfather might have caused worse tensions at home. Father Townsend was recognizing that the rift between the two cultures was a lot wider than the Swinomish Channel separating reservation from town. And Mark felt like he was somehow flailing in the middle of it. His mind flashed back to his dream from the night before and the warning from the old Indian grandmother: *what the water brings us, it also takes away in time*. Were the two connected? In his own mind, yes. But in reality?

The boat docks in the basin were lit by lamps lining the walkways. With the moon's added light, the yachts gleamed at their moorings. Mark circled the golf course and parked next to one of the docks, but stayed in his car, staring out at the floating pleasure boats.

Touring the *SinCan*, although fascinating, might also have been a mistake. What did the Swinomish people think of fifty-five feet of incredible wealth floating in the midst of their modest fishing boats? Eddie Walking Boy called the luxury cruisers pukers. He had watched Mark stepping off the *SinCan*, his borrowed skiff dwarfed by the huge power boat. Mark had to admit that he had felt safer and a lot more comfortable on board the *SinCan* than he did sitting in Eddie's boat, water lapping just below the lip of the gunwale. As a Jesuit priest, his natural sympathies lay with the Indians. But as a white man, the niceties in his own culture provided him a comfortable and safe shelter. Perhaps, Mark mused, Shelter Bay was meant to refer to more than just the dredged-out harbor in front of him.

He backed out of the parking lot and headed out of Shelter Bay. At the Indian cemetery he turned left, away from the Rainbow Bridge and into the reservation. The Indian settlement looked dark and quiet. Mark cruised slowly down the street, examining the houses along the sides of the road. He wondered about the lives of the people sleeping inside. What were their dreams? Their nightmares? The community's tall totem pole loomed up in front of his car, pale blue in the moon light, its totem figures indistinct and mysterious. Father Townsend turned onto Sneeoosh Road.

He had gone no more than a quarter of a mile before bright blue lights began flashing behind him. He spotted the police car in his mirror and angled his car to the side of the road. An officer's approaching footsteps crunched in the gravel as he unrolled his window. Then a bright flashlight shone in his face as someone behind it studied his features.

"Aren't you Father Townsend?"

Mark squinted into the light, trying to see past it.

"Yes, I am."

The officer turned the beam down to the car's side, bouncing light back onto himself. Mark recognized the policeman.

"Your name is Jennings, isn't it?"

"That's right. Mike Jennings. We met the other day."

"I remember. It was on the beach with Mrs. Olsen."

"Kind of late to be out, isn't it, Father?"

"I was having trouble sleeping," Mark explained, "and thought I'd take a drive. Is there a problem?"

"Not really," the tribal policeman replied. "But you didn't signal when you made that turn back there and an unfamiliar car driving slowly through the rez—that was a good excuse to stop and check you out."

Father Townsend lifted his eyebrows at the policeman's explanation, but said nothing.

"Just checking to make sure everything's all right."

"Do you have much trouble on the reservation?" Mark politely asked.

The policeman shook his head, then shrugged as if trying to decide. "Drinking. Some theft. Drugs once in awhile. Fights on the weekend. Not much more than that. Olsen's was the first murder on tribal land."

"You're pretty sure Greg Patsy did it." As hard as he tried not to, Mark let a note of skepticism creep into his voice. Jennings picked up on it immediately.

"You don't?" he asked the priest. "Everything points to him. Olsen ran through Patsy's net just the day before and Greg threatened to get even. There was no love lost between those two. And we found the murder weapon hidden on Patsy's boat. Ballistics verified it. Patsy's prints all over it. He admits he was out in his boat, fishing right out in front of Pull and Be Damned at the same time

Olsen's watch stopped. A couple of residents saw an Indian setting nets where Greg said he was and they described a boat that looks like Greg's. That gives him motive, means, and opportunity. It'd be hard not to arrest him.''

"Did anyone actually see him shoot Dutch?"

"No."

"Did your witnesses see Dutch Olsen's boat?"

"A lot of boats cruise through there," Jennings argued. "They wouldn't necessarily notice. But someone setting nets would attract attention. It's still early in the year, even for spring Chinook. And folks are pretty touchy about the Indians' fishing rights around here. They keep an eye on them."

Everything the policeman was saying made sense. Anger is a motive strong enough for murder. Father Townsend knew that from experience. *I was so angry I could have killed him!* Hours spent in Saturday afternoon confessionals had dumped just about every exclamatory fault into his ears that was imaginable. And while no one had ever actually confessed a murder to him, there were plenty who had given the dark deed more than a passing thought. Plenty of people—husbands, wives, children, even other priests—had mulled over the mortal act's advantages. Usually out of anger.

Something about Jennings's scenario still felt strange to Mark. But without more information he had no way of formulating a question that might help clarify matters for himself.

"Let me ask you about something else," the priest requested. "Do you have much problem around here with people trying to steal Indian artifacts?"

Jennings was puzzled. "Like what? There isn't a whole bunch around here that anyone would want. Most of the old and really good stuff was buried with people's ancestors long ago.''

"I don't know," answered Mark. "I just wondered if people came on the reservation looking for old stuff."

"There's a little of that. They caught some kids one time, getting set to cut one of the figures out of the totem.

Some of the local boys took care of that one. Another time they caught a couple of jerks from California with shovels in the cemetery. But nothing big time, not around here.''

"I was just wondering," Mark assured him. "Some places have real problems with that."

"Yeah, I guess they do."

The two men bid each other a good night. Jennings, almost as an afterthought, cautioned the priest to drive carefully. As Mark pulled back onto the road, he saw the police car make a U-turn, heading back toward the center of the settlement. Father Townsend continued on out Sneeoosh Road for another mile or so before stopping and turning around. He was suddenly tired of driving.

He was almost back to the same spot in the road where Jennings had stopped him when his headlights caught a sudden movement off to his right. He turned sharply into the middle of the road, fearful of a deer bounding out in front of the car. But this was no deer. Two figures were hurrying along the roadside, one behind the other. The leader was a middle-aged Indian man with long black hair, wearing a heavy blue parka. Mark caught only a glimpse of the one behind him, as the man in front quickly tried to shield the other person from the car. But he saw bright cloth, feathers, fur, and what looked like bone. And where the head was supposed to be, a veil of beads.

Mark was already past them, searching in his mirror for another look at the strange figure at the side of the road. But there was only the darkness behind him.

They had to be participants from Seeowyn, he realized. One of the babies, out for whatever reason, being guided by a babysitter. Father Townsend was chilled by the sudden encounter, although he had spent hours watching the same veiled figures dancing next to the fires in the Swinomish smoke house the night before. But coming across one unexpectedly, in the middle of the night like this, was a little frightening. His own spirituality made room for spirits, both good and evil. And he sensed the presence of both in this dark place. It was time to go home. Mark knew he would not sleep, but he had seen and heard enough for one night. He reached the end of the road and turned back toward Shelter Bay. He made sure to signal this time.

TWELVE

Dutch Olsen's funeral was not until two o'clock in the afternoon. Despite staying up half the night, Father Townsend was awake early. He was planning on heading back to Seattle that evening and there was plenty he wanted to do before then. Mark lingered long enough for a cup of coffee and glass of juice with GrandSam and Nan, then headed out the door.

Linda Patsy was not an early riser. Nor was her daughter, Jesse. They were both still in bed when Mark stood on their porch at 7:45, impatiently ringing the doorbell. Timidly, Linda peeked from behind her door at the tall priest standing on the step, tugging at the ends of his mustache impatiently.

"Father Mark? What are you doing here?" She opened the door a bit wider, self-consciously pulling her faded blue robe a little tighter around her body.

"Can I come in?"

She looked back at her messy living room in dismay. "I guess so."

He sat at the kitchen table while she made them tea. Dirty plates were piled next to the sink and the garbage can needed emptying. Mark had the impression that any sense of order in the Patsy household was put on hold as long as Greg remained in jail. It looked like Linda and Jesse were going through the motions, living moment to moment. He wondered how long they could sustain themselves like this.

"I'm sorry for coming by so early," Mark apologized. "I guess I should have called first."

"It's okay." Linda managed a slight smile.

"I'm heading over to Anacortes this morning and wanted to talk to you first."

"To see Greg?"

"No, I want to visit the museum."

Linda Patsy glanced at the priest to see if he was joking. He was bent over the table, intently drawing on a paper napkin. Apparently he was not kidding. She set a cup of tea down in front of him. Mark glanced at it but continued drawing. When he was finished he turned the napkin around and slid it across the table towards her.

"Does this look like anything you've seen before?"

He had drawn an oblong, slightly rounded shape with four holes more or less in the center.

"A button?" Linda guessed.

Mark scowled down at the napkin and pulled it back. He studied it for a moment, flipped the paper over and drew a similar shape, slightly larger this time, with two of the holes a bit larger than the other two.

"It's bigger than that," he explained, "about twelve to fourteen inches long. Made out of wood. Cedar, I think. And there's two of them."

Linda looked at the paper napkin again, puzzlement wrinkling her brow.

"I don't think it's anything I've seen," she finally said. "Is it important?"

Mark shrugged. "I don't know, I thought they might be. Maybe something used here on the reservation?"

"That's possible, Father, but you'd have to ask someone else. I'm Colville, from over near Omak. Until I met Greg, I'd never even heard of Swinomish. There's still a lot about the tribe and how they do things that I don't know about."

If the two carved boards Mark discovered in Olsen's

shack were Indian in origin, he realized they probably belonged to the Coastal Salish. A Colville from the other
side of the Cascade Mountains would not necessarily recognize them.

''What about Eddie?'' the woman suggested, ''He
might know what they are.''

Eddie Walking Boy lived alone in a small cabin off
Reservation Road on the way to Anacortes. Before heading out there, Father Townsend swung by the fish processing plant, on the off chance that Eddie might be
around the boats. He saw one fishing boat pulling away,
but there was no other activity on the docks. Wandering
over to the SinCan building, Mark stuck his head inside
the open doorway. The front office was nothing but a
small room with a couple of desks, three file cabinets, and
four metal folding chairs for visitors. A large color poster
on one wall identified the various species of fish found in
the icy waters of Puget Sound. Another wall held a bul-
letin board littered with official-looking notices and an-
nouncements. A passageway opposite the entrance led to
the back of the building. He was just starting back when
he heard voices coming towards him.

Li Kuhn Suu and Colin Petty were arguing over a list
of figures on a clipboard. They both stopped talking and
walking when they spotted the priest.

''Father Townsend,'' Li Kuhn greeted Mark, ''what a
nice surprise. What brings you to SinCan so early?''

''I was looking for Eddie Walking Boy. Has he been
around?''

The Asian looking questioningly at his partner, who
shook his head.

''I guess not. Colin and I are the only ones here at the
moment. I don't believe I have seen Eddie since he picked
you up on the dock yesterday morning.''

''I saw him later,'' Colin interrupted. ''He dropped
Patsy's kid off.'' He shot the priest an accusing look. ''But
you weren't with 'em.''

''No,'' Mark acknowledged. ''I came back with someone else. I guess maybe I'll check his house.''

"Yes," Li Kuhn replied. "If he is not here, that is usually where you find him. Unless, of course, he is helping someone with fishing."

Eddie was not fishing. Following Linda's directions, Mark turned into a narrow dirt drive exactly six-tenths of a mile past a dirty white clapboard church on Reservation Road. Thick green growth pressed in on both sides of the driveway; the priest's car was swallowed up by brambles and ferns. Eddie's small house sat thirty yards back, on land cleared out of the middle of a dense stand of tall fir trees. The survivors, like silent witnesses to their fallen companions, surrounded the perimeter of the yard, only about fifteen feet away from the house. If any ever toppled, Walking Boy's cabin would be reduced to rubble. Mark spotted Eddie sitting on a battered kitchen chair in front of his small house, sipping coffee, wrapped in a Cowichan sweater a size too large for him. The morning had started out drizzly and cold, but a thin beam of sunlight had worked its way through the cloud cover and the trees overhead in a brave effort to warm the spot where Eddie was sitting. He looked almost like he was waiting for the priest. He stayed in his chair as Mark climbed out of his car.

"*?Us-chal chuwh*" Eddie greeted him. "That means, 'How are you?' " He got up and motioned Mark to take his place on the chair, resettling himself onto a wood chopping stump that was out of the beam of sunlight. "You want coffee?"

"No thanks, Eddie."

The two men sat silently looking out at the clearing in front of them. The quiet was comfortable, almost meditative. A jay momentarily dived to the ground, about ten feet in front of them. But realizing he was not alone, he quickly lifted himself, flapping into a dense grove of alder trees where he proceeded to loudly scold the two men for being there.

"Your grandfather does not like Indians much."

Mark could feel his face begin to redden. "I think he was nervous about who was coming up on them."

"Maybe."

"He thinks Greg Patsy killed his good friend."

"Not all Indians are Greg Patsy," offered Eddie.

"No," Mark admitted. "I'm sorry he met us that way. It was wrong."

Eddied nodded and sipped his coffee, turning to search the alders for the blue jay. "Some of us think it was a mistake to lease the land for Shelter Bay," he said. "All those big houses and the pukers—they remind some people of how much we don't have. Some others say that what is most important is our land, and now we don't have that." He glanced over at the priest for just a moment. "That was one pretty place. Lots of wild stuff in there: foxes, eagles, ducks, geese, deer, even a black bear. Most of them are moved on now. Some of us think we're poorer because of it.

"Our elders say that when an eagle flies over you, that you are being blessed. And if he circles back around and flies over you again, it means he is watching over you— sort of for protection." Eddie paused. "No matter how much cash you got, you can't buy an eagle to fly over you."

Eddie turned back towards Father Townsend. "I know your grandfather's feelings," he said. "Sometimes I have them myself."

Mark reached inside his jacket, pulling out the sketch he had drawn for Linda Patsy.

"I saw something out there at the shack," he said, handing the napkin to Eddie, "and I wondered if you might know what it is. There were two of these, actually."

Eddie studied Mark's drawing.

"Buttons?"

The priest told him to turn the napkin over to the better drawing on the other side, again explaining that they were a lot larger and carved out of wood. Eddie studied his sketch much longer this time.

"I might," he said finally, hesitantly. "But I need to ask someone else. Can I keep this?" Eddie folded the drawing into his own pocket. "Where did you say you saw these?"

Mark described finding the two carvings wrapped in the blanket inside of Dutch Olsen's cabin. He recounted for the young man what he knew about Dutch's hobby of searching for lost treasures stashed by early-day smugglers. The Indian nodded knowingly.

"Yeah, I know about them," he said. "They were all around here. But I never heard of any gold or anything."

"Evidently Dutch thought some of it is still hidden on some of the islands around here."

Eddie Walking Boy offered the priest a wry smile as he stood up. "That man didn't need gold," he informed Mark in a solemn voice. "What he needed was an eagle watching out for him."

The Anacortes Museum was housed in the town's former library, one of the old Carnegies built just after the turn of the century. This one was erected in 1909, according to the date chiseled into the cornerstone. Made of red bricks, someone had decided to spruce the building up by painting it a dull gray. A tall row of steep cement steps led up to the front door, but a sign pointing to Research directed Father Townsend around the side, to a door in the basement.

The small cluttered office was deserted, but Mark could hear movement in the next room. A plastic name plate on the desk informed him the museum's researcher was Miss Pamela E. Harcotte. There was a small old-fashioned desk bell placed next to the name, so Mark rapped it twice. A woman's voice in the other room loudly called out to him, acknowledging the bell.

Miss Pamela E. Harcotte was a tall, willowy blonde. Tall, willowy, blonde, and about seventy-five years old. She was wearing dark green corduroy pants, a gray I ♥ Anacortes sweatshirt, and blue canvas deck shoes. Her very blonde hair swooped out in stiff flips from both sides of her head, just above her ears. They looked like wings. Miss Harcotte was wearing thick glasses with bright red frames and a pair of thin white cotton gloves.

"You'll have to come back," she said peevishly, "we're not open to the public until one o'clock." Straightening her shoulders, she clasped her hands in front of her and raised her chin defiantly, prepared to rebut whatever arguments this stranger tried to hand her. "You'll have to come back later," she repeated.

"I'm sorry, I didn't know your hours."

"One o'clock until five, Thursday through Monday."

Mark tried warming her with a smile. "I have a funeral to attend this afternoon, and am heading back to Seattle after that."

Miss Harcotte gave a tiny shake of her head and the massive twin wings of hair bobbed in response. "I understand. But I'm in the midst of rearranging my archives and my documents are disarrayed. It would be impossible to find anything. I'm immensely sorry."

Mark doubted if Miss Pamela E. Harcotte ever allowed anything to come even close to disarray. She did not seem the type. But she appeared determined to stand her ground. He tried offering her another smile.

"Maybe I could just ask you a couple of quick questions," he proposed. "Then I'll be out of your . . . way." He had almost said hair.

"If they're quick ones." She bent her waist stiffly and leaned forward expectantly.

"I'm staying over in LaConner," Mark began, "and have heard a couple of stories about smugglers . . ."

"Oh, Lord!" Miss Harcotte crowed, "Another one!"

"I beg your pardon?"

"What is going on in that village by the slough?" she asked dramatically. "You're the fourth person in a month." She bustled over to her desk and grasped pen and paper. "Your name?"

"Townsend. Mark Townsend."

"I'm sorry Mr. Townsend, but I simply don't have time right now. You'll have to come back some other day."

"It's Father Townsend."

"I beg your pardon?"

"I'm a Jesuit priest. My name is Father Mark Townsend."

She was about to fly away. Her wings fluttered furiously as she began bobbing her head excitedly.

"A Jesuit! That's absolutely delightful!" she enthused.

"One of my oldest and dearest friends is a Jesuit—Father William DeAngelo." Yanking off her cotton gloves, she dragged a chair directly in front of Mark. "Sit down, Father, please sit down! Why didn't you tell me you were a Jesuit? How's Father Willie?"

For nearly thirty years, Father William DeAngelo had worked as the Jesuit archivist. Originally assigned as a librarian at Gonzaga University in Spokane, Willie had managed to parlay the Jesuit Provincial's request to catalog and store a few boxes of Jesuit memorabilia into a full-time career. He began by collecting documents pertaining to the Jesuits and their works in the Pacific Northwest, but very quickly expanded his search to include not just anything even remotely connected to the Jesuits, but just about everything else that related to the history of the Catholic Church in that part of the world. Before he retired, Father DeAngelo had filled an entire warehouse with crates of artifacts, books, documents, and photos. Which prompted one Jesuit wag, during an evening's rec room banter, to immortalize the line, "Willie's lust is dust." And as his collection mushroomed and his fame spread, Father Willie found himself befriended by just about every librarian, historian, and museum curator in the region.

Miss Harcotte was obviously one of Father DeAngelo's biggest fans. As she settled in behind her desk, she rhapsodized about her dear old friend. Mark listened and smiled patiently.

"But listen to me go on!" Pamela (it was Pamela now) exclaimed. "I'm just so thrilled to have a Jesuit visiting my little collection here. Of course this is nothing compared to Father Willie's." Her golden wings twitched with excitement. "But!" She raised a dramatic finger. "You're here for other purposes, aren't you, Father? Smuggling. That was it." She cocked her head and fixed him with a quizzical, expectant smile.

Mark swallowed. "Yes," he replied, preparing to explain his reasons.

"We have Smuggling," she cut him off. "Box S dash 38. Let me get it. Meanwhile, Father, if you wouldn't mind, I'll just ask you just to fill in one of our little requisition forms.'' Miss Harcotte slid a piece of paper and a pen across the desk at him, leaving him to complete the form while she raced into her storage room.

He barely had time to pen his name before she returned, cradling a gray box big enough to hold a large sheet cake in her arms. ''S dash 38!'' she pronounced, settling it carefully on the desk.

''That was quick. Your files can't be in too much disarray,'' Mark observed.

''Not these. As I said, they've been very popular lately.''

''Why is that?''

''It's a mystery, isn't it?'' Wings trembled. ''For the last few years, Smuggling has had only one regular visitor. But I've heard that that poor unfortunate was recently murdered. Now all sorts of visitors are requesting S dash 38.''

''Mr. Olsen. Yes, I know about him. That's whose funeral I'm attending.''

''It's awful, Father. You wonder what in the world is happening to us. The poor unfortunate man.''

''Did he come here often?''

''At least once a month. His last visit was . . .'' She was consulting a blue binder. ''. . . March fifteenth. Less than three weeks ago. He visited Smuggling, Swinomish, and Goat Island. S dash 38; S dash 50; and I dash 21.'' She slapped the binder shut.

''You said there were other people interested in Smuggling?''

''Robbins, Larry.'' She was reading from the binder again. ''S dash 38 on March twenty-second. And then Smith, Bill. S dash 38 on March twenty-fifth. Robbins also returned on March twenty-sixth and visited Swinomish and Goat Island. Then Smith returned on March twenty-ninth. Curious, this. He examined the same materials: Smuggling, Swinomish, Goat Island.'' She set the binder down. ''I suppose they're all partners.''

''I know Larry Robbins,'' Father Townsend told her. ''But Bill Smith doesn't ring a bell. I don't suppose you'd have a requisition form from him, like the one I filled out.''

"Oh but of course I would. However!" she exclaimed, arching her eyebrows, "I treat those with confidence. It's procedure." Her frown said no, but the wings, the wings said yes. "But perhaps in this case an exception might be in order."

Mark was not sure why an exception was in order, but he eagerly accepted the retrieved form she handed him. Bill Smith lived at 1234 First Street in LaConner. His phone number also ended with 1234. He had listed his specific area of interest as family history. The Jesuit suspected Smith's family history was as bogus as his residence.

He spent the next hour and a half poking through the box labeled S dash 38, as well as the ones marked S dash 50 and I dash 21. Miss Harcotte had fitted him with a pair of white cotton gloves like her own before bringing him the boxes. Invoking the name of her oldest and dearest friend once more, Pamela Harcotte informed the Jesuit priest he would be allowed to study the contents of the boxes alone while sitting at her own desk. This was highly unusual, she observed, but she did need to attend to the disarray. Mark thanked her for the privilege and plunged into the first gray box.

Most of the materials collected on smuggling were newspaper accounts about some of the men who had made their living in the late 1800s and early 1900s by sneaking Chinese laborers into the United States from Canada. In 1881 the Canadian government gave permission to the Onderdonk Construction Company to import seventeen thousand Chinese from the South China province of Kwang Tung to help lay railroad tracks across the Rocky Mountains. When their labors for Onderdonk Construction were finally ended, many of the unemployed coolies became desperate for work. They were told that there were plenty of jobs in the United States, if only they could find a way across the border. Enter the smugglers. And as more and more Chinese arrived in the states to toil for the mines, fisheries, lumber mills, and railroads, a growing market developed for Chinese wine and opium. While their white counterparts would retire to the local tavern at the end of a workday, the Chinese would crawl into smokey dens for a relaxing pipe of the opiate. So the accommodating smugglers gleefully began running liquor and narcotics, too.

Mark read through several of the life stories he found in the box. He recognized Ben Ure's name from one of the islands across from the beach where Dutch's body was found. A renegade called Old Man Harris apparently smuggled a lot of the Chinese, or Celestials, as they were referred to back then. And there were several stories about Clarence O'Rourke, the "King of Smugglers." All of them seemed to have had hideouts scattered throughout the islands of Puget Sound. Father Townsend found references to caches of gold and opium but they seemed pretty vague, sort of like lost treasure maps and abandoned gold mines—the kinds of stuff legends are made of.

The next box he opened was S dash 50, and it contained historical accounts of some of the early Swinomish tribal members. There were two or three dozen photographs, too: faded, stained images of faces solemn with dignity, staring rigidly into the camera with dark eyes that looked like they had never blinked. Although the large box was nearly empty, it felt to Mark like the weight of an entire people lay inside. He searched for some scrap of information that could have tied S dash 50 to S dash 38. And although a couple of the smugglers had married Indian women, there did not seem to be much commerce between the two groups. The Swinomish pretty much stuck to themselves, subsisting mainly by hunting and fishing. He found one old printed map in the Swinomish box that indicated all the areas where the people went to forage. The penmanship was difficult to read, and in places the brown ink had faded to a mere trace, but Mark recognized several familiar spots where the tribe used to collect food. There were beaches marked on the map where they gathered clams and oysters, forests where deer were hunted, and tidal flats full of geese and ducks. A beach close to Pull and Be Damned Road was labeled with an Indian name. Beneath it someone had translated, *this means "Nice Beach" in Indian.* Mark found it easy to imagine an earlier time, when the people would have traveled to the nice beach to bathe and relax. Houses, roads, shops, even the Rainbow Bridge did not yet exist. Cedar canoes would have been the only way to cross the slough, and the tribal smoke house would have been the largest structure anywhere around.

The third box Father Townsend examined contained materials on Goat Island, a tiny island located at the southern mouth of the Swinomish Slough. I dash 21. This was, by far, the fullest box. And for good reason. According to the first document Mark studied, the U.S. Army had established a fort on the island in 1909 as part of the Puget Sound Harbor defense system. In all his years of visiting GrandSam and Nan, Mark had never heard anything about a fort. He dug deeper into the box.

The military site was named Fort Whitman and had been established to help prevent enemy ships from penetrating coastal waters. A number of similar defenses were built around the same time: Forts Casey, Ebby, Worden, and Flagler. Goat Island was the only site through Deception Pass however, and on the lee side of Whidbey Island. Although smaller than the others, Fort Whitman had contained some heavy fire power. According to the documents, four cannons had been mounted on a bluff overlooking the water. Each gun weighed twelve thousand pounds and was designed to rise up above the crest of the bluff to fire, then to quickly lower back into its hidden position.

Mark found a General Site Plan in the box, detailing the locations of the guns as well as the other buildings. There were barracks for the troops, a mess hall, latrines, officers' quarters, even a theater. A small ferry shuttled between the island and LaConner and in the summertime, picnics for the town were sponsored by the fort. Baseball games were organized between the soldiers and the young men from the town. Mark Townsend was amazed: apparently, an entire garrison had been squirreled away on a small island less than 130 acres in size, less than two miles from LaConner, at the end of the Swinomish Channel. Intrigued, he continued reading.

The fort was manned through both world wars, but in 1949 was turned over to the Washington State Game Department. The Army Corps of Engineers continued to maintain two rock quarries on the island. The guns were dismantled and the fort abandoned. The island remained deserted and isolated and eventually most of LaConner seemed to forget about Fort Whitman. Eventually Goat Island was turned over to the Boy Scouts as a campsite.

Father Townsend leaned back in his chair and rubbed his eyes. The small island's big history was fascinating, but he could not make any connections with either smugglers or the Swinomish. The three subjects appeared almost totally unrelated. And yet Pamela Harcotte said all three archives had been researched by three different men within the last month. One of them was dead and another had to be an alias. He closed the lid on I dash 21 and stood up.

"All through, Father?" Miss Harcotte appeared from her archives, brushing dust from her sweatshirt.

"Yes, thank you, Pamela. I appreciate your letting me in here."

"Father," Pamela E. Harcotte looked down through her red framed glasses and gave him a coy smile, "it was my pleasure. I hope you were able to find what you were looking for."

He gave her a noncommittal nod. "There are two questions maybe you could help me with," he said.

She shook her wings in anticipation. "Ask away!"

"Have you ever seen anything like this?" He quickly sketched one of the two cedar boards with four holes carved in the middle. "They're carved from cedar and are about a foot and a half long."

Miss Harcotte studied the sketch and shook her head. "No, I don't believe I have. Perhaps they're Native American in origin."

"That's what I think too. My second question has to do with the name of a road . . ."

"Pull and Be Damned?"

"Yes, that's the one."

She trilled delightedly. "Pull *or* Be Damned, Father. It's misnamed. The original phrasing was *or*, not *and*. It has to do with the horrific tidal action through that particular stretch of water. Deception Pass is just beyond the passage, and it's such a narrow opening and there's so much water passing back and forth. If anyone tried rowing through there when the tide was running strong, they had to pull hard or be swept away. Hence the saying: *Pull or be Damned.*"

Father Townsend grinned with delight. "Miss Harcotte—Pamela—you are an angel! Thank you so much."

The researcher of the Anacortes Museum stood waving good-bye from her basement doorway as Mark got into his car. As he drove away he waved one last time to his angel with wide wings of very solid gold.

THIRTEEN

Dutch Olsen's funeral was being held in the Little Chapel at the Safe Harbor Mortuary in Mount Vernon, a twenty-minute drive from LaConner—a twenty-minute drive at any time of year other than during the Tulip Festival. By the time Mark had returned to Shelter Bay to change his clothes and then negotiated his way past the tulip fields and down the highway-turned-parking lot, the service was already underway. His grandfather was sitting in the front with five other pallbearers, on a pew between his friend, Larry Robbins, and four other elderly gents in dark suits too snug for comfort. Nan Mary was sitting halfway back, next to an aisle. She had saved an empty place in the pew for him. Mark squeezed in and gave her an apologetic smile. Nan grasped his hand in hers and turned her attention back to the speaker.

A middle-aged man in a dark blue suit of some indeterminate shiny material was at the podium, eulogizing Alfred "Dutch" Olsen. Like every other minister of the Word, Mark listened with one ear tuned for content and the other for presentation. Both ears were wanting. The man continuously referred to the deceased as Alfred instead of Dutch, and was building a word portrait based primarily around Olsen's work at the oil refinery. The decedent's occupation provided the preacher with plenty of opportunities to speak to his makeshift congregation about the need that everyone has to refine what is crude in life, converting it into riches. *Like the oil running down Aaron's beard* was a phrase he used more than once. His captured listeners started squirming in their pews when he exhorted them to burn off their excesses with the fire of holy works. And he lost them completely when he began comparing the various types of salvific grace to the relative merits of different weights in motor oil: 10–30, 10–40, etc.

Nan Mary gave Father Townsend a worried look and leaned into him, "I don't think Pastor Goodman knew Dutch too well," she whispered. "He never was much of a church-goer."

Mark finally gave up trying to follow the preacher's endless oily analogies and tuned out. This would become one more story for Bad Moments in Liturgy, when Jesuits took turns swapping tales over drinks in the rec room on a slow night. This one would pale however, compared to some of the all-time greats. There is an oral tradition of stories that gets passed along from Jesuit rec room to Jesuit rec room, and no matter how many times they are recounted, the classics are always appreciated. And when younger Jesuits are around, you know there is always one or two of the new guys still capable of being scandalized.

Despite the somber setting of Safe Harbor's Little Chapel, Father Townsend's face broke into a wide grin as he recalled a Jesuit companion's tale about a funeral where the family showed up with their dead mother in the back of a pickup truck. They carted her casket into the tiny rural church and plopped it on the floor in front of the altar, informing the bewildered priest that they needed some praying done before they took her back to the family farm for burial. The Jesuit did what he could under the circumstances, offering some hastily composed prayers and a blessing. Afterwards the family asked if he would object if they leaned the casket upright against the altar for a picture of him with mom. Father politely declined.

There was also the tale of the newly ordained priest

conducting his first funeral. Five minutes before the liturgy he was informed that the dearly departed had undergone a sex change several months earlier, so half the congregation would recognize the deceased as Michael and half as Michelle. Lots of luck, Father!

Mark had even found occasion to recount his own recent experience at St. Joseph's, when they opened the casket of a murder victim at the end of the Funeral Mass to find a knife sticking out of the corpse's chest.

Nan was tugging on his sleeve, and with a sudden start Mark realized that everyone around him was standing. Pastor Goodman had ended his eulogy and piped-in organ music was preparing them for two verses of *"Amazing Grace."* He stood with the others and cleared his throat.

After the funeral had ended and GrandSam and the other pall bearers had loaded their friend into the hearse, Mark huddled with his grandparents for a moment in front of the mortuary. The two of them would be accompanying Dutch to his gravesite and then returning to Jeanne Olsen's house for a reception and buffet; Mark however, was planning to bow out.

"I thought I'd head back to the house and change," he told them, "and then maybe visit a couple of folks on the reservation."

His grandfather gave him a disapproving scowl but said nothing.

"Are you still planning on going back to Seattle tonight?" his grandmother asked.

Mark nodded.

"We'll see you before you go, won't we?"

"Sure." He pecked her on the cheek and made his way through the throng of mourners to offer the widow his condolences.

As he returned to his car, a clock chimed three o'clock. If he was going to get away tonight, Mark would have to make tracks. But once he reached the outskirts of Mount Vernon, the roads once again clogged with tour buses and sightseers and the tulip traffic slowed to a crawl. Even though it was a weekday afternoon, the roadways throughout Skagit Valley were lined with people who had flocked here to see the tulip fields. And the flowers were beautiful, Mark had to admit. The sun had burnt through the overlay of clouds and warm light cast a glow onto the bright, colorful fields. Acres of tulips stretched out in radiant rows of red, yellow, white, pink, and purple. Majestic Mount Baker stood shining in the distance, while old red barns with oak trees growing alongside nestled in the center of some fields. It was picture perfect. And every man, woman, and child had abandoned their cars with camera in hand to prove it. Father Townsend's fingers drummed the steering wheel impatiently as he tried negotiating his way through the traffic back to LaConner. He spotted a bumper sticker on the back end of a truck belonging to one disgruntled local who was obviously fed up with the whole mess. *Nuke the tulips,* it pleaded.

An hour and fifteen minutes later, he was back at his grandparents, nerves frayed. As quickly as he could he changed back into blue jeans, a Pendleton shirt, and tennis shoes. Then he called Walking Boy. Eddie was home and expecting his call. Yes, he now knew what the cedar boards were and was anxious to talk with Mark about them. There were two elders who also wanted to speak with Mark about the boards. They agreed to meet at Eddie's in an hour.

Linda Patsy was not home when Mark called, but her daughter was. Jesse did not know where her mother was or when she might return. Yes, she would tell her mother that Mark had called.

"Are you still trying to help my daddy?"

The child's question caught him by surprise. Sometimes, when you get caught up and lost in a project, you can forget what motivated you in the first place. Father Townsend had never met Greg Patsy and he did not know if he would even like the man. But he had a growing conviction that an injustice was being done to him; and without ever explicitly intending to take up the cause of Jesse Patsy's daddy, the priest had set off to try to make things right. After he hung up the phone, Mark sat at his grandparents' kitchen table, twisting at the ends of his mustache as he silently reflected on his role in the events of the last few days.

There was no doubt that one of his objectives was to try and figure out what had happened to Dutch Olsen. Initially he was responding to his grandparents' own pain around the death of a close friend. His grandfather was worried about Dutch's widow, Jeanne. While at the same time, his grandmother was worried about her house-keeper's husband, arrested for the murder. And like most priests, Mark found himself trying to respond to every-one's hurts at once. In the process, he had managed to anger his grandfather plus draw down the wrath of Sister Teri Carter. At the same time, he also had to acknowledge that he was neglecting his parishioners and pastoral duties back at St. Joseph's in Seattle.

Father Townsend passed his hand in front of his eyes and groaned. Why do things have to become so damn complicated? Years ago, when he had fantasized about becoming a priest, he had imagined himself celebrating the sacraments and spending quiet, reflective moments in prayerful harmony with his Creator. But the reality was far from that idyllic, peace-filled fantasy. There were times when the stress, the ambiguity and the complications made his religious vocation feel much too difficult to sustain. Mark knew there were easier ways he could be spending his life—with the love and companionship of a wife, happy times with children of his own, and the leisure to pursue and care for his own needs and interests. Maybe he had made a mistake. Maybe he was wrong.

He leaned across the table and grabbed the phone, quickly dialing his parish in Seattle and asking the recep-tionist to put him through to Father Morrow. He waited impatiently while she rang Dan's office.

"Dan, this is Mark. Listen, I just need to know how things are down there. I'm caught up in an awful mess and am not really sure what to do about it. But I'm feeling strongly tempted to chuck the whole thing. And usually when I begin feeling that way, it means dark forces are trying to steer me off course. Help me out, buddy."

For the next twenty minutes Father Townsend answered

his Jesuit friend's questions and listened to his counsel as the two of them reviewed the situation together and discerned Mark's next steps. When he hung up the phone, Mark Townsend was back on track. Dan Morrow was able to remind him of a primary Ignatian principle: *In time of desolation*, St. Ignatius counseled, *we should never make any change, but remain firm in our resolve.*

An old dark green Ford Fairlane was parked in front of Eddie Walking Boy's ramshackle house when Mark arrived. He saw no sign of Eddie or the two elders he was to meet. But a voice called out a greeting to his knock at the door, so Mark let himself inside. The living room was dark and full of shadows and his eyes took a moment to adjust to the dimness. Two people were sitting close together on a couch and Father Townsend recognized one as the old woman who had spoken to him in front of the tribe's smoke house a couple of nights earlier. A white-haired man, as old as she, was sitting next to her. Eddie's voice came from the kitchen.

"I'm getting tea, Father. I'll be right in."

He introduced himself to the couple on the couch. The old woman's hand felt soft and cool and fluttered briefly like a small bird against his palm before she withdrew it. The man shook Mark's hand only a little longer, and his touch was similarly light. He said his name was Simon. His wife's name was Ida.

Mark took the chair next to the couch and waited for Eddie to appear. The two elders were content to sit silently, their eyes resting on some spot across the room. The silence, strong as it was, did not feel oppressive or uncomfortable. Indeed, it would have felt awkward if Mark had tried to make small talk while they waited for their host to serve them their tea. Eventually Eddie came in carrying a pot and four mugs, placing them on a low table in front of his guests. He returned to the kitchen for sugar and milk before settling himself into a straight-back chair he pulled alongside of Mark. The four of them quietly stirred their tea, taking tentative sips.

"So," Eddie began, "you went to the funeral?"

"Yes. With my grandparents." The old woman turned her head to look at Mark. "There was a pretty good crowd."

"A lot of people knew him," Eddie observed. "Lots of whites."

More silence as they drank coffee.

"It's good to have sunshine after all that rain," Eddie said.

"I drove by the tulip fields on my way," Mark said, "and the light was beautiful."

"Yes, it would be." Eddie set his coffee down. "Grandmother says the salmon berries will be good this year. Their flowers have already dropped."

"Fishing, too." The old man was speaking. "Spring Chinooks come when you see those salmon berry flowers." His wife nodded her head.

"Simon knows more about fishing than the rest of us put together," Eddy said respectfully. "I never bother putting out nets until he says it's time."

"But no more fish," said Simon. "Not like it was. Too many greedy people. The salmon know that and they left. Too bad for us." Ida nodded again.

The four of them sat quietly in the darkening room. Eddie offered more tea to his guests. When he was done pouring he turned to Father Townsend.

"I showed Simon and Grandmother the drawing you gave me. They say those cedar boards belong to the tribe."

"I thought they might," replied Mark. "Can you tell me what they are?"

The old man answered him. "Squa-de-lich. From our traditional ways."

"They were used by one of our medicine people," Eddy told him. "He's dead now."

"Squa-de-lich and Tus-tud helped our people find the food we needed for each year," Simon explained.

"Tus-tud is a staff," Eddie explained. "They are very strong medicine. Only certain people are given the power to care for Squa-de-lich and Tus-tud. They were strong medicine to the man who owned them."

For the first time, Ida spoke. Her voice was low and solemn and both Simon and Eddie listened respectfully as she conversed in her own dialect. When she was done, Simon translated.

"Fires are built for Squa-de-lich and Tus-tud," he told Mark, "and we burn salmon and berries in the smoke house fires. And many prayers are said."

"When you are not using them, where are Squa-de-lich and Tus-tud usually kept?"

Simon turned to his wife for a response, but the old woman kept her eyes on the floor in front of her and said nothing. Finally, Eddie cleared his throat and answered the priest's question.

"Their keepers hide them in safe places," he told him, watching his grandmother's face as he spoke. "No one is supposed to know where they are."

"But they'd be here on the reservation?" said Mark.

"Yes," Simon spoke up. "They are kept by those of us who use them. But when that person dies, the cedar boards are taken away and put where they can be safe and left alone. But now you tell us you have found them." The old man turned his eyes onto Mark Townsend's face. "Where did you see these, Father?"

The old man's stare was unwavering and Mark was forced to look away. He turned to Eddie instead with his reply.

"I only saw the boards," he informed them, "not the staff. They were in Dutch Olsen's hunting shack."

Eddie looked at him impassively. Mark could feel Simon's eyes still fixed on him. No one said anything.

"They were wrapped in a blanket."

"Please bring them to us." Grandmother's voice sounded clear and strong, but it came so quickly and so unexpectedly that Mark wondered if she had really spoken. He turned back to the old woman, but her head was still turned down, her eyes on the floor.

Eddie walked him to his car and thanked him for coming. "We hope you can return the Squa-de-lich to us," he told Mark. "Otherwise we will have to send someone ourselves. And after what has happened with Greg, it would probably be better if you could get them yourself.''

"Eddie, could Greg Patsy have known about those boards?''

"Sure,'' the young Indian answered. "They're part of Seeowyn—our old ways. Everyone who does Seeowyn would have to know about them.''

"Would Greg have known where they were hidden?'' asked Father Townsend.

"I doubt it.''

"But if he did?''

"If he did,'' Eddie hesitated before answering further, "it would mean he was one of their Keepers. His job then would be to protect them.''

"No matter what?''

Walking Boy laughed nervously and gave the priest an uneasy smile. "I don't know what you mean by that, Father.'' With that, he turned his back on the priest and went into the house.

FOURTEEN

St. Ignatius of Loyola left plenty of guidelines and sage counsel for his troops. One of his oft-quoted admonitions advises Jesuits to go out of their way to put the best interpretation on other people's actions and words. More than just giving them the benefit of the doubt, Ignatius wanted his men to work off of the assumption that the intentions of others were pure and holy.

Father Townsend tried, but he was having a difficult time finding anything pure and holy about stealing Swinomish sacred objects. The two cedar boards he uncovered in Dutch Olsen's hunting shack had to have been put there by one of three men: Dutch himself, Larry Robbins, or his grandfather. Or any combination of those three. As much as he hated to, Mark had to consider the possibility that GrandSam was one of the culprits. He knew his grandfather had no great love for things Indian, but would the old man go so far as to steal the cedar boards?

Maybe the three of them had merely stumbled across them during one of their searches for smuggler's gold. Perhaps they had no idea what they had. Mark certainly did not know when he first uncovered them. But then why carefully hide them wrapped in a blanket? Maybe the men had decided they should take them to the shack for safe keeping. Maybe someone else had found them and sold or given them to Dutch. Or Larry. Or GrandSam.

Maybe the best interpretation, in this case, was not going to fly. Mark was back where he started. The Squa-de-lich he saw at the shack had no business being there and Father Townsend had now been formally asked by tribal elders to arrange for their return.

The harder Mark tried to extricate himself out of this situation, the deeper he seemed to be getting. He was beginning to feel like some prehistoric beast who had wandered into the La Brea tar pits. The more he struggled, the deeper he sank.

"Pull and be damned is right," the priest mumbled to himself, steering his car down Reservation Road. Daylight was fading fast and Mark flipped on the headlights. Ahead of him, a startled deer bounded out of the road and into the deep underbrush alongside. Mark eased off of the gas, suddenly aware of how fast he was speeding.

He had already resigned himself to spending another night in LaConner. There was no way he could return to Seattle with the unfinished business at hand. Eddie Walking Boy had made it clear that unless Mark found some way to return the Squa-de-lich quietly, tribal members would take care of the matter themselves. That could possibly end up involving GrandSam. Father Townsend was willing to do just about anything he could to avoid that. And there was one other small matter left unresolved. Linda Patsy's husband was still in jail, charged with the murder of Alfred "Dutch" Olsen.

No lights were on at the Patsy house. But through the living room window Mark could see a flickering glow against one wall. The television was on and he was pretty sure he knew who was watching. Peering through the picture window from the front lawn he spotted Jesse, curled on the couch, her legs tucked tightly up to her chest. Her small face was bathed in the TV's blue light. The youngster was sucking her thumb, just like a much smaller child.

He rang the doorbell and waited. He could hear her

small feet on the other side of the door, but it remained closed. "Who is it?"

"Jesse, it's me, Father Townsend. Can I come in?"

"My mom's not here."

"Would it be okay to visit with you while I wait?"

The lock clicked and the door slowly opened. He could see the damp smudges of hastily wiped tears.

"I'm watching TV."

"Can I come in and watch with you?"

The girl made no reply but padded back to her spot on the couch. Mark closed the door and followed, taking a chair facing the set. Robin Williams was doing something weird with balloons.

"What's the show?"

"*Mork and Mindy,*" Jesse replied. "He's funny."

"I like it when he talks to his boss at the end," the priest said.

She looked at him with something verging on interest. "You watch this show?"

"I used to," Mark admitted. "It was on a long time ago."

"I never saw it before this year."

They watched the space alien's antics in silence until commercials started, then Jesse jumped off the couch.

"You want to eat something?" she wanted to know.

"What do you have?"

She headed for the kitchen, her voice trailing behind her, "Peanut butter with carrot and celery sticks. Mom won't let me eat candy before dinner."

"Where is your mom?"

"Seeing Daddy again." Mark could hear a stool being dragged across the kitchen floor. "In a couple of days he's going to go to a jail in Seattle. Mom says that's too far to visit him so she's seeing him up here instead." Jesse dashed back into the room with her snacks, plopping onto the couch just as the program resumed. She dipped a celery stick into the jar and offered it to Father Townsend.

"I imagine it doesn't feel very good to know your father's in jail."

The girl turned her face away from Mark, towards the

TV, and bit into a carrot stick. He waited for her reply.

"Not very good," she mumbled. "I try to keep it out of my head, but it always comes back." She swallowed and took another bite of carrot. "I wish we were having school because then I'd have to be thinking about something else."

"When does spring break end?"

"Next Monday. I can't hardly wait."

The room was suddenly awash in bright, white light as a car pulled into the cul-de-sac. They heard the engine stop in the Patsy driveway and Jesse bolted from the couch. She threw herself against her mother's legs as Linda opened the front door, burying her face against her mother's breasts.

Linda Patsy looked haggard. She managed a weak smile when she spotted Father Townsend, but there was no energy behind it. She shifted a brown shopping bag from one arm to the other in order to rub her daughter's back. Bending down, she kissed the top of Jesse's head. "Hello, sweetheart," she softly cooed, "have you been good?"

Mark reached out and took the sack from the woman's arms and carried it into the kitchen. The sink was filled with dirty dishes and a pan of cold food sat neglected on the stove top. Life in the Patsy house was continuing to unravel.

Mother and daughter were snuggled together on the couch when Mark returned to the living room. Linda Patsy smiled her thanks at him.

"How's Greg?" he asked.

"Okay, I guess. They're taking him to Seattle in a couple of days. He's not too happy about that."

"Why can't he stay in Anacortes?"

"Because he's Indian," she said, making no attempt to disguise the bitterness in her voice. "Everything we do becomes a federal case. Greg comes under the U.S. attorney's office and that's in Seattle." She looked up at the priest and then gently placed her hands over her daughter's ears. "He's real scared, Father."

"Is there any chance of bail?"

She shook her head. "They already issued a warrant to

hold him without bail. He's a flight risk they think, because we live so close to Canada and because a lot of Greg's family are on that side of the border.''

A Jesuit at Seattle University moonlighted as a chaplain at the King County Jail and Mark made a mental note to call him when he got back into Seattle.

"You remember that drawing I showed you? I found out what it was.''

"Your trip to the museum paid off then.'' Linda was idly combing her daughter's hair with her fingers while she talked.

"Yeah, but not for that. A couple of the elders were able to identify the carvings. They're called Squa-de-lich.''

The woman nodded. "I recognize the name,'' she said. "Part of the harvest festival for Seeowyn. I've never seen them used, though. Those boards would be pretty old, I think.''

"The tribe kept them hidden for safe keeping,'' Mark told her. "But I don't know who would have been in charge of them.''

"I'm afraid I can't help you, Father. Like I said, I'm Colville.''

"What about Greg? Would he have had anything to do with them?''

Linda's head snapped sharply up at the priest's question and she stared hard at him with bright eyes.

"Jesse, honey, I bought turkey pot pies for our dinner. They're in that bag in the kitchen. Why don't you run in and pop those in the oven, would you please? Set the temperature at 375. Make sure the other dial says bake.''

Her daughter slowly got off the couch and went into the kitchen. Linda waited until her daughter was out of the room.

"I'm not sure what you're asking, Father.'' Her tone was firm and cold.

"I'm trying to find out how those carvings got into Dutch Olsen's shack,'' Father Townsend replied. "I just wondered if Greg . . .''

"You just wondered if Greg might have stolen them.''

"No, Linda . . ."

"I think so, Father. I think you've found some tribal property that white men have and now you're looking for an Indian to blame. Isn't that about right?" She stood up from the couch.

"Please, Linda," beseeched Mark, holding out his hands, "that's not what I meant."

Jesse was standing in the doorway to the kitchen, watching them.

"You're asking if Greg had access to the boards, if he could have taken them. Maybe you think he sold them to Dutch Olsen." Her voice was loud and angry. "Maybe Greg killed the guy for more money. Isn't that what you're thinking, Father?"

"Mommy!"

"No, Linda, it's not." Mark was standing, trying to calm her. "I'm not thinking that."

"I think you need to leave."

"Please, Linda."

Jesse had started to cry.

"I would like you to. Now." Linda Patsy was opening her front door. "I don't think you're helping us," she declared. "Please go."

The door closed firmly behind him and the lock clicked. Mark could hear Jesse crying and Linda trying to soothe her. He moved off the porch to his car, parked at the curb. As he started to get in, he noticed its back end tilting oddly. He had a flat tire. Father Townsend stooped to examine the tire and found a deep slash in the rubber. He stood back up and looked around. Far down the street, passing under a dim streetlight, he could see a figure hurrying away. Mark could not swear to it, but it looked like a woman wearing a long blue skirt, with sandals on her feet.

By the time he had changed the tire and driven back to his grandparents', it was a quarter past seven. GrandSam and Nan were in the living room, watching *"Wheel of Fortune."* His grandfather looked up and Nan stood when Mark came in.

"We thought you were lost," Sam said, his eyes drifting back to the television.

"Have you eaten?" his grandmother asked worriedly.

"I did," Mark lied. That was easier than trying to refuse the plate of food he knew would be forced upon him. His stomach was too upset for eating.

"Jeanne said to thank you for attending the funeral. The poor woman, I think she's wrung out from all the stress." Nan pressed her lips together. "I feel so sorry for her."

"Yeah," GrandSam added, "me too."

"I think I'm going to stay up for another day or so, if that's okay."

His grandmother beamed. "That's wonderful, Mark. We'd love it if you could stay all the time. You know you're welcome here anytime."

Father Townsend gave his grandmother a quick kiss on the cheek. "I'd better call the parish."

Rather than call the house and risk getting Dan Morrow, Mark called the church office. He knew no one would pick up the phone after hours. The days of omnipresent housekeepers or even an answering service were past.

"You have reached the offices of St. Joseph's Catholic Church . . ." Helen Hart's loud, shrill voice announced. The problem with leaving a message on the parish's answering machine was having to wait while their receptionist's recording recited the long list of Mass times, both daily and weekend, and then raced through three available phone numbers in case of an emergency. The lengthy announcement was necessary but frustrating to listen to. Doubly aggravating when you were calling long distance. The mechanical beep at the end was blessed relief. Mark left a quick message for the parish staff, informing them his return would be further delayed, and hung up.

He quickly dialed a second number. The phone rang only twice before it was answered by a live voice.

"Eddie, this is Father Townsend." Mark was speaking quietly, hoping that Pat and Vanna, the game show hosts, were keeping his grandparents' attention riveted to the

TV. "Can you borrow your friend's boat tomorrow morning?"

Eddie thought he could.

"When is the tide high enough to get us through Hole in the Wall?"

The two men agreed to meet at 6:30 in the morning at the Swinomish dock. Mark had decided it was time to reclaim the Squa-de-lich.

FIFTEEN

Drumming on the roof meant rain. And lying in the dark, Father Townsend could hear a lot of drumming. He rolled over and focused on the red glow of the bedside clock. Six o'clock. There was always the chance that Eddie would cancel because of weather, but Mark knew he could not risk it. He took another moment before climbing out of bed, pausing long enough to offer up whatever the day would bring. In twenty minutes he was out the door and headed towards the Swinomish dock. No coffee, no rain gear—this was going to be a fun trip.

Eddie had both items waiting for him. Mark found him at the end of the dock, his small boat bobbing in the choppy waves of the channel. Although it was past sunrise, the heavy cloud cover was keeping the morning dark and gloomy. The river was cloaked in a thin veneer of fog, making the shops and buildings on the other side look vague and indistinct. The young man was draped in a dark green poncho and he had managed to spread it out to cover both his body and most of the seat he was on. Mark's poncho was laid across the seat in the middle, keeping it dry.

"Great day for a boat ride, huh, Father?"

Mark grunted and climbed into the little skiff. Eddie

waited until he was seated with his poncho on before handing him the thermos of hot coffee. Then reaching behind him, he pulled the cord to start the engine. They were soon bobbing into the middle of the channel, heading towards Hole in the Wall. Rain fell in torrents and the small motorboat was being roughly tossed around by the waves. Mark looked around for life jackets and finally spotted two faded orange ones floating in the oily puddle that sloshed in the bottom of the stern.

Eddie was small enough so that his poncho kept him protected. Although Mark sat hunched over, there was still plenty of his body left exposed and he could feel his clothes growing wetter by the minute. Spray from about every sixth or seventh wave flipped above the bow, spattering Mark's back. Eddie was doing a good job of sliding between most of the bigger waves, but one caught him unaware and sloshed across the bow, washing against Mark's back.

"Sorry!" he called out. Mark gave him a morose look which the Indian found hilarious.

"You probably don't get to do this much down in Seattle, do you?"

The priest shook his head. "It's not in my job description, no."

"If we let the weather keep us off the water," Eddie said, "we might just as well give up our boats. The fish don't care, they're wet anyway. If we want to eat salmon, it means we have to get wet."

"How much fishing is done for subsistence?" Mark questioned the Indian. "I thought most of what you caught was sold commercially."

Walking Boy nodded. "Now it is. But unfortunately, the runs are so thin that there isn't much to sell. Most of what we keep for ourselves are the kings. They're the best eating anyway."

Out of the foggy murk behind them Mark saw a large boat bearing down. He pointed past Eddie's shoulder. The Indian turned around and looked, then made a quick adjustment, steering their boat toward the shoreline. Mark could see several figures moving about inside the cabin. The cruiser was cutting back its speed.

"I think they see us," he said.

As it cruised past he could see the name, *SinCan V*, on the side. The side door slid open and a jacketed arm waved at them. Mark started to raise his in reply, but he could feel rain hitting his thigh and quickly lowered the poncho back over his torso.

The big boat's wake had reached their tiny skiff and was lifting them up, sliding them perilously close to the rocky shoreline.

"Damn pukers anyway," Eddie swore. "Why the hell can't they move over!" He turned to cut back across the *SinCan*'s wake, hitting the waves just off forty-five degrees, slicing through them as smoothly as he could as he tried to fall in behind the center of the yacht's wake. "That must be Suu's tour group."

"What tour?"

"I heard him talking yesterday," Eddie explained. "A bunch of business types were coming in from Asia and he was planning to take them out on a cruise today. Too bad they chose such a lousy day to do it. They'll probably go out Deception Pass and then on up north into the islands. Stick around and we can meet them coming down the other end of the channel this afternoon. Maybe they could take another try at swamping us."

"Thanks. Once is enough."

The weather was not the greatest for cruising the San Juan Islands. The rain and low clouds would keep the *SinCan*'s passengers inside the cabin as they sailed through some of the most scenic parts of the Pacific Northwest. Suu's Asian guests would be forced to squint through the yacht's windows if they wanted to keep dry and still see anything. But after Mark's tour of the luxury boat, he did not imagine anyone would suffer too greatly. Plenty of food and drink would be available in the well-stocked galley, and the view outside the windows would look just fine from the plush seating in the main cabin. Father Townsend had to admit that wealth did have its privileges. When he professed his vow of poverty eighteen years earlier, he never realized it would one day translate into choosing to drown in a ten-foot open dinghy against lounging inside a fifty-five-foot yacht.

"There's the Hole." Eddie was turning their craft directly for the center of the opening in the rocks in front of them. Once through, the water on the north fork of the Skagit flattened out. Now the raindrops were making flat ringlets where they struck the smooth-flowing water. The river's pull was much weaker and Eddie did not have to fight the currents as much, enabling him to cut back on the throttle. The engine adjusted immediately, quieting down.

Once in the river it did not take them long to reach Dutch Olsen's cabin. Both men were searching ahead to see if another boat might be tied in front of the floating shack. Father Townsend was well aware that he was about to commit the same crime his grandfather was guilty of: breaking and entering. Except in GrandSam's case, the old man was breaking into the shack as Dutch's friend to make sure everything was safe. Mark and Eddie were there to steal—plain and simple. Despite the fact they were taking back what rightfully belonged to the tribe, Mark's religious sensibilities still left him feeling uneasy.

Eddie showed no hesitation. As they drew near he gunned the engine and they roared toward the shack. Just before it looked like they might plow headlong into the floating logs, the Indian cut the engine and swung the boat back toward the river's center. Momentum carried them forward and as the boat settled they slowly drifted sideways into the log boom. Both men leaned across and grabbed dock lines, tying the boat in place. Eddie clamored out first, offering a hand to the priest, rocking unsteadily as he tried to balance himself in the center of the skiff.

"Careful," the young Indian warned, "you don't want to fall in."

"What difference would it make?" Mark replied. "Could I get any wetter?"

Walking Boy gave the priest a wicked grin as he helped him up onto the landing. The door to the shack was padlocked. They tried the windows on each side of the cabin and those were locked tight, too. Neither one was very eager to try breaking the door, so they began looking in the obvious places for a key. One had to be hidden somewhere.

"What do they keep it locked for anyway?" wondered Eddie, "It's just an old shack."

Mark did not mention the guns he knew were kept inside. "Keep looking," he urged, "it has to be around here somewhere."

"It'll be attached to something like a cork or plastic bobber," the Indian predicted, "in case they drop it overboard. So look for something that floats."

Mark found it. The key was beneath a small piece of weathered driftwood that looked like it had been casually tossed against the house. A strand of fishing line kept the key tied to the wood.

The shack was dark and cold and looked the way it had when GrandSam, Larry, and Mark had left it two days earlier. The Jesuit crossed quickly to the cot in the far corner, hunting for the blanket he had picked off the floor. It was gone.

"Check the other cots," he instructed Eddie. "It's one of those old green army blankets. The boards are wrapped inside."

Only one of the cots had a blanket like that, and there was nothing in its folds. The boards were missing. The two of them roamed through the one-room shack, checking shelves, looking under old clothes—anywhere where the Squa-de-lich could be hidden. But the boards were not there.

"You're sure they didn't have them when you guys left?" Eddie questioned the priest.

"Positive."

"Then someone has been in here since then."

. Mark stopped his searching and stood next to the table in the middle of the room, slowly turning and studying the inside of the cabin. As far as he could remember, things looked exactly the way they had left them two days before. Except of course, for the missing blanket.

"Come on," the young Indian urged, "no use hanging around here."

Eddie turned their boat back toward the opening into Swinomish Channel. Both men were feeling disappointed and they moved down the river in silence. The only sounds came from the outboard motor and the rain hitting against their ponchos. Walking Boy cautiously steered them through the opening between the river and the channel. Once on the other side, he turned to the left. Mark was lost in his own thoughts and it took a minute or two before he realized they were heading away from La-Conner. He looked back over his shoulder, toward the mouth of the channel.

"Where are you going?"

Eddie tipped his head towards the channel's entrance. "Just out there a ways, not too far."

The priest could feel impatience and irritation rising inside him. The trip out to the shack was a waste of time. He was cold and wet and wanted to go back to his grandparents' where he could take a nice long, hot shower. Instead, they were heading in the opposite direction for no reason that Mark could discern. Eddie Walking Boy seemed oblivious to the weather as he kept peering into the rain ahead of them, holding the outboard's handle with his right hand and ignoring the priest's scowl.

The waves increased as they neared the channel's mouth. Skagit Bay was broken with white chop and their small boat bounced roughly across the heavy waves. Reluctantly, Mark poked his arms out from beneath his poncho to grab a hold onto the boat's sides. A rogue wave lifted them above the water's surface, then just as suddenly dropped them back down with a jarring thud. This was beyond stupid, the priest decided, it was turning dangerous. He was about to ask Eddie to turn around when the Indian spoke.

"You been on Goat Island yet?"

Mark shook his head.

"So you've never seen the fort."

"Fort Whitman? I read about it at the museum."

The Indian grinned. "Reading and seeing are two different things." He was turning the boat starboard, curving them toward the southern side of the island. "It's not too far." He pointed to a bluff rising about seventy-five feet above the island's rocky shoreline. "Up there, behind those trees, is where they hid their cannons."

There was nothing to see except the steep, rocky side of the bluff and on top, the sinuous red limbs of a few madronna trees growing along the edge of a stand of tall firs.

"Why don't we do this some other time," suggested Father Townsend, "when the weather's better?"

Eddie shrugged. "We're here now." But he continued following the shoreline, keeping about thirty feet out from the beach. "You can get to the fort from there," he pointed to a narrow strip of rocky beach, "but you have to climb up a cliff by rope. It'd be pretty muddy. There's another place down a ways. It's further to walk, but safer." He fell silent as he studied the shore.

Mark shivered inside his poncho. The boat's constant rocking was making him queasy. This was almost as bad as flying in an airplane, he decided. He kept his eyes glued to the island, trying to ignore the churning waves beneath him. His companion studied him as he began guiding the boat closer into shore.

"Cheer up," Eddie reassured him. "There's covered places at the fort. We can build a fire and warm up before heading back."

They did not pull their boat up onto the shore. Eddie said the tide was slack and would soon start running back out. The boat might shift and move a little then, but it would be easier than trying to drag it back down to the waterline. He secured the bowline around the roots of a massive tree truck, bleached white and half-buried in the gravel beach. Fastening a small blue daypack beneath his poncho, he led Mark up a trail into dense woods.

The trail was overgrown and wet boughs impeded their progress. The men moved slowly, keeping their heads turned downwards to avoid getting slapped in the face by a wet limb. The ground was rough, broken up by small gullies and hillocks. Rotted tree trunks had crashed across the trail in spots. They were able to step over the smaller ones, but there were two or three so thick that they had to climb over them. One massive fir was almost four feet in diameter.

"The army left some of the old growth," Eddie told Mark, "but they used most of it for building docks and things." He pointed off towards the northeast. "There's a rock quarry up at that end."

"No one uses this island now?"

"Nah," the Indian ducked under a drooping, low hanging limb. "The Scouts set up camp here in the summer, and kids like to come over and explore around, but no one lives here." He turned back and grinned at the priest. "There's no electricity, so you couldn't use your micro-waves and VCRs. Can't live without those, you know."

Slowly they threaded their way through the quiet woods. The two of them fell silent as they hiked, partially to conserve energy but also because the silence around them was impressive enough to curtail idle chatter. Walking Boy occasionally stopped to point out a plant or tree he recognized. When he knew it, he also shared the Indian name with Mark. They had been walking for about twenty-five minutes when Eddie pointed to a dark square shape through the trees.

"That's part of the fort," he informed Mark. "We'll start seeing buildings now."

He led the priest over to the structure. It was some sort of small bunker, about ten feet square, made of thick concrete. A thick metal door was frozen open on rusty hinges. There were no windows. Inside it was dank with moss growing across the floor and up the walls. A couple of crumpled beer cans lay in one corner.

"There's more interesting stuff further up," said Eddie, leading the way.

As they moved further on the terrain changed. The ground became flatter, with less undergrowth. And the trees thinned out. They were moving through an area that had once been occupied. More and more footpaths criss-crossed in front of them. The shapes of more small buildings began appearing through the trees and there was litter scattered across the ground. Eddie marched them past a small pile of broken red brick. Mark bent and grabbed a piece as he walked by, but it was just brick with crumbling white mortar and he soon let it drop. All around was evidence of the army's encampment, although there was nothing of value in sight.

They left the cover of the trees and entered a clearing. In front of them rose a thirty-foot concrete wall, formed into a half circle. The floor of the bunker was also poured concrete, with a round elevated base about eight feet across and set into the center. The rusted threads of massive iron bolts were anchored in the concrete. Whatever they had once secured was now gone.

"A cannon mount," Eddie informed Mark. "There's four of them," he added, pointing to the left and right of where they stood. "They used to have them aimed out across Skagit Bay. The guns were on lifts, so if an enemy boat came in through Deception Pass these big honkers could rise above that wall and blast them out of the water. Then they'd duck back down."

"Incredible," the Jesuit exclaimed, half to himself.

Father Townsend was enough of a romantic to imagine himself emerging from jungle thickets into the site of some lost city in a remote corner of the world. Blackberry vines and thick moss were growing over the concrete and brick. There were dark, foreboding doorways and small windows of black emptiness staring out at him. The only sound was the dripping rain as his eyes searched the ruins in front of him. Stairs led up to the tops of the bunkers. There were rusted iron rings set into the walls and pieces of pipe and iron railing scattered around. He crossed the circular floor and peered into a doorway leading into a concrete hall. Enough light filtered in from the doorway and small windows to let him move about inside. Like the other outbuilding they had inspected, this place was cold and dank. He was in a long narrow room that stretched back into the darkness. He could not tell how far back it might extend. The remains of a campfire sat in the middle of the floor in front of the entrance; blackened chars of wood and ash. Nearby were two squat logs, makeshift stools for whomever built the fire. Behind one of them lay a tattered blue stocking cap. Cigarette butts littered the floor and graffiti covered the wall space opposite the doorway. *Class of '89 rules!* was sprayed in large faded red letters on the gray concrete. Beneath it, in crayon, a dissenting author had responded: *'89 sucks!* There were lots of names too. From the signatures and messages scrawled on the concrete, it looked like half of the kids from LaConner had visited the abandoned ruins of Fort Whitman to scratch their messages into crumbling concrete: *Jeff was here! Jenny is cute! Dan the Man. John loves Pam. Jesse loves Ryan. Vern and Beans forever. Kim loves* . . . the other name was smudged.

Mark backed out of the room, blinking as he reemerged into the daylight. His companion was on the other side, piling an armful of wood against a concrete overhang.

"I'll build a fire," Eddie said. "Look around if you want to. There's more on both sides."

"Do you know how many soldiers this place used to hold?"

"I don't, maybe a hundred. It got built right before World War I and was used until after the second war. My grandfather remembered playing baseball against the soldiers' team. And that was way back."

While Walking Boy concentrated on building his fire, Mark continued his wandering. He climbed to the top of the bunker. Trees had grown up, but through them there was still a view of Skagit Bay, with Whidbey Island off in the distance. He wandered across the top, pausing to peer down into the three other placements. They all looked the same: half circles with the empty cannon mount sitting in the middle. Each was littered with five decades of debris, but Mark was still able to imagine a garrison of men moving below while lookouts posted watch over the waters in front of them.

By the time he returned, Eddie's fire was burning brightly. They stripped off their ponchos and sat close to the flames, letting the heat warm them. The steam rose from their wet clothes. Eddie had brought along his Thermos of coffee and from the pack under his poncho, produced a sack of sandwiches. The priest realized how hungry he was and eagerly accepted the Indian's food.

"In the past this was a place where our people came," Eddie said, swallowing a bite of sandwich. "They used to gather shells and hunt ducks out here." He slowly sipped his coffee. "They called it *Kewdust'atab.*"

"What's that mean?"

The young Indian shrugged, then grinned at him. "Place where you gather shells and hunt ducks, I guess."

"Touché," Father Townsend acknowledged.

"Some things don't mean any more than just what they are."

"You're a philosopher, too," Mark told him.

"Not really. But lately it seems like everything that's Indian has to have some special meaning to it. Hell, sometimes frybread is just frybread."

Mark nodded. He realized the same thing could be said about priests. But sometimes bread and wine are just bread and wine.

They finished eating but continued huddling by the fire. The chill had left and Mark's clothes were almost dry, however he was still reluctant to head back out into the rain. But Eddie tossed the paper sack into the fire and stood to pull on his poncho so Mark followed suit.

"Don't forget your pack," he told Eddie, bending over to lift it. As he did so, the top flopped open and a pistol fell onto the concrete. Quickly Eddie scooped it up and hurriedly stuffed it back into his pack.

"What the hell are you doing with that?"

"Nothing," the Indian muttered.

"I mean it," Mark insisted. He stared hard at the Indian and could feel his temper rising. "Why'd you bring a gun?"

"I didn't know what was going to happen at that shack." Eddie's face was flushed. "I didn't know if someone would try and stop us."

"So you brought a gun?"

The Indian shrugged. "And I didn't know what we'd find here, either. It's better to be safe."

"What does safe have to do with anything?" countered Mark angrily. "I didn't think we were doing anything so dangerous that we'd need a gun. Were you thinking my grandfather and Larry Robbins would ambush us?"

Eddie kicked at the fire but made no response.

"He's my grandfather."

There was still no answer.

Mark turned to look around the clearing. "And what? You thought maybe the soldiers had come back here?"

Eddie raised his head and blinked.

"Why the gun, Eddie?"

"Come on," Walking Boy said in reply. "I want to show you something." Turning his back on the priest, he began walking quickly into the woods.

SIXTEEN

Father Townsend studied Eddie's back as they traipsed through the sodden woods. As near as he could tell, they were following the same trail that they had come in on earlier. The Indian made no effort at conversation, but kept moving determinedly ahead. Mark had watched him stuff the pistol back into the bottom of his pack, but it made him nervous to know Eddie had it on him. As he reflected on it, he realized how little he actually knew about the young man leading him through the woods. He also realized there was no one on God's wet green earth who knew he was on this island with Eddie Walking Boy. If anything were to happen . . . he let the rest of that consideration go unexpressed; better not to think such thoughts. With a sudden wave of relief he remembered the *SinCan* cruising past them in the channel. At least there were witnesses who could place him with Eddie. Although a lot of good that would do if . . . Again, better not to think on it.

The two men had been moving through the woods for about fifteen minutes, at a much quicker rate than when they hiked into the fort. Mark figured they were probably less than ten minutes away from the beach where they had landed. He hoped that was where Eddie was leading him.

But trails kept intersecting theirs and the woods were so thick that he had no way of knowing where they were. The bits of sky he could see through the trees were thick with dark gray clouds and gave no sense of the sun's direction. Mark was lost in a maze of tall trees and thick brambles.

"Where are we headed?" he tried out on the silent back in front of him.

There was no answer at first, then without turning, Eddie replied, "It's not much further."

They continued hiking in silence. The rain seemed to be letting up a little. They were climbing a small hill, following a narrow path, heavily overgrown with thin, leafy vines. Suddenly Mark's left foot struck something solid and without warning he tumbled to the ground. The undergrowth was thick enough to break his fall, but his face was washed by the fronds of a dripping fern and he lay still for moment on the muddy trail before Eddie's hand reached down to help him up.

"Are you okay, Father?" he said, his voice sounding solicitous. "There's a lot more rocks around here, so you've got to walk careful."

"I'm all right," Mark said gruffly, more embarrassed than anything else. His poncho was coated in mud and leaves and he brushed at the front of it, dirtying his hands in the process. "What a mess," he complained.

"We're almost there," Eddie assured him. They set off once more.

They hiked up another hundred feet or so when Eddie called back over his shoulder, warning the priest to watch his step. Eddie paused when they reached the top of the hill, looking down at the path in front of them.

"It's real steep here," he cautioned, "so go careful. Try grabbing onto the branches as you go down. They'll slow you so you won't slip. Let me go first and wait so you don't get hit by any limbs."

With that the young man set off down the trail, slipping in the mud but managing to stay on his feet to the bottom. Mark waited at the top until the trail was clear, then began inching his way down the muddy pathway. He could feel his feet slipping beneath him, but by keeping a firm grip on the limbs poking out on both sides of him and planting his feet sideways, he managed to make it down without mishap. The ground was noticeably more rocky at the bottom and they had to slow down to pick their way across the rough, uneven ground. After another five hundred feet or so, a wide clearing opened in front of them. About seventy-five feet across, it formed an open circle filled only with sky overhead. There were no trees growing in the opening and only a thin ground cover of ferns and weeds. Both men paused at the edge. After coming through the closed darkness of the woods, the light in the clearing was startling.

"Over there," Eddie nodded and struck out across the open ground. Mark followed him to the other side. As they neared the center he realized they were in a shallow depression, and all around them the trees stopped right at the raised lip of the concavity. At a few feet away from the exact center, Eddie dropped to one knee. He was kneeling in front of the narrow opening to a cave sloping into the earth. The entrance was about five feet across, and maybe six feet high—large enough for a person to easily pass through. The young Indian picked out a rock and lobbed it into the center of the hole. Mark heard it bounce against stone, followed by a splash.

"There's water down there," Eddie pointed out unnecessarily. "But you can wade through. It gets wide further back and goes a long ways." He looked up at the priest. "I never went all the way back in there."

Mark knew there had to be some significance to the cave, but he has having trouble understanding what it might be. Then it came to him.

"This cave," he said, "is this where your people hid the Squa-de-lich?"

Eddie Walking Boy gave the Jesuit an incredulous look, then threw another stone down the hole. This time Mark barely counted one second before he heard it bounce and land with a splash.

"You kidding?" Eddie turned back to him. "You think we'd put them in where there's water?" He shook his head. "This is an old mine. A long time ago they took out some ore that had travertine in it. Folks got real excited, but there wasn't very much in there and it wasn't very good, so nothing much was ever done." He stood back up and looked at the trees surrounding them. "But it's a pretty cool place, isn't it?"

"So what's the point?" Mark's patience was wearing thin. Eddie seemed to sense what the priest was feeling and he turned to face him directly.

"We never hid anything in the cave," he told the priest, "but pretty near to it. Our people considered this a holy place." He turned on his heels and headed towards the trees. "Come on."

Mark followed him back into the dense woods. There was no apparent trail and the two of them had to climb over fallen trees and through thick brush. They only went about thirty feet before Eddie stopped in front of a tall, thick fir. The tree was obviously old growth, soaring straight and high above all the surrounding ones. The base was a good five feet in circumference.

"This is where those cedar boards were put," Eddie told him in a quiet voice, sounding almost as if he was afraid of being overheard. "But that was after the fort closed and everyone left the island. They brought them over here where we thought they'd be safe."

Eddie knelt at the base of the tree and, carefully sweeping the fronds of a large fern into his arms, bent them to one side. He was exposing a large natural cavity that went under the tree's roots. There was more than enough room for the two cedar boards Mark had found in Dutch Olsen's shack.

"Our people used to come to *Kewdust'atab* to hunt and gather shells," Eddie said, releasing the fern and letting it spring back into place, "but they also thought this was a good place to pray. You priests go away on retreats sometimes, yeah?" Mark nodded. "Well, we came here." He stood and brushed his hands before leading Mark back toward the clearing. "That's spring water in the cave," he continued, "and good-tasting. Some of our elders say it's good medicine. When the whites tried mining in there we figured this place was ruined. But since then it's gone back to the way it was before.''

They were back at the center of the clearing now, and the two of them unconsciously were turning in a full circle. The tall trees surrounded them on all sides, silent green guardians towering above them. Above the tree tops the sky was a soft, thick blanket of cloud. The rain was falling as a light mist now.

"Some who believe in Seeowyn say they have seen spirits of our ancestors here.'' Eddie's voice was almost a whisper again. He was speaking in a reverent tone and Mark had the sudden impression of standing in the center of a cathedral. This was a holy place—he could feel it. And his nervous fear of being alone on the island with Eddie now turned into feelings of awkward embarrassment.

"So whoever took the boards must have found them here," reasoned Mark.

Eddie nodded.

"So they knew about this place."

He nodded again.

"So either they're Swinomish who know what this place was used for, or . . ." The priest stopped speaking and turned back towards the mouth of the cave, tugging at one side of his thick mustache as he stared into the dark hole.

Eddie waited and watched, knowing Father Townsend was sorting something out in his own mind. He would speak when it was time. After another minute, Mark turned back to him, his mouth forming a small, tight line.

"Either a Swinomish or someone who somehow knew exactly where to look."

"That's what Grandmother said," Eddie told the Jesuit. "But how would they know where to look?"

"S dash 50 and I dash 21." Father Townsend's mouth relaxed as Eddie frowned in puzzlement. "The museum in Anacortes has boxes of files about both the Swinomish and Goat Island," he explained. "And there's certainly enough in those files to make the connection. Especially if you know what you're looking for."

"That'd take some work, though."

"It sure would," agreed Mark. "I looked in those files for a couple of hours and never made the connection. Someone else read through that same stuff, only he knew what he was doing."

"But why bother," wondered Eddie, "unless you were interested in Seeowyn?"

"That's a good question," the priest admitted. "I wish I knew the answer."

The beach was less than five hundred feet away from the clearing, in the opposite direction from which they had come. Mark was puzzled why they had hiked nearly half-way through the island to the fort before Eddie led him back across the island to the cave. But he let it go. The young man must have had his reasons.

The tide had turned and started back out. Their small boat had drifted to the end of its tether, but eventually the water ran out, leaving it sitting high and dry on the gravel beach. The two men set to work tugging and dragging it back into the shallow water. For such a small craft, the weight felt immense and Mark's arms and shoulders were soon tightening in protest. Scooting the boat into water deep enough to float it meant soaking both their feet and lower legs. The cold was numbing. By the time they were back in the boat and able to use their paddles to push out into deeper water, both men were wet and muddy up to their thighs.

Eddie was having trouble starting the motor. He pulled the starter rope several times, stopping to adjust the choke, trying again. The engine sputtered but failed to catch. Eddie pulled a few more times.

"What's the matter with it?"

"I'm not sure," the Indian replied. He yanked on the rope again.

"Maybe it's flooded." Mark was guessing. He knew nothing about engines.

"I don't think so," Eddie sniffed. "It doesn't smell flooded." He lifted the gas tank and shook it, then disconnected the fuel line and shook it over the side of the boat. "There's probably water in the line," he told Mark.

He reattached the line, adjusted the choke, and pulled again. After a few tries the motor sputtered to life and caught hold. Eddie quickly pushed in the choke and leaned on the throttle, steering them away from the shore. "It was water," he called to Mark. They were making a wide arc back toward the mouth of the channel. Father Townsend looked back, past Eddie, watching the shoreline of Goat Island receding behind them. There were still too many unsolved puzzles and he had the uneasy sense that the answers to most of them were back on the island.

When engaging in a contemplation, Ignatius counselled his Jesuits not to be too anxious to leave one scene for another. Stay with it until you've sucked everything out of it that you can, he urged. Don't be too eager to move on until you're satisfied you've found what you're seeking. Mark Townsend knew he had not yet found what he was seeking. But the problem, he realized, was in not knowing exactly what it was that he was seeking.

The engine's drone thickened suddenly, choked, coughed twice, and then stopped. Their boat fell back off the crest of water it was riding, settling heavily into the gray wash behind their stern. They were drifting in silence. Eddie turned and started working on the motor, doing all he could to revive it. Mark sat in the bow, not knowing enough to offer any suggestion or help.

"It's got to be water in the line," he could hear the Indian mumble.

They had not had time to move into the mouth of the Swinomish Channel, so were still adrift in Skagit Bay. By fixing his eyes on a point on the shore, Mark could tell that the tide was carrying their small boat westward, and that they would soon drift past the channel's opening. He felt only slightly nervous. The water, after all, was well traveled. Although there were no boats around at the moment, he was confident someone would eventually see them. But he was a little surprised at how quickly they were drifting. Eddie continued struggling with the motor back in the stern.

"Any luck?" Mark called back.

The Indian shook his head, then looked up and around, studying their position in the water. "We're in the current now," he observed, bending back to his work.

Their boat seemed to have picked up speed. Mark tried guessing how far they might have drifted. The channel's mouth looked to be about a quarter of a mile behind them.

"The tide moves pretty fast through here, doesn't it?" he observed.

Eddie looked back up, the disconnected fuel line dangling in his hands.

"That's Pulled and Be Damned right off that point," he said, motioning to a spot on the shore in front of them. "The tide's going to carry us right around there. Hope Island is up ahead of us about two miles."

Mark turned in his seat to stare at the shoreline ahead. They were too far out for him to be able to pick out any recognizable sites, but he knew they had to be drifting toward the area of beach where Dutch Olsen's body was found. He tried looking for anything familiar, recalling the last time the two of them had been in this area together. Meanwhile Eddie had reconnected the line and was pulling on the starter. He repeated his rituals with the choke and starting rope, making minute adjustments between each pull. After four or five tries the engine caught. He shifted gears and Mark could feel the surge as they once again began to move forcefully through the water. He looked back at Eddie as he prepared to make his turn around toward the channel. Mark turned back to the beach, and then back to Eddie again.

"Turn it off!" he hollered. "Turn off the engine!"

"What?"

Mark leaned toward the stern. "Just for a minute, please. Turn it off."

Walking Boy looked doubtful. Nevertheless, he cut the engine and they settled quickly back into the water, although they were hardly sitting still. The tide's current continued carrying them in a forward direction.

"What happens if you can't restart the motor?" asked Mark.

This priest had water on the brain. Eddie wondered if

Father Townsend might not be suffering from hypothermia.

"We keep drifting," he replied.

"And then what?"

"What do you mean?" the Indian answered impatiently. "We just keep drifting. Either we'll wash up on shore somewhere or we'll keep going."

"Yeah? How far?"

He had no idea what the priest was getting at, but his questions were stupid.

"If the tide kept going out it could carry us right through Deception Pass," Eddie told him. "That's probably what would happen eventually, even if we didn't go all the way through on this tide change. It might take awhile but yeah, we'd probably go out Deception Pass. Don't worry though, someone would find us before then."

Mark shook his head in frustration. That was not what he meant. "Would the same thing happen if we jumped out of the boat?" He grabbed the edge and for one brief moment Eddie wondered if the priest was actually going to jump overboard. He leaned forward to stop him.

"Unless it were an emergency I wouldn't try it," Eddie cautioned. "Like I say, someone would find us." He leaned back when Mark let go of the boat's side. "That water's cold. You could die before you made it to shore. It'd be better to stay in the boat and wait for help."

"If you did die," Mark persisted, "would your body drift out with the boat?"

He looked at the priest and then turned to study the shoreline as he tried to picture what Father Townsend was proposing. Finally he turned back.

"I don't think so," he said slowly. "In fact, I know you wouldn't." Intent on his explanation, Eddie leaned forward in his seat, using a finger to diagram on the bench that separated the two men. "See, our boat is drifting on top of the water." He sketched as he spoke. "But your body would be at least half submerged. Or maybe all the way down. You'd be drifting slower, so the boat would go out ahead of you." He leaned back and once again looked toward the shore.

"What happens if the tide changes while you're float-ing?"

"If the tide started coming back in?" Eddie's eyes were still on the shoreline.

"Yeah," said Mark. "If the tide came back in."

Walking Boy turned back to the priest, finally under-standing. "You'd probably wash up," he said flatly, jerk-ing a thumb towards the beach.

Now it was Mark's turn to study the shoreline. They were still too far out to pinpoint exactly where Dutch Ol-sen's body was discovered lying on the rocky beach at low tide. But their boat had continued moving in the tidal current and he knew they were getting close to the spot. The body had washed up almost directly off their star-board side. He looked from the shore back toward the mouth of the Swinomish Channel, which was now out of sight, around the point in back of their boat.

"Olsen's body was somewhere over there," Mark stated, pointing at the beach. He shifted around in his seat. "But they found his boat out there, around that island."

"Hope Island."

"Okay. Now if his body's here, and his boat is over there, that means Dutch went in one direction while his boat drifted in another. What's that tell you?"

The Indian was beginning to see where the priest was going with all of this.

"If his body washed up on shore, then there was a change of tide—either going out or coming in. And if his boat was down around the island, that'd mean an outgoing tide carried it there."

Townsend was nodding in agreement. He waited until Eddie was done speaking, then picked up where the young man left off.

"I think the tide changed while the body was still in the water," he said. "High tide carried him into the beach and left him there when it went back out. Meanwhile his boat was still drifting and eventually moved around Hope Island, toward Deception Pass."

Eddie Walking Boy looked over to the beach, then down toward Hope Island, trying to visualize what Father

Townsend was describing. What the priest said made sense.

"All right," he said finally. "But I can't see what that solves."

"Where was Greg Patsy fishing?"

Dawn broke, and a wide, toothy grin spread across Eddie Walking Boy's face as he finally understood the priest's logic. Greg Patsy did not kill Dutch Olsen. At least, not the way the police described.

"Patsy was fishing for spring Chinook," Eddie said, "somewhere between here and Hope Island. The fish come in Deception Pass and right up through here, which is where we set our nets."

"Right where they found Olsen's body," Father Townsend added.

"But if Greg had killed him out here, like they say, then the old man's body would have drifted further down, nearer to Hope Island. It couldn't have been clear up here."

"So Olsen had to have been killed even further up, closer to the mouth of the channel," Mark asserted. "His body drifted down to here and then the tide shifted and washed it up on shore. Meanwhile his boat, which you said drifts faster, had already been carried on down toward the Pass."

"That means Patsy didn't do it," Eddie crowed in triumph.

"Not exactly," Mark corrected. "It means he didn't do it here."

Eddie restarted the engine and they turned around, heading back toward the opening of the Swinomish Channel. On their way, the two men shouted back and forth over the engine's drone, speculating on the exact location of where Dutch Olsen's boat might have been when he was shot and fell into the water. Walking Boy knew much more about the local tides and currents, and as he moved them toward the channel's opening he became more and more convinced that they were nearing the spot where Olsen was murdered. Mark turned in his seat to face the bow, watching the water in front of them. He could hear

Eddie's voice behind him but he let it meld into the same white noise as the motor, focusing his attention on the view.

They were drawing closer to the tall black pilings that lined the mouth of the Swinomish Channel. On their starboard side floated a red can buoy, marking the safe passage for boats cruising in or out of the channel. On their port side were the mud flats, only exposed at low tide. Power boats never ventured across them for fear of running aground, although every once in awhile newcomers to the region would fail to read their charts and try a shortcut into the channel. Their shortcut usually cost them long hours in the mud, waiting for the next high tide.

If Mark and Eddie's calculations were right, then Dutch Olsen's murder occurred much closer to the Swinomish Channel than to the beach off Pull and Be Damned Road.

Walking Boy was steering them into the channel now. Further ahead, Mark could see the narrow passageway leading back into LaConner. The Hole in the Wall, opening into the Skagit River, was also up there. On their port side was the open water, leading back toward Pull and Be Damned, Hope Island, and Deception Pass. And on the other side, as they slid into the channel's mouth, loomed the shrouded, high green bluffs camouflaging the abandoned fort on Goat Island.

SEVENTEEN

Father Townsend nervously parked his car next to the curb on the opposite side of the street. Both doors to the duplex across the way were clearly visible. A small child's tricycle lay on its side in front of the apartment on the right. And slouching against the corner of that end of the building were the wasted brown remains of last December's Christmas tree.

A stucco pot sprouting with tulips was arranged next to the door of the apartment on the left. And as Mark watched, he could see the dark shape of someone inside passing in front of the window.

"Sweet Jesus, get me through this," he murmured, getting out of his car.

As he approached the porch, he could hear the ethereal notes of a flute playing a haunting, aboriginal melody. Father Townsend recognized it as the work of R. Carlos Nakai, a Native American flutist. He heard the doorbell ring over the music and a few seconds later the sound of the flute was stopped. Mark braced himself as he heard the door's deadbolt being drawn back.

Sister Teri Carter looked less than happy to see the tall priest standing outside her door.

"Father." That was the extent of her greeting.

"Can I come in?"

Grudgingly she opened her door wider and stepped back, allowing the priest inside. She stared pointedly at his grubby, mud-caked clothes, but Mark offered no explanation.

"Would you mind taking off your shoes?"

Her apartment was filled with the scent of smoldering sweetgrass. Mark followed the nun down a short hallway. Her living room was small and tidy. One wall was almost entirely covered by a large, pale blue star quilt. Two large and crowded bookshelves filled one of the remaining walls. A glass door opened onto a small patio outside. He could see her spotless kitchen.

"Would you like to sit down?" Sister Carter motioned to one of three wooden chairs. A narrow and low coffee table held the burning braid of sweetgrass, its pungent smoke drifting upwards from one end. "I can make some tea, if you like," she offered, trying to sound polite.

"Thank you, no."

When Mark had seated himself she chose the chair across the room from him. She was wearing the same type of long denim skirt she had on last time he saw her. But instead of the blouse she was wearing a pink sweatshirt. Like Mark, she was in her stocking feet. Hers looked dry.

"I was hoping you could help me with some information," Mark began.

Sister Carter sat quietly, watching the priest with interest, her lips pressed together. He waited a moment, then took a deep breath and continued.

"I know you want me off the reservation," he acknowledged, "and I plan to leave soon. But I'm pretty sure Greg Patsy is innocent, and with a little more time I think I can prove it. That's the only reason I'm still around. I'm not here to get in your way."

Sister Carter folded her arms and continued studying the priest. There was a glimmer of interest in her eyes. Interpreting that as an encouraging sign, Mark leaned forward in his chair, his elbows on his knees and his hands clasped together, almost as if in prayer. His dark brown eyes were wide open and expressive. He kept them fo-

cused on her, in spite of his nervousness. He was trying
to keep his voice soft and polite.

She cleared her voice. "Can you understand why I
haven't wanted you here?"

Mark ducked his head. "Some of it, yes, I think so."

She sat waiting. He looked at the sweetgrass burning.

"It's got to be hard, living here alone like this," Mark
said eventually. "I know a lot of Jesuits who've done
graduate studies, and every one of them says that it's an
isolating, tough time." He looked back up at her. "You're
here as a religious woman and as an anthropologist. I
don't imagine you've made too many friends on the reservation. A nun who has come to study them would not
be made too welcome, I guess."

"That's part of it," she grudgingly admitted, her eyes
watching him intently.

Father Townsend took a deep breath and continued,
"And I'm a priest. Most people welcome us wherever we
go. They open up their homes to us, feed us, and make
us feel welcome. They tell us their deepest secrets." She
was still staring at him. "I guess in your opinion, you do
all the work and I get all the glory."

She stirred in her seat. "There's more to it than that,"
she said uncomfortably.

"I'm sure there is."

"There's a pattern of abuse, Father Townsend. It has
nothing to do with you personally. Not really. But by being a priest you're part of those same clerical, hierarchical
structures which have oppressed both women and native
peoples for centuries." Her voice was tightly knotted with
the passion of her feelings. "I came here to get away from
that. Don't get me wrong. I love the Church. It's the men
who run it I have trouble with. The doctoral studies are
only an excuse for staying up here, I could care less about
the degree. I came up here to get away from all of you.
Do you understand? If I have any hope of staying in religious life, I have to stay outside."

Mark let the woman talk. Tears began to flow as she
told about the pain she felt living as a religious woman in
the Catholic Church. The feelings and thoughts she was

expressing were not new to him, but she made the hurt and the brokenness sound personal and he found himself squirming in his seat, unable to keep his own experiences separate from this nun's personal anguish. Teri Carter had been much easier for Mark to dismiss when she was just another angry nun. Listening to the torment she felt as she found her religious identity merging with that of Native Americans was not as easy for the priest to ignore.

By the time she was finished sharing her story, the afternoon had stretched into early evening. Both Father Townsend and Sister Carter had lived in religious life long enough to know that there were no easy answers to the painful issues they were discussing. Neither one tried to pretend that anything was being resolved as they sat across from one another in the nun's tiny living room. Teri Carter's vocation, like Mark Townsend's, was rooted in two thousand years of church tradition. They both recognized that there are times when tradition can prove to be as much a curse as it is a grace.

In the end, they sat in silence. The small room was dark with shadows as daylight faded. Sister Carter's face was lined with exhaustion. She had poured out so many hard and bitter feelings, trying to get this priest to understand. And in the end she was not sure it mattered. She knew if there was ever to be any peace, it would have to come from within. Certainly no priest could ever give it to her.

"You said you needed help," she said at last, returning to the reason for Father Townsend's visit. She reached across and flipped a switch. The room was suddenly and harshly lit by a bright overhead light. Mark blinked several times as his eyes tried to adjust.

"Do you know if there is much of a market for artifacts from around here?"

"You mean Swinomish?"

"Hmmm." The light was still bothering him. "Are there collectors in LaConner?"

Sister Carter shook her head. "Not that I know of. Once in a while you'll hear of buyers coming up from Seattle, trying to get the people to sell them things."

"What kinds of things?"

"The usual," she replied. "Anything that's old and Indian. Everyone wants medicine bundles, of course."

"Has much been stolen? Or just disappeared?"

She pursed her lips. "I'm not really sure, no one seems to talk about it much. At least not around me." She paused, waiting for some response. But Mark remained silent. "I think some things have disappeared, though. There've been murmurings. I think some might even suspect that I'm involved." Again she waited, almost challenging Mark to speak up. "How does this tie in with Greg Patsy?" she finally asked.

"I'm not sure," Father Townsend admitted. "But I think the man who was killed possibly might have been looting old Indian sites."

"You mean Dutch Olsen?" she said incredulously. "I can't believe that!"

Her reaction caught Mark by surprise. "Why?"

"He had nothing to do with the Swinomish. I can't believe he'd be interested in their artifacts."

"What if he was selling them off?" proposed Mark. "Maybe as a way of getting even?"

The nun shook her head. "I didn't particularly like the man, but somehow that just doesn't sound like him. Maybe, but I doubt it."

Sister Carter seemed fairly convinced of Olsen's innocence. Mark was still not, but he decided to let it go. He asked if she knew anyone who collected Swinomish artifacts.

"I could probably find out," she told him. "Someone back at the university would probably know some names. Do you want private collectors, dealers, or museums?"

"How about all three?"

Father Townsend's grandparents were halfway though their dinner when he walked in the back door.

"Oh Mark, look at you!" Nan was up from the table and bustling towards him. "Where have you been? We haven't seen you all day!"

His grandfather remained seated at the table, his eyes fixed on his grandson.

"I was over on Goat Island with Eddie Walking Boy."
He looked down at his mud-caked pants. "The tide went
out and we had to pull the boat back into the water. I
guess I should have taken these off outside."

"You go on in the bathroom," Nan scolded. "I'll get
you a robe."

Mark was turning towards the hall when Nan called
back after him. "Someone called for you a while ago."

"Do you know who it was?"

"No, he didn't leave a message. He just asked if you
were here."

"It was probably Father Morrow," Mark guessed. "I'll
call him in a bit."

While his wife got Mark a robe, GrandSam went back
to eating his dinner.

The rerun of *"I Love Jeannie"* was an old one and
Mark had seen it before. He was sure his grandfather had
too, but the old man watched it intently. Nan sat through
it with them, but as soon as the show was finished she
returned to the kitchen to start the dishes. GrandSam
picked up the TV's remote control and began surfing
through the channels.

"How about a game of chess?" Mark challenged him.

"If you want," his grandfather replied, clicking off the
set.

Mark set the game up between them. He drew white
and led off.

"That Goat Island is quite a place," he said. His grandfather studied the board.

"Hmmm. Is that so?"

"Have you ever gone over to see that old fort?"

The old man moved a pawn and shook his head.
"Nope. I've never been on Goat Island."

It was Mark's turn to move. "Really? I would have
thought you and Dutch would have explored over there."

"Nope. We never made it over there." GrandSam cautiously lifted his knight, then set it back down. "Dutch
didn't think smugglers used Goat Island. Too close to
town. Besides, the army was all over that island when they

had the fort.'' He moved another pawn instead.

Mark's rook advanced to the middle of the board.

''There's a pretty secluded beach around the back side of the island,'' he observed. ''Smugglers could have gone in there and no one would ever see them unless they were sailing right by.''

''Dutch didn't think they went there,'' his grandfather said firmly.

The two of them played on in silence. Sounds of Nan's dishwashing drifted in from the kitchen. Mark lost his bishop.

''What about Larry?'' he finally asked.

GrandSam tightened his grip around Mark's bishop. ''What about him?''

''Did he ever go to Goat Island?''

''How the hell would I know?'' GrandSam dragged his queen across the board, leaving his king exposed.

''You sure you want to make that move?'' Mark asked him.

GrandSam looked down at the board and then up at his grandson. Realizing his mistake he slammed the bishop down. ''Do you want to talk or play chess?''

Father Townsend studied his grandfather's stern face a moment, then said quietly, ''Let's talk.''

They moved down the hallway into Mark's room, closing the door behind them. Sam sat on Mark's bed while his grandson leaned against the dresser. The two of them faced off.

''What is it, Mark? What's this about?'' The gruffness in GrandSam's voice was almost completely gone, replaced by caution and worry.

Mark told his grandfather about uncovering the cedar boards wrapped in the blanket in Dutch Olsen's shack. At the time he did not know their significance, he explained, but they looked like something that might have come from the Swinomish tribe. GrandSam listened in silence as his grandson recounted his attempts to find out what the boards meant. Mark described his visit to the Anacortes Museum and told him about finding the three names written in Miss Harcotte's registry of visitors. Then he recounted his meeting with Eddie Walking Boy and the two elders, when he was finally told about the Squa-de-lich.

"They belong to the tribe," he told GrandSam, "and they want them back."

Next Mark told him about his trip back to the shack with Eddie Walking Boy that morning, finding the hidden key and going in to reclaim the cedar boards. When they could not find them, Eddie took him to Goat Island and showed him where they had been hidden.

"I don't know how you guys ever found them," Mark concluded.

His grandfather stood up from the bed. "I told you, I was never on Goat Island!"

"But you knew about the boards."

The old man's shoulders sagged and he sat back down on the bed.

"I knew," he confessed. "I didn't know what they were, but I knew they were probably Indian." He looked back up at his grandson. "I didn't think they were anything special, Mark."

"Who found them?"

"Larry did. I didn't know anything about them until we went back to the cabin after Dutch's death. I found them kind of like you did—accidentally. Robbins wasn't going to say anything about them, so I asked him. And he told me he'd got 'em over on the island. One time when he was poking around on his own."

"With Dutch?"

GrandSam shook his head. "I don't think so. No. I think Larry went over there by himself."

"Olsen wasn't looking for Indian artifacts?"

Again he rose from the bed, this time in his friend's defense. "No, not Dutch. He was always after that lost treasure. He could care less about the Indians. Larry was the one interested in that stuff. Whenever Dutch told us he found a new place he wanted to explore, Larry wanted to know if any Indians had lived nearby. He told Dutch he was more interested in them than in smugglers."

"And you say Dutch never went over to Goat Island?"

"Not with me, he didn't. I knew he was reading up

about the place, but he never said anything about taking a trip over there.''

"So when you guys went out hunting for treasure, Larry was looking for artifacts,'' Mark guessed.

"I didn't know for sure if that's what he was doing,'' his grandfather protested. "Those Squa things were the first time I ever saw him bring something back.''

"Where are they now?''

"I don't know. When we left the cabin, Larry left them there, wrapped in that blanket. Maybe he went back and got them later on.''

"They belong to the tribe, GrandSam. I want to get them from Larry and give them back.''

"Tonight?'' His grandfather looked at his watch.

"Let's go do it now,'' Mark urged him. "Before it's too late.''

Neither man knew it, but it already was.

EIGHTEEN

Larry Robbins lived by himself in a small house at the far end of Shelter Bay. When GrandSam and Mark arrived, the front of his place was dark. They could see no lights, although Larry's car was parked beneath a covered carport. The digital clock in Mark's car blinked at 8:10.

"He can't be in bed this early," his grandfather claimed.

Mark pulled up directly in front, his headlights aimed at the house. They could see that the front door was wide open. GrandSam started out of the car.

"Wait!" his grandson cautioned. "Let's wait a minute."

Mark kept his headlights turned on while they examined the front of the house. There was no movement that they could see, only the open door.

"Something could be wrong," GrandSam said. "I'm going inside."

"Maybe we ought to call the police," suggested Mark.

"I want to see if he's in there," GrandSam said, opening the car's door.

His grandfather quickly walked inside the house and Mark followed. His own inclination would have been to hold back and move cautiously, but GrandSam was already charging ahead. He flipped on the hall light as he walked in, calling Larry's name.

"It's Sam, Larry. Where the hell are you?"

Together they searched the house for Larry Robbins. But there was no sign of him. Things generally seemed in place and undisturbed; it was as if the owner had simply disappeared into thin air. They found the back door opened too, and went out to look around the narrow fenced yard behind the house. Further down the street a dog began to bark, but they saw nothing in the yard. Mark went back out front and looked inside Robbins's locked car.

"Anything?" his grandfather asked, standing just inside the front door.

"No." He rejoined him on the porch. "I think we should call the police."

GrandSam nodded in assent. "Phone's in the kitchen. Why don't you make the call."

An open door in an empty house was hardly considered an emergency. But then the Swinomish reservation was not a hotbed of crime, either. By the time the 911 call was relayed to the tribal policeman who was patrolling around the west end of the reservation, ten minutes had elapsed. It took the tribal policeman another ten to get to Robbins's house. He pulled in next to Father Townsend's car and he could see the priest standing underneath the porch light, watching anxiously.

"Father Townsend," Mike Jennings touched the brow of his cap as he stepped onto the porch. "We meet again. You're becoming a very familiar face around the reservation."

"I came with my grandfather to see his friend," Mark explained, "but he's not here."

The two of them moved into the living room. There was noise coming from the kitchen and Jennings gave the priest a questioning look as he started toward the sound.

"My grandfather," Townsend explained.

GrandSam was opening drawers.

"Are you looking for something, sir?" Mike Jennings

moved up behind him. Sam looked back and slid open another drawer.

"Just checking around," he replied.

"Why don't you come out in the other room with us," the officer suggested in a polite but firm voice, "so we can figure out what's going on."

The story was complicated, and with GrandSam's interruptions it took Mark twice as long to tell Mike Jennings the basic facts. Larry Robbins, a friend of Dutch Olsen's (*and mine!* Sam interjected) seemed to be missing. Mark had reason to believe that Larry might have something belonging to the tribe. (*He probably just found it*, claimed Sam.) When they came to talk to Robbins, they found the front door wide open. (*And the back one!* Sam reminded his grandson.) Things looked a little suspicious so they decided to call the police. GrandSam nodded his agreement.

Mike Jennings glanced around the room. "Can you tell if anything is missing?"

"That's what I was just checking," GrandSam told him.

Jennings pulled out a pad and began jotting a few notes. "Nothing seems disturbed," the policeman observed. "No furniture moved or anything." He wandered away from them, poking his head back into the kitchen before moving down the hall and into Robbins's bedroom. They could hear him opening and closing closet doors.

"He's not going to find anything," GrandSam whispered to Mark. "I've already looked. There's nothing."

The officer finished his search and rejoined them. "I don't see anything that would indicate a break-in," he reported. "Nothing seems out of place." GrandSam gave Mark his I-told-you-so look.

"It's possible that the man who lives here is dealing in stolen artifacts," Mark informed Jennings. "And he may also have some tie-in to Dutch Olsen's murder."

The cop leaned back and studied Mark's face, chewing on the end of his pencil.

"That's quite a leap you're making, Padre," he finally decided. "I think I'd have to see some more evidence before I could investigate further. Without a search warrant, about all I can do right now is secure the premises and wait for Mr. Robbins to come home. Oh, and in case you forgot, we've already got our murder suspect.''

Mark could feel his grandfather's eyes boring holes into his back. Then he heard his irritated voice behind him.

"Father Mark has been trying to help Greg Patsy's wife, Linda," GrandSam said to the policeman. "Now it's possible my friend might have picked up something belonging to the tribe, but Larry would no more hurt Dutch than I would. I think my grandson is wrong.''

Jennings was nodding his agreement, tucking his notebook back into his pocket.

"Why don't we lock up the house for Mr. Robbins and see what happens," he suggested. "I'll keep an eye on the place. If he's not back in a day or two, we'll take another look around. How's that?''

For Mark, that hardly seemed like enough. But he realized that both legally and logically the policeman was probably right. For now, there was nothing more they could do. Tomorrow morning he would have to tell Eddie Walking Boy that he thought he knew who had taken the Squa-de-lich, but that the man and the boards had both disappeared. Father Townsend wondered how the Indians would react to the bad news.

Nan was sitting in front of the TV, wearing her robe and with a book in her lap when they returned home. Mark knew she was sitting there waiting for the two of them, and a wave of tenderness washed over him. He plopped onto the couch next to her, grabbed her cold hands, and pecked her on the cheek.

"You weren't worried, were you, Nan?''

"Me? Not at all. I was watching this silly show." She faked a yawn. "Mercy! It must be my bedtime. But first tell me what you and your grandfather found.''

He told her about their search of Larry Robbins's house, finding the doors open but no sign of the owner. He had just finished telling her how the police had come and helped lock the place back up when GrandSam came into the room after changing into his pajamas and robe.

"Your grandson thinks Larry had something to do with Dutch's murder," he growled. "He's got him pegged both as a thief and a murderer."

"That's not true, GrandSam. That's not what I said."

"It sounded that way to me," his grandfather retorted. "And to that cop, too."

Mark started to argue back, but he felt Nan's gentle squeeze of his hand, so he swallowed his words and remained silent.

"What we probably need is a good night's sleep," his grandmother suggested to both of them. "I'm sure things will look clearer in the morning."

Before either man had time to respond she was up off the couch and kissing Mark goodnight. She hooked her arm in her husband's as she hobbled from the room.

"Come on, old man," she cajoled him, "it's time for your beauty rest."

Father Townsend smiled to himself as he heard them shuffling down the hall to their bedroom. They were a remarkable couple. He picked up the remote control and was about to begin channel surfing when Nan poked her head back into the room.

"I almost forgot," she said apologetically, "that man called for you again. I asked if he was Father Morrow, but he just hung up. I'm sorry."

Dan Morrow would have identified himself—Mark was certain of that. But just to make sure, he dialed the Jesuit residence. Their phone in Seattle rang four times before his own voice informed him no one was available to take his call. He waited until the message was over, then left word that he was still in LaConner and hung up.

As tired as he felt, Father Townsend was having a hard time getting to sleep. Too many images kept pushing sleep aside. As he reexamined the day's events, beginning with meeting Eddie at the dock and ending with the phone call from some mystery man, Mark realized almost everywhere he went and everything he did was met with frustration. They did not find the cedar boards in Dutch

Olsen's shack; nothing on Goat Island offered any clue to their whereabouts; Larry Robbins was gone, presumably with the Squa-de-lich; the police were not terribly interested in finding him; and he had managed to get GrandSam mad at him again. Mark saw those all as negatives, and for a few minutes he allowed himself to feel their weight. Then, as he was taught to do from his earliest days at the novitiate, the Jesuit began examining his day for positives. He found a deeper trust and respect for the young Indian man he had spent most of the day with. And Eddie trusted him enough to reveal where tribal members had hidden the Squa-de-lich. And although they might not have found the missing boards, they did know who took them. They also knew something more about Dutch Olsen's murder that might, in turn, end up helping Greg Patsy. Finally, Mark remembered the gentle feelings he felt for Nan Mary, and the satiny touch of her cheek when he kissed her goodnight. He squeezed his eyes closed and breathed a prayer of gratitude. And finally, with the peace, came gentle sleep.

"Sam! Sam!"

Nan's shrill yell filled Mark's dreams. But these were not dreams. She was screaming again.

"Sam!"

Mark heard loud thumps and his grandfather's muffled voice. There was a sound of breaking glass and a sudden loud explosion that sounded like it was right outside of Mark's bedroom door. He scrambled out of bed, throwing open the door into the hall. Everything was still black, but he could smell the acrid stink of gunpowder in the air. He heard his grandmother moaning.

"Nan?" Mark called out, feeling his way down the dark hall.

"Mark." His grandfather's voice. "She's over here."

"Where's the light switch?" Although wide awake, he was still too confused to know exactly where he was.

"The lights aren't working," GrandSam said.

"What happened?" His knee struck something soft and his grandfather grunted.

"Careful," GrandSam warned. "Mary's right here."

Mark squatted down beside his grandfather. His eyes were open wide now, adjusting to the darkness. He could see the outline of Nan's body on the floor in front of them.

"Was she shot?"

"No," his grandfather said. "That was me. I shot at the guy who attacked her."

"Where is he now?" Mark raised his head, straining to see down the dark hallway.

"I think he's gone. I heard him running." GrandSam was cradling his wife's head in his arms. "Mary. Nan. Are you okay, honey?"

She did not reply. Mark got to his feet and carefully stepped around her body. Cautiously, he moved out into the living room, looking around him for any sudden movements. His heart was beating so loudly he could hear nothing else. He felt a cool breeze and saw the front door was open. Outside, the night was calm and quiet.

Along with the lights, their phone was also dead.

He recalled the magnetized flashlight Nan kept attached to the side of her refrigerator. The batteries were weak, but there was enough of a beam to lead him back to the hallway. GrandSam was still holding his wife's head in his lap. He squinted when Mark shined the beam in his face. He moved the beam down to Nan's pale face, and they could both see the thin red slip of blood flowing from her temple.

Mark handed GrandSam the light. "I'm going next door for help."

His grandfather turned the beam back onto Mark. "You'd better put some clothes on first," he suggested.

NINETEEN

Mary Townsend was carefully loaded into the back of LaConner's aid car. She was conscious and appeared to be okay. The wound on her head had stopped bleeding, but the medics were concerned she might have suffered a concussion. She was struck with a vase lifted from the living room by her unknown assailant.

For the second time that night, Mike Jennings was talking with Sam Townsend and his grandson, the priest from Seattle who was popping up around the reservation just a little too often. The casual demeanor the officer had exhibited at the Robbins house was gone now—he was all business as he investigated the attack on Mrs. Townsend. The main circuit breaker in the Townsend's garage was turned off and the phone line cut. Someone had jimmied the lock on their front door and entered the living room. Mary Townsend claimed that was the sound that got her out of bed. She thought it was her grandson, Mark, and went out to see if he was okay. She could remember moving down the hall; without her leg brace she had leaned against the wall for support, but after that everything else was lost to her.

Sam Townsend's .22 pistol was found lying in the hallway next to where he said he had knelt to help his wife.

Jennings found a small hole in the wallboard of the hall, near the entrance to the living room. It was six feet, seven inches up from the floor and looked about the size of hole made by a .22. The old man was lucky he had not shot his wife. As far as Jennings could see, and from what the Townsends said, that was the only shot that was fired.

"Mike, can you come outside?" His deputy, Matthew Joseph, was signalling to him. He followed the deputy out the side entrance, through the passageway between the house and the garage. Joseph led him out to the front of the garage and then across the lawn, shining the way with his flashlight. Near the edge of the Townsends' lawn they stopped. A small blue backpack was lying in the grass.

"There's a gun inside," Matthew Joseph informed him.

"Don't let anyone near it," Jennings ordered.

A voice behind him said, "That's Eddie's."

Father Townsend had followed them into the yard. The priest's hair was still rumpled from sleep and he was barefoot. He had on a pair of blue jeans and a blue T-shirt that he was wearing inside out and backward. The label was sticking straight out just beneath his throat and bobbed whenever he spoke.

"Who is Eddie?" Jennings asked him inquisitively.

"Eddie Walking Boy," the priest said, staring down at the pack. "That's the same pack he had with him this morning. He had a gun in it then, too."

Jennings took Joseph's flashlight, bent down and peered inside the pack. "Did you happen to notice what kind of gun it was?"

Father Townsend shook his head. "I don't know guns," he said. "It was short and had a brown handle."

"Grip," Matthew Joseph corrected. "It's a .38."

Jennings looked again, then stood back up. "You're sure this is the same pack."

Father Townsend nodded grimly. "Positive."

The policeman let out a long, deep breath. "Father Townsend," he said, shining the light in the priest's eyes, "do you have any theories on how Eddie's pack could have ended up in your grandparents' front yard?"

"Unfortunately, none besides the obvious one," Mark replied, squinting back at Jennings.

The tribal policeman turned back to his deputy. "You'll probably need to go find Eddie," he ordered. "When you do, take him back to the office and wait for me there. But first record and bag this pack. Be sure and check to see if the gun's been fired." He waved his hand toward a knot of people standing in the road in front of the Townsends' house. "And ask those folks to go home, would you please? I don't know what the hell they think they're going to see here. Tell them to go home."

As the deputy set about his chores, Jennings turned his attention back to Father Townsend. He noticed the man was shivering and suggested they move back into the house. Sam Townsend would ride to the hospital with his wife, but Jennings had more questions he needed to ask the priest.

Mark made them coffee and they sat at the kitchen table. With Nan and GrandSam both gone, the house felt foreign to him, like he did not belong in there. He was glad for Mike Jennings's company, although the policeman was behaving in a very cold and detached manner. He allowed Mark to tell the story his own way, only stopping him when he needed to ask a question for clarification.

"Eddie didn't say why he was taking you to the island, then?" Jennings was asking.

"No, he didn't. He just said there was something there he wanted to show me."

"Which was . . . ?"

"I told you," Mark said. "We hiked in to the fort and then he showed me where they had hidden the boards. That was back by where we'd beached our boat."

"And that was it?"

"Yeah. Wait. No." Jennings raised one quizzical eyebrow. "The Squa-de-lich were hidden near an old mine in the middle of a clearing. Eddie said that area was considered a sacred place in the old days. And there was water in the bottom of the mine. He threw a rock in and you could hear it splash."

"And when exactly did you see him with the gun?"

"That was at the fort," Mark told him. "We ate a sandwich, and when we went to go I picked up the pack and the gun fell out."

"And he didn't explain why he had it?"

"Just that he wasn't sure what we'd find." Mark thought a moment. "And he was nervous about going back to Olsen's shack." He shrugged at the policeman. "I already told you what happened the first time we went."

"Yeah—your grandfather and Robbins and the guns—I remember." Jennings's fingers were drumming a tattoo on the side of his coffee mug. The policeman was scowling. Mark waited, realizing the policeman was trying to work things out for himself.

"There's a question you haven't asked me yet," Mark finally told him. "It's the same one that's bugging me."

Jennings took a sip of his coffee. "Oh? And what question is that?"

"If Eddie Walking Boy wanted to hurt me, why didn't he do it on the island? Why wait until tonight?" Mark was pulling at his mustache as he spoke. "That doesn't make sense to me. I mean, that would have been the perfect place. No one knew we were there. For that matter, he could have just shot me in the boat and dumped me in the water."

"Like Olsen."

"Exactly," Mark agreed. "If that was what he wanted to do."

The two men sat for a while longer, but it became clear that the rest of Mike Jennings's questions would have to wait until after they had found Eddie Walking Boy. Discovering his pack with the gun in the Townsends' yard tied him to the night's events. But what neither the policeman nor the priest could decide was what the Indian's motive might have been for breaking into the Townsends' home.

Mark was anxious to get to the hospital and check on Nan and GrandSam, so after a few more questions Jennings agreed that the rest could wait. He cautioned Mark to double check all the windows and doors before he left, although both of them knew that if someone was determined to get back into the house, they could. He warned the priest to be careful and said goodnight.

Before he left for the hospital, Mark turned lights on in every room of the house. The police had already arranged for the phone company to come in the morning to repair the severed line. The main thing right now was to rejoin Nan and GrandSam as quickly as possible.

He took Reservation Road to Anacortes, slowing down when he drove past the driveway that turned into Walking Boy's place. There were no lights that he could see, and no sign of the deputy's patrol car. Mark wondered if they had already taken the Indian in for questioning. He was still finding it difficult to imagine Eddie breaking in and assaulting Nan. That did not make sense. But it was his pack in the yard, Mark was certain of that. Past the driveway, he pressed hard on the gas, hoping the tribal police were too busy to watch for speeders on Reservation Road.

TWENTY

Nan was already admitted into a room and asleep when Mark arrived at the hospital in Anacortes. The doctors who checked her thought she might have suffered a slight concussion and they wanted to keep her overnight, then run a couple more tests in the morning. Mary was tired and frightened and had no energy left to protest. Sam promised he would stay with her, and the nurses arranged an extra bed in the room so he could sleep next to his wife. But he was wide awake and pacing the hallway outside Nan's door when Mark found him.

He looked every day of his eighty-two years. Under the hard glare of the fluorescent lights his skin looked loose and gray and his eyes were red. Like Mark, he had thrown on whatever clothes were close at hand after the attack. His shirt was untucked outside his pants and he was still wearing his bedroom slippers. Mark noticed his hands were trembling, and when he spoke, GrandSam's voice sounded weak and fearful.

"Did you lock up the house?" was the first thing he wanted to know.

Mark nodded and led his grandfather to a couch further down the hall. He offered to get him something to drink, but Sam said no. He told Mark that Nan was sleeping, that she might have a concussion, that he was staying the night with her. His energy ran out and the old man stared vacantly at the floor. Mark wrapped a consoling arm around his grandfather's shoulders.

"The police said it was an Indian who broke in," Sam said thickly.

"Maybe," Father Townsend replied. "They found Eddie Walking Boy's backpack over by the garage."

"With a gun."

"Uh-huh." Mark could feel his grandfather's muscles tense briefly. His body shuddered and then relaxed. "But I can't figure out why he would have done it. It makes no sense."

"It's those damn boards," GrandSam claimed. "He thinks I have 'em."

Mark considered the possibility and realized his grandfather might be right. Walking Boy had no way of knowing the two of them had gone to Larry Robbins's house and found the doors open and the owner missing. He might have suspected that Mark was covering for his grandfather to avoid implicating him in the theft of the Squa-de-lich. Eddie could have decided to take matters in his own hands. Or else, Mark considered, others were growing impatient and had ordered him up to the Townsends' house.

But the Jesuit still had a hard time believing that Eddie Walking Boy had come to the house to harm him. He had Mark on the island and in the boat just hours earlier, with any number of opportunities to do whatever it was he wanted. But going after his grandfather at the house in the middle of the night, when he knew Mark was there, made no sense either. Nan, he was now convinced, was merely an innocent bystander. But unfortunately, his grandmother was a light sleeper and was the one who heard the intruder breaking into the house. Presuming the noises she heard were coming from her grandson, she had innocently hobbled into the hallway to see if Mark needed help. He closed his eyes and remembered her lying on the floor, the thin ribbon of blood on her head shining bright in the flashlight. A defenseless old woman. Mark's right hand involuntarily tightened into a fist.

He opened his eyes and unclenched his hand as he heard footsteps approaching. A nurse, wearing white cotton pants and a light blue smock, offered him a sympathetic smile as she continued down the hall. Father Townsend turned to GrandSam and realized the old man was sleeping. Gently, he shook him awake. He leaned against his grandson as Mark eased him off the couch, down the hall, and into the darkened room where Nan lay sleeping. Father Townsend quietly helped his grandfather undress and then tucked him into the bed next to his wife's. Before he left, Mark offered a silent prayer over the two of them.

The eastern sky was turning light by the time he left the hospital. The night was nearly over. When he reached his car he started to unlock the door, then hesitated. There was a phone in the hospital lobby, so he retraced his steps to call the office of the Swinomish tribal police.

Mike Jennings answered on his cellular phone. Both Matthew Joseph and he were still in their cars, searching the reservation for Eddie Walking Boy. He could not have gotten far, the policeman insisted over the phone. They had checked Eddie's house but it was dark and empty. There was no indication that the young man might have fled. His pickup was still parked in front, and the small boat he usually borrowed was tied at the dock. Still, Jennings assured the Jesuit, it was only a matter of time before they found him.

"My grandfather thinks Eddie came looking for the Squa-de-lich," Mark said over the phone. "He may think GrandSam has them."

"Does he?" the policeman asked bluntly.

"We've already told you that," Mark answered evenly. "Larry Robbins took them." The priest was tired and he could feel his anger rising close to the surface. Jennings was only doing his job, he reminded himself.

The policemen were checking Eddie's relatives and friends, waking them to ask if they had seen or heard from

Eddie in the last few hours. No one had, they said. But Jennings admitted it was unlikely that anyone would tell the police even if they had. The Swinomish was a small reservation, where almost everyone was either a relative or friend. The policeman was convinced someone was hiding Eddie Walking Boy. He was equally convinced someone would eventually let slip who that was.

Mark told him he was about to leave the hospital and head back to LaConner. He agreed to meet Jennings for breakfast in town, but first he wanted to stop at the house to shower and change his clothes. After hanging up the phone he found his way out to his car and was soon back on the highway, heading toward his grandparents' house. The lights at the oil refineries in Fidalgo Bay looked bright and festive as he drove east, but Mark barely noticed them. Traffic was nonexistent and it only took a few minutes for him to reach the turnoff onto Reservation Road. The morning's pale light had not yet spread far enough to reach the narrow road flanked on both sides by tall trees, and he slowed down to negotiate the road's curves in the near darkness. As he drove, the priest found himself searching the edges of the road, watching for some movement or sign of human life. He half expected to see Eddie suddenly materialize, frozen in place like a deer in front of his headlights.

The Swinomish Reservation might be small, but someone growing up there would know plenty of places to hide. And there were enough roads and waterways into and out of the reservation for a friend or relative to help Eddie escape.

Despite the dark, Mark knew when he was near Walking Boy's house. He slowed down so that he could peer down the dark drive as he went past. A light inside the house fell directly onto the pickup parked in front. So Eddie had not driven off; Jennings was right about that.

He was already past the house and picking up speed when he remembered something else the policeman had told him. Eddie's house was dark when they checked it before. No lights were on. Mark made a cautious U-turn in the middle of the road.

His car's tires crunched in the gravel as he drove slowly along the side of the road. He cut his lights as he neared the drive turning into the house. While still a few yards off he turned off his engine and carefully eased open his door, quietly closing it behind him. Mark knew what he was about to do was stupid, and he hesitated by the side of his car to study the area around him. There were no houses nearby and no other way that he could summon help. He would have to go in by himself. Besides, he reasoned, if the man was inside, he could be preparing to leave at any moment. A couple of short miles down the road Mark had just driven and he would be out on the highway. And there were enough nearby turns so that he could head in any of several directions. His mind made up, Townsend started creeping towards the house.

There was still enough darkness for him to stay near the trees and hopefully, out of sight. He thought if he could just get a glimpse through the lighted window he might be able to see what Eddie was doing inside. He moved alongside the truck and placed his hand on the engine's hood. The metal was cold and damp. Mark eased around the vehicle's back side. His left foot broke a small twig and there was a loud crack. He quickly ducked down behind the truck. After waiting a few moments, he cautiously started moving to the corner of the house, edging slowly toward the window. A stack of firewood was piled directly below it, and Father Townsend had to lean his weight across to peer inside. Resting one hand on a cut log, he put his other against the house to balance the rest of his weight. There was still no way to see very much.

Mark was looking into the small front room where he had sat with Eddie and the two elders. He could see the couch and the chair next to it. The doorway into the kitchen was out of his line of sight, but another doorway leading into Eddie's bedroom was open. Only the one light, coming from the kitchen, was on. Slowly he lifted both hands, leaning back from the house. Perhaps there was a kitchen window in the back. Trying to be more careful of where he stepped, Mark moved around the corner, into the back.

There was a window, with nothing in front of it this time. He was able to steal directly beneath it and then slowly raise his head above the sill. The kitchen was empty. There was no sign of anyone inside. Mark straightened and allowed himself a deep breath. Perhaps Jennings was mistaken about the house being dark. Or else the policeman had gone inside to look, then left the light on. In either case, the house appeared empty now.

When he turned back around, the light spilling out from the kitchen window was shining on Eddie's legs. The priest gasped. He was in a tree about twenty feet away. Mark could only see the Indian's legs and feet poking beneath the lower limbs. He tried to run, but was rooted in fear. The Jesuit was an open target, standing exposed in front of the lighted window. There was no way Eddie could miss him. Mark stood waiting for the Indian to jump down and confront him, but the man in the tree did not move. Mark hesitated, then slowly stepped forward.

Eddie's hands hung limply down at his sides. His head was dropped nearly to his chest, held up only by the thickness of the coarse rope around his neck. Mark could not see the Indian's features very well, but he looked angry.

"Oh, God," the priest moaned, half in prayer and half in pain.

He backed away from the tree, still staring at the legs as he stumbled toward the house. He would call Mike Jennings and tell him that he could stop searching for Eddie Walking Boy.

TWENTY-ONE

They took forever getting the body down. Mike Jennings was the first one on the scene and after a quick look at Eddie's hanging corpse he turned his attention to Father Townsend, peppering the priest with continuous questions. Although he never did say it out loud, the officer felt uneasy that it was the Jesuit who had discovered Walking Boy's body, especially after the attack at the Townsend house just a few hours earlier. This same priest figured in Dutch Olsen's death, Larry Robbins's disappearance, the Townsend assault, and now Walking Boy's death. Like most policemen, Mike Jennings was more than a little uncomfortable with coincidences. When he was finished asking all the questions he could immediately think of, Jennings radioed his deputy, Matthew Joseph, then turned his attention to a closer examination of the body. Daylight had fully arrived, and the house and surrounding area were light enough to view the scene plainly.

An aluminum ladder leaned against one side of the fir tree, tall enough to reach the lower limbs. The rope around Eddie's neck was an ordinary three-eighths-inch sisal. There were varying lengths of it all around the yard; the young Indian seemed to use a lot of it. One end was tied securely to a thick limb at a point near the trunk of the tree and the other, in a slip knot around the Indian's neck. Both the young man's neck and face were swollen and a dark, reddish-purple color. His shoes were five feet off the ground, about four feet down from the lowest limb, and another five from the higher limb where the rope was tied. The fir's bark along the top of the lower limb was broken and scuffed from the weight of standing on it.

When Matthew Joseph finally got to the scene, he compared his own notes with Jennings's. The deputy had first checked Eddie's house at 2:35 in the morning, approximately half an hour after Mike Jennings had told him to bring Walking Boy in for questioning. No one answered his knock, and Joseph had checked both the front and back doors, finding them locked. No lights were on inside the house. Walking Boy's pickup was parked in front, and the engine had felt cold to his touch. He had reported his findings to Jennings via radio and then started his search through the reservation. Mike Jennings stopped at Eddie's house at 3:30, again checking to see if the young man was around. Like his deputy, he had searched in both the front and back of the house. No lights were on. Jennings had also driven by about an hour later, but seeing nothing different, had not stopped.

The undertaker's van from Anacortes arrived as the two policemen were comparing notes and Jennings ordered them to wait. There were still diagrams and pictures to make before the body could be taken down. Meanwhile, Father Townsend leaned heavily against a corner of the house, watching silently. He had told Jennings as much as he knew and now all he wanted to do was go back to his grandparents' and sleep for a few hours. His legs felt like bags of cement pulling him to the ground. Eddie's suicide was a tragedy, but there was nothing more he could do here. Meanwhile the undertaker and his assistant returned to their van and sat waiting patiently. They got paid whether they were working or waiting.

Jennings led his deputy back to the tree and the two men stood a few feet from the body, studying Walking Boy's corpse and the ground beneath his feet. Mark Townsend watched as Jennings pointed up into the tree.

Joseph started climbing the ladder. The deputy carried a camera with him, photographing both the lower limb and the higher one, where the rope was tied. Curious, Father Townsend sidled next to Jennings to watch the proceedings. The policeman glanced at the priest.

"Tell me again, Father, where were you when you first saw the body?"

Mark pointed back to the house. "Over there, near that window."

"And then what?"

"At first I waited. I could only see the legs and I thought he was sitting on a limb," Mark recounted for the policeman. "I didn't know he was hanging until I got closer."

"How close did you come?" Jennings wanted to know.

"About halfway," said Mark, gesturing to a spot midway between the house and the tree.

"At any point did you come over and stand next to the body?"

Mark shook his head. "As soon as I realized he was dead I went to call you."

"You didn't come over to feel his body? To check for a pulse?"

He wondered what Jennings was getting at. Had Eddie still been alive? Was there a possibility Mark could have saved his life? Mike Jennings saw the troubled look on Father Townsend's face.

"I'm asking because there are footprints underneath the body. I wondered if they were yours."

For the first time, Mark looked down at the muddy ground beneath the Indian's dangling feet. He could see the faint indentations the policeman was talking about, but was not sure of their significance. He looked back at Jennings.

"And there's interesting marks where the rope's tied to the tree limb," Jennings continued. "It's cut through the bark up there."

Mark was still confused. "I'm not sure what you're saying," he told the policeman.

Jennings gave him a small, tight smile. "Well, that

makes two of us. But Matthew and I are beginning to wonder if this is really a suicide or just made to look like one.''

''You mean someone could have hung Eddie's body up there?''

''Possibly. That would explain the footprints underneath. And if you stood on that lower limb and pulled the body up to where it is, the weight of Eddie's body could have caused that rope to cut into the tree like that. It's possible, I guess,'' the policeman mused, staring back up into the tree.

Matthew Joseph was climbing back down the ladder.

''There's a lot more we need to do here,'' Jennings informed the priest. ''But we should know one way or the other before we're done. You can go on home if you like, Father, but I may have some more questions for you later on.''

Mark was not sure he understood. But the policeman had already dismissed him with a nod of his head and turned his attention back to his deputy. Mark stumbled back toward his car. He was feeling confused and light-headed. His thoughts were jumbled, he knew he was not thinking straight. But if he understood Mike Jennings correctly, Eddie Walking Boy's death might be murder, not suicide. Numbly he climbed into his car, which was still parked on the shoulder of Reservation Road, and drove slowly home.

The Townsends' phone was not working yet, so Mark called the hospital from a neighbor's house. When he was finally connected with his grandfather, GrandSam informed him Nan was still sleeping. The doctors had not done any of their tests, he said, so he was not sure when they would be ready to come home. But he would call when they were. Meanwhile, he urged his grandson to get some sleep.

That was easier said than done. Exhausted, Father Townsend kicked off his shoes and stripped off his clothes. Falling across his unmade bed, he buried his face in the pillow, trying to will himself asleep. But as tired as he was, he could not sleep. He wound the blanket around himself. The images and emotions of the last day and a half were crowding in on him. Mark squeezed his eyes tightly shut, trying to clear his mind of the confusing sequence of events.

He knew there were connections. There had to be. Olsen and Robbins and Walking Boy. GrandSam, too. Connections, but also missing parts—the Squa-de-lich and Larry Robbins. And he was so tired. If he could sort it all out. If only things were as neat and organized as the tidy boxes in Miss Harcotte's archives. A place for everything and everyone. Swinomish in one box, Smuggling in another, Goat Island in a third. Nice and tidy. Father Townsend rolled on his pillow and eventually sank into a deep but troubled sleep.

The moment he awoke—before he even opened his eyes—Mark knew something was wrong. His heart was beating wildly. He tried holding his breath, listening for sounds. He knew he was in the guest bedroom at GrandSam and Nan's, but this was not night. Cautiously, he half-opened one eye. Daylight. A door in his brain opened wide and the memories of the past day and night came spilling out. Relieved just to be able to remember, he rolled onto his back, opening his eyes wide.

In the doorway, three pairs of eyes were staring at him. Mark blinked and stared back.

"Are you okay, Father?" Linda Patsy looked worried.

Mark sat up in bed and nodded. Her daughter, Jesse, stood in front of her and Sister Carter was peering in over her left shoulder. The three of them made no move to enter the room, but continued looking at him. He felt his blanket slip below his naked chest.

"We heard about your grandmother," Sister Carter offered by way of explanation. "And about Eddie."

"We tried calling," Linda continued, "but your phone isn't working. I thought we better check to see if Mary needed help. We knocked, then I used my key."

Jesse stared at the priest sitting in the bed with her big dark eyes and said nothing.

"She's still at the hospital," Mark managed to say, still

not completely awake. "GrandSam's with her."

Linda bit her lower lip and nodded. Her concern for Mark's grandmother was evident from the expression on her face.

"You look like you need coffee," Sister Carter said. "Mind if I make some?" She quickly turned and headed for the kitchen without waiting for the priest's reply.

Suddenly embarrassed, Linda leaned over her daughter. "Come on, Jesse, let's let Father get up." She began backing out of the doorway. "We'll wait in the kitchen," she told him.

Mark waited until they were down the hallway, then climbed out of bed. He lived in an all-male environment at the parish house, and was unaccustomed to having women show up at his bedroom door. During his first years of Jesuit training he had sat through several exhortations about clerical etiquette, but his novice master had never covered the protocol for an occasion such as this. Hastily he pulled on his jeans and a T-shirt. Still in his bare feet, he padded into the kitchen.

"If you don't mind, I'm going to take a quick shower," he told the women.

A shave and a shower does wonders for the soul. Mark felt almost human again when he reemerged. They were waiting for him at the kitchen table and Sister Carter poured him coffee. She waited until he took a sip, then spoke.

"Tell us what happened last night."

As briefly as he could, Mark described the recent events, starting with Nan's cry for help and ending with his discovery of Eddie Walking Boy's body. They listened without interruption. He did not tell them that Mike Jennings had questioned how Eddie actually died. Linda waited until he finished before she said anything.

"That doesn't sound like Eddie," she finally declared, vigorously shaking her head. "He wasn't that kind of man."

"To kill himself?"

"To break into here and attack Mary. He wouldn't do that," she insisted.

"What about suicide?" Mark said.

"I don't know," she admitted, "but it doesn't sound like him."

Sister Carter waited until they were through discussing Walking Boy's death. "I called my friend at the university," she informed the priest.

"And?"

"And she's sending a list of dealers and museums. I asked if she knew anyone who collected Swinomish specifically, but she didn't."

Linda was listening to their conversation with interest. "Do you think Eddie was selling artifacts?" She sounded doubtful.

"No, not Eddie," Father Townsend assured her. "But I think Larry Robbins was. He's the one who took the cedar boards. I'm pretty sure of that."

"Those were on Goat Island!" Jesse chimed.

All three adults looked at the child.

"How do you know that?" her mother asked.

The girl shrugged. "Saw them," she replied, suddenly turning shy.

"Jesse," said Mark, "when did you see them?"

She squirmed uncomfortably in her chair and looked down at her lap. All three grownups were watching her. Linda laid an arm around her daughter's shoulder and drew her close.

"Sweetheart," she spoke in a low, soothing voice, "this might be something important. Maybe it can even help your daddy. Can you answer Father's question? When did you see the boards on the island?"

Jesse avoided looking up, but answered softly, "Angel showed me during camp-out."

"Angel is her cousin," Linda explained to the priest and nun. "Her father is a strong believer in Seeowyn. He'd know about the boards."

Mark remembered reading the students' names scratched onto one of the walls at the abandoned fort. Jesse's name was included there. "And Angel knew the hiding place," Mark guessed. The child nodded in reply.

"Did she show you anything else during your camp-out?" he coaxed.

"The place where they mined," she mumbled quietly. Mark was pretty sure she meant the travertine mine Eddie had shown him. "And where they hid their whiskey." She said it so quietly he was not sure he heard it.

"I'm sorry? What'd you say?"

Jesse looked up at the priest's face across the table and repeated, "Where they hid whiskey. The cave in the rocks."

Mark leaned back in his chair. Eddie had not shown him any cave. He was searching his memory, trying to recall the scraps of paper in the museum's box on Goat Island. There was nothing about hiding whiskey in a cave, not that he remembered. But what the girl was telling them made sense. Smugglers could have used a cave on the island during Prohibition. Canada was not that far away. And with a fort full of soldiers nearby, there would have been plenty of customers for bootleg whiskey. GrandSam had told him Dutch did not believe smugglers used Goat Island, but Olsen had to have visited the island at some time.

He gave the young girl a wide grin. "You knew something I didn't, Jesse."

She smiled happily back at the priest.

"Would you remember where that cave was if you were on the island?"

Jesse assured him she would.

"If there's more artifacts on that island they belong to the tribe," Sister Carter told the priest. Her tone of voice left no room for discussion. "You can't take anything."

Mark decided to ignore her remark. "I've been trying to figure out the connection between Dutch Olsen, Larry Robbins, and Eddie Walking Boy," he told them. "And because of what happened here last night, I have to include my grandfather and myself. That's five." He laid one of his hands on the table top, spreading his fingers out. He drew three of them together as he continued, "Dutch, Larry, and GrandSam were all at the hunting shack, but they were also on the island." He grasped his two remaining fingers. "That leaves Eddie and me. And both of us have been to Olsen's shack and also over on the island. Now Olsen and Walking Boy are both dead and Larry Robbins is missing. And Eddie tried to attack GrandSam and me.''

"You can't prove that!" Sister Carter objected.

Mark frowned at her, about to argue. But the nun made a good point.

"You're right," he admitted after another moment. "We presumed it was Eddie because of his backpack and the gun. But I can't prove it was him." Mark looked down at his hand. "But if it wasn't . . . ?"

"Larry Robbins!" The nun's choice was clear.

Father Townsend grabbed the end of his moustache and began twisting. "Maybe," he grudgingly conceded, "but why would Larry want to break into GrandSam's house? And where would he get Eddie's gun?" Mark shook his head. "That doesn't feel right to me."

Teri Carter looked at the priest with derision. "I didn't think you Jesuits worked off feelings," she jeered. "What happened to cold, rational logic?"

Mark was readying a sarcastic answer when Linda Patsy nervously cleared her throat. "But what about my husband?" she asked both of them. "He wasn't at either place. Greg was just fishing over by Pull and Be Damned. He wasn't on the island or at Mr. Olsen's shack."

"I don't think Greg's involved in this at all," Mark tried to reassure her. He glanced down at the little girl next to her. "Your daddy didn't do anything wrong, Jesse, I'm sure of it."

"But they found the rifle on his boat," Linda reminded him.

"Anyone could have put it there," he countered.

"Just like with Eddie's gun," the nun chimed in.

She was right, of course. If someone was capable of hiding a rifle on Greg Patsy's boat, someone could certainly drop Eddie's pistol and backpack on the Townsends' front lawn. Especially if Eddie Walking Boy was in no condition to object. Perhaps the tribal police were right in their suspicions. Perhaps the Indian's death was not a suicide after all.

When his visitors finally left, Father Townsend went to work tidying the house. He rinsed dirty cups and put them in the dishwasher. Finding his grandmother's vacuum in a closet, he started on the carpets. A trail of dried mud and leaves littered the floor from both entrances, through the living room and down the hallway. A house full of police and medics can leave a horrible mess. He sucked up as much of the grime as he could. Afterward Mark made up his grandparents' bed, then started on his own.

He found it easier to think when his hands were occupied. While he straightened the sheets and blanket, his mind replayed bits of conversation and scenes from the past few days. The lives of both Dutch Olsen and Eddie Walking Boy had come to tragic ends. Neither man's death made any sense. Mark picked a pillow off the floor. Was violent death ever intended to make sense? What did it mean if a life was ended before its time? He sat on the edge of the bed, holding the feather pillow in his hands.

They make the end a means, Ignatius once warned his followers, *and the means an end. So as a result, what they ought to seek first, they end up seeking last.*

The Jesuit slammed his fist into the pillow.

TWENTY-TWO

"Careful!!"

Mark lunged to grab onto the dock as Jesse started to clamber into the boat. Sister Carter, sitting in the bow, scowled at him.

"I think the child knows how to get into a boat," the nun scolded him. "You don't need to bark at her."

Jesse flopped down onto the middle seat between the nun and the priest, smiling at both. She seemed perfectly at home around boats, no matter how small they were. Father Townsend handed her a bright orange life vest.

"What's this for?" she asked.

"I want you to put that on, Jesse," Mark told her.

"No way!" The child threw the vest down. "Those are for babies! My daddy never makes me wear one."

Mark shifted uncomfortably inside his own orange vest. His own faith in the bulky life saver was shaky anyway. He was never really convinced the ill-fitting vest would actually keep him afloat, but this was not the time to try a test. He was about to head down the cold and wet Swinomish Channel with a belligerent nun and a ten-year-old girl, hoping to navigate his way to Goat Island in a boat that was a little bit longer than his bed. Father Townsend looked with longing at the *SinCan*, tied to the other dock.

The huge yacht looked as big and solid as the Vatican. He spotted the skipper looking out at them and debated once again about asking Mr. Kuhn Suu for a ride to the island. Mark knew as much about driving a boat as he did flying a plane. But if St. Peter had enough faith to walk on water, the priest figured he could at least try floating a boat across it. As Sister Carter began untying the bow line he suddenly recalled that the sainted apostle had sunk.

"God help us," he muttered, yanking on the cord to start the outboard motor.

Linda Patsy was willing to let her daughter accompany Mark to the island to find the cave the young girl had described that morning. If it was a hiding place for smugglers at one time, there was no reason why it could not be a hiding place again. Eddie Walking Boy did not seem to have known about it, otherwise he certainly would have shown it to Mark when they visited the island the first time. The Indian had not hesitated to reveal the hollow place where the Squa-de-lich were hidden. So he would have had no reason not to show Father Townsend the cave.

Despite his grandfather's assurances, Mark was pretty sure that both Dutch Olsen and Larry Robbins were exploring Goat Island, each searching for his own kind of treasure. Both men, independent of each other, had visited the Anacortes Museum and asked to see the contents of box I dash 25 on Goat Island. As had a third man, the mysterious Bill Smith.

For years Dutch Olsen roamed around the islands searching for lost gold cached by early-day smugglers. Mark's grandfather had often accompanied the old-timer, more out of friendship and fun than any real hope of finding lost treasure. But the younger Larry Robbins, Mark now believed, went with them for a different reason. Collectors of Native American artifacts were paying big money for anything Indian. So while Dutch and Grand-Sam hunted for their gold, Larry Robbins tagged along, keeping his eyes peeled for anything he could steal and then later sell.

The Swinomish Channel was calm and they were making good progress. Mark tried to keep them near the center, where he figured the water was deepest. He was not concerned about running aground, but he did worry about hitting rocks submerged just below the water's surface. Jesse was twisting back and forth, trying to watch both shorelines at once. Sister Carter turned in her seat, keeping her eyes on the view in front of them.

When Mark asked Jesse's mother if he could take her to the island to look for the cave, Sister Carter announced she would go along too. Demanded was a better word. At first, Mark supposed that she wanted to come as a chaperon. And for that reason he had not objected. There were too many accusations being leveled against priests, and Father Townsend preferred not to put himself in a position where his motives or behavior might be suspect. But the more he thought about it, the more he was convinced that Teri Carter refused to believe his only interest was in trying to resolve some of the questions about the deaths of Dutch Olsen and Eddie Walking Boy. The woman's own insecurities and possessiveness held her captive. And as long as Father Mark Townsend remained on the Swinomish Reservation, she was not going to rest easy. Mark had no idea what they might find on the island or in the cave, but he felt sure that Sister Carter was tagging along to make certain that nothing belonging to the tribe would be removed.

The island was in front of them now, and he could see the pilings from the former dock poking above the water next to shore. There was no place for them to land on this side, so Mark continued on, steering their boat to the east as he followed the island's steep shoreline. He looked back over his shoulder, toward the point of land off of Pull and Be Damned Road. Somewhere between Goat Island and there, he was sure of it, Dutch Olsen was murdered. The priest was certain he had the chain of events down pat. The strong pull of the outgoing tide swept both the submerged body and the empty boat beyond the point. Both drifted toward Deception Pass, but at different speeds. When the tide reversed its flow, Olsen's body washed up on shore while his fishing boat was pushed back away from the narrow Pass.

"Watch where you're going!" Sister Carter yelled at him. "Can't you see those rocks?"

They were closer to shore now, and the dark wet shapes of several large rocks jutted above the water. Mark swerved to avoid them and cut back his speed.

"Turn more to the right," the nun directed. "There's rocks here, too."

He could not see them, but he did as she ordered. A gravel beach sloped toward them, with a long, bleached log stretching out into the water. A seagull rested on top of it, nervously shifting its weight from one webbed foot to the other while it suspiciously eyed the approaching craft.

The bow dug into gravel while they were still several feet from the beach, so Mark quickly cut the engine. Small waves lapped against the boat's metal sides, but their craft remained firmly stuck.

"One of us is going to have to get out," Sister Carter announced.

"I'll do it," said Jesse, jumping to her feet. The girl's movement rocked the boat.

"Sit down," the nun told her. "Father will pull us in."

Mark rolled his pants up to his knees but kept his tennis shoes on. The water was icy cold and he could feel the slippery gravel shifting beneath his feet. Teri Carter handed him the bow line as he waded toward the beach, towing the boat behind him. Jesse and the nun moved back to the stern, allowing the boat's bow to float higher. Father Townsend gave two more strong tugs, pulling enough of the boat onto the beach for Sister Carter and Jesse to step out without soaking their feet.

Jesse was already racing toward the trees as Mark finished tying the line.

"Wait up," he called after her. "Let's stick close together, Jesse." He rolled his pant legs back down.

Teri Carter sniffed the cold, salty air suspiciously. "How far is it to the mine?"

"Not far," Mark told her. "Through those trees over

there." They picked their way across the rocky beach to-gether. In front them, Jesse threw stones at the seagull perched on the log until the exasperated bird flew away.

"Come on," the girl called impatiently. "Hurry up!"

When they reached the tree line, Mark hesitated. "I think the clearing is this way," he said doubtfully.

"I know where it is," Jesse assured them. "I'll show you." And she plunged straight into the woods.

Father Townsend and Sister Carter did their best to keep up with her. But she was young and small and able to dodge most of the branches and vines that impeded the progress of the two older and bigger people. They could hear her though. Jesse was not quiet. By the time they reached the oval clearing, the young girl was already lean-ing into the entrance to the mine shaft.

"Jesse!" Mark's voice rang out in the silence. "Get away from there! Now!"

The girl backed quickly away, her mouth forming a round O of surprise. She was not used to being spoken to in such tones.

"That doesn't look very safe," Sister Carter told her with the proper tone of restraint in her voice. She looked pointedly at the priest. "Father's worried you might fall."

The child shrugged and skipped away.

"That's the mine?" the nun asked.

Father Townsend nodded. "There's water inside," he told her. Together they crossed to the edge and peered into the darkness. Mark kicked a loose stone into the mouth and they listened until they heard the splash. He pointed toward the top of the tall fir growing near the edge of the clearing. "The Squa-de-lich were hidden at the base of that tree." He started to lead the way. Jesse had found something to occupy her attention at the other side of the circle. Mark took one last look at the girl before plunging back into the woods. He did not want to have to search the island for a missing child.

Once at the tree, he pushed aside the ferns growing at the base and showed Sister Carter the hollow where the cedar boards were kept. The earth inside was firmly tamped and the bottom was lined with dried grasses. The hollow was deep enough for a big dog or small child to lie down inside. Mark let go of the ferns and they sprang back into place.

"Pretty clever," the Sister observed. "I wonder how Robbins ever found it."

"Either he discovered something at the museum that identified this place or else someone showed it to him. There's no way he could have found it on his own."

Teri Carter was looking back toward the clearing.

"It's certainly a good enough hiding place," she mused. "I'm sure the people thought the boards were safe over here."

"Eddie told me the tribal members never came here when the fort was open," Mark informed her. "But once the soldiers left they started coming back."

"It's a pretty setting," the nun admitted, looking around her. "I can see why they came here."

They got back to the clearing just in time to see Jesse about to disappear into the woods. Sister Carter gently called her back before Mark had time to shout.

"Are you able to remember where that cave is?" the nun asked the girl. Jesse nodded. "Will you take us there?"

She led the two adults out of the open circle, back into the woods. The contours of the ground rose at a gradual incline. Thick undergrowth pressed in on both sides of them. They seemed to be following a narrow, winding trail through the growth. The path was too narrow to have been made by humans and Mark worried what sort of animals could have found and forced their way through the thick bracket growing around them. At the top of the rise they could just make out a thin view of the water, but Father Townsend had no sense of what direction they might be facing.

"We go down there," Jesse announced, pointing in front of her. "Angel found a deer's head by it. She said bears ate the rest, but I didn't believe her." She looked into Sister Carter's face for reassurance. "But there's no bears here. Are there?"

Mark caught himself turning to inspect the narrow path behind them.

The three of them descended the small hill, still following the narrow game trail through the undergrowth. As they drew closer to the bottom, the ground leveled and the space around them began to open up. They could see a rocky beach through the trees in front of them.

"It's over by those big rocks," Jesse said, pointing to a place where part of the hillside had tumbled onto the beach, ending in a huge pile of stone. The girl began clambering over the rocks and the nun and priest did their best to keep up. Jesse slipped down behind a large boulder and they heard her cry of discovery. "I found it!"

Rounding the same boulder, Mark and Teri found themselves at the entrance to a dark hole, about five feet in height and three feet wide. The inside of the cave turned pitch black beyond a few feet, so it was impossible to see how far back the tunnel might extend. Mark reached into the pocket of his coat for the flashlight Linda Patsy had lent him, flipping it on and shining it into the cave.

The ground outside the cave was strewn with rough rocks, but inside the earth was dry and sandy. Stooping over, Mark stepped two feet into the cave's mouth and knelt down on one knee. Faint impressions of footprints fell under his beam of light. He stood again and aimed his flashlight back into the darkness.

"I want to look a little further," he told them.

"Me, too!" Jesse's voice thrilled with excitement.

"We'll stay close behind you." Sister Carter's voice sounded hollow as she stepped inside the cave.

They moved slowly, Mark pausing to turn his light and illumine the way behind him for the others to follow. The cave's tunnel curved gradually to the left, burrowing back into the hillside. The air inside was cool and dank with moisture, although the ground remained dry. About thirty feet back they lost sight of the cave's entrance, although light from the opening continued to reflect off the rocky walls behind them. Father Townsend pointed his light in front of them, searching the darkness. A part of the cave's floor looked different from the area around it and Mark slowly made his way toward it, playing his light across the surface of the sand. He found more footprints and near the side of the wall, straight and flat indentations in the sand. Something heavy had once been left on that part of the cave's level surface.

"There was something here," he told the others, moving his light across the markings etched in the soft sand.

"Hold it still," Sister Carter ordered him. "You're making me dizzy, moving that around so much." Mark did as he was told, slowing the flickering light.

"What's that?" the nun's voice said. "Hold the flashlight still."

Mark turned the light back and a glint from something shiny reflected back. Jesse scrambled forward and grabbed it. The young girl took one look at the object in her hand and tossed it into the darkness in front of her.

"It's just a book of matches," she informed them.

"I'd like to look at that, Jesse," Mark told the child. "See if you can find it again." He aimed the flashlight into the darkness in front of her, trying to light the way.

Jesse did as she was told, carefully stepping over a pile of rocks and searching for the matchbook in the shadows in front of her. Suddenly the child let out a piercing scream and raced back to Father Townsend's side.

"There's a man," she told him, quaking. "He's lying back there."

Sister Carter knelt down and hugged the child against her as Mark carefully crept forward, splaying his thin light across the ground in front of him. He stepped over the same mound of rocks Jesse had crossed and looked down.

Larry Robbins was lying on his stomach with his face turned towards Mark. His arms were tied behind his back, and even from several feet away Mark could see the large wound in the back of the man's head, clotted thick with blood. Near the dead man's feet Mark saw the matchbook. He picked it up and held it beneath his light, examining the cover. Pocketing it, he quickly picked his way back to Sister Carter and the girl.

"We have to get out of here," he said hurriedly, urging them towards the mouth of the cave.

"What is it?" Sister Carter's voice sounded thin and strained.

"I think we might have been followed," he told the nun. "We've got to get off the island."

TWENTY-THREE

"Looks like we're too late," Mark whispered.

The *SinCan* was anchored seventy-five feet out from the beach. Li Kuhn Suu stood on the flying bridge, peering along the shoreline with binoculars. Meanwhile, Colin Petty was rapidly approaching the beach in the *SinCan*'s small dinghy, his bulky frame bending over a pair of oars which he was wielding with fierce determination.

Father Townsend, Sister Carter, and Jesse Patsy watched the scene from behind a thick stand of ferns growing along the edge of the woods. Their own small boat sat in plain sight a few yards in front of them, but there was no way they could get to it without being seen. Mark could feel Jesse's small body trembling as she leaned against his side. He wrapped his arm around her as they watched Petty rapidly drawing nearer.

"How did you know it was them?" Sister Carter asked.

"That book of matches in the cave was from the *SinCan*," the priest explained. "When I saw the ship's name I knew they were involved."

"One of them killed that man back there?"

"Yes, I think so," Townsend murmured, watching as the dinghy drew closer to the beach.

"We have to hide." Teri Carter's voice was firm, but

still full of fear. She grabbed Jesse's arm and began edging backward.

Mark followed them a short distance into the woods, but then stopped. "You two go on," he told the nun. "I'm going to stay here."

"What do you mean?" Sister Carter snapped at him. "They'll kill you." Jesse began to whimper and Mark knelt down beside her.

"You've got to be brave," he told the child, "and be real quiet. You and Sister Carter go hide yourselves. Pretend it's a game. But don't come out until Sister says it's safe." He stood back up. "Go on," he ordered the nun, "find someplace to hide. I'll be careful."

A look of doubt swept across her face, but she grabbed Jesse's hand and ran quickly down the path that led back to the clearing. Mark returned to his hiding spot above the beach and parted the ferns. Colin Petty had already landed and was pulling his dinghy alongside their own boat. He dropped the boat's line on the rocks without bothering to tie it, and bent to reach back inside his boat. When he stood back up he was holding a black pistol and what looked like a two-way radio. That was confirmed when Mark saw the man speaking into it and on the *SinCan*, Kuhn Suu lifting a similar device to reply. Petty pocketed the radio but kept the gun out, holding it lightly in one hand. He stood relaxed on the beach, looking confidently around him. From his stance, it was obvious that he expected no resistance from a priest, a nun, and a small girl. After another glance at the woods, he set off down the rocky beach, heading toward the cave. Mark figured he would search for them there first and then begin working his way back to the clearing. He stayed hidden in the same spot, watching as the burly man moved further away. Meanwhile Li Kuhn Suu remained on deck, watching his partner through his binoculars, occasionally sweeping them back and forth along the shoreline for some sign of movement. Mark remained still, crouching out of sight.

He watched as Petty rounded the beach and disappeared. He was about to move, but then decided to wait another five minutes. Checking the time on his watch,

Mark resolved not to make a move until all the time was up. He watched nervously as the second hand swept slowly around. By then he figured the man had to be at the cave. No doubt he would spot their footprints in front of the opening and follow them inside, hoping he might catch the three of them still in the cave and dispose of them as easily as Larry Robbins.

Time was up. Boldly, Father Townsend stood up from his hiding place facing the *SinCan*. Slowly he began walking onto the beach, heading towards the boats. Kuhn Suu spotted him immediately. He stared through his binoculars as the priest marched defiantly across the rocks toward the boats. Lifting his radio, he called for his partner. Mark could not make out what he was saying, although the sound of the excitement in his voice carried across the water. He was jabbing one arm at Mark as he shouted directions into the radio. Townsend was at the boats and reached inside their own first, disconnecting the gas line between the engine and the tank, then grabbing the boat's single paddle. Li Kuhn Suu had him fixed in his binoculars, watching his every move. Next he removed both oars from the *SinCan*'s dinghy. Then he turned his back on the yacht and with his arms full, headed back for the shelter of the trees. Father Townsend was halfway back up the beach when the first shot rang out. Startled, he dropped his boat's fuel line. It fell on the rocks as a second shot was fired. He heard the bullet ricochet off a nearby rock. Hurriedly grabbing the fallen hose, he began running awkwardly for the trees. He should have known Kuhn Suu would have a gun. Another shot was fired. He felt the impact as the bullet split the blade of one of the *SinCan*'s oars, tearing it out of his arms. He left the shattered pieces of wood on the beach and dashed wildly for the safety of the thick stand of fir, still cradling the oars and hose in his arms. Behind him he could hear the Asian's voice again, loudly yelling for his partner.

Mark dodged further back into the brush, heading away from the clearing and toward the ruins of the old fort. The long oars were awkward to carry and were slowing him down, so he jettisoned them along with the gas line in a thick growth of brambles and continued running. After about fifty yards he changed his course and headed back toward the shore. He had to make sure Kuhn Suu knew which direction he was heading. Sister Carter and Jesse had headed in the direction of the clearing, so he knew that he had to do something that would draw Petty away from there. Mark reemerged from the trees onto the beach and raced a dozen yards along the rocky shore until he was certain he had caught Kuhn Suu's attention. Then just as suddenly, he dodged back into the trees. He was not going to give the man another opportunity to shoot at him.

Petty would be in pursuit by now. He would not try to chase Mark along the rocky beach, but would cut back through the island's middle towards the fort, expecting to gain distance on the priest that way. That route would take him dangerously close to the clearing and Mark hoped Jesse and Teri Carter would remember his warning and remain hidden. He ran faster. Unless he reached the abandoned fort before the other man, he would have no opportunity to hide himself.

The trail he was on was unfamiliar, but he had a sense he was running in the right direction. He was trying to watch where he was running, avoiding rocks, logs, and holes that could trip him. The last thing he needed now was a sprained ankle. An accident like that would mean certain death if it allowed Petty to catch up to him. Mark was running too hard and his heart was beating too loudly for him to hear anything behind him. He could only hope that Petty had indeed gone directly to the cave, and that the distance from there to the fort was greater than the distance he needed to cover. The ground was beginning to slope upward and Mark was racing as fast as he could through the thick woods. He was breathing hard now, and hoped it was not much further to the fort. He had no way of knowing where Petty might be and he was tempted to stop and listen for the burly man. But he forced himself ahead. He had to reach the fort and find a place to hide.

The square, squat shape of one of the outlying bunkers materialized through the trees. But it stood alone and was too small. Mark pressed on, dodging through the trees,

racing as quickly as possible over the broken ground. He
passed a pile of broken bricks and mortar, a sure sign he
was getting close.

Father Townsend arrived at the far end of the ruined
gun emplacements. He could see the circular base that
once held one of the huge guns, and knew there were three
others in line to his right. Pockmarked along the bunkers
were the gaping black holes of dark, empty rooms. When
he first came to this place with Eddie Walking Boy he
had not spent much time exploring them, but he knew
there were connecting tunnels between the various compartments honeycombed throughout the emplacements.

Mark slowed at the second mount, examining the site.
He would make his stand here. Suddenly he heard a loud
snap, and he willed himself to stop and listen. He could
hear a crashing in the woods. Petty was getting close.

There were three doorways leading into the bunker. The
ones in the center and to the right still had heavy iron
doors attached. The priest made his choice and ducked
into the center doorway. He was plunged into immediate
darkness. The light fell only a few feet onto the cement
floor inside and Mark could not tell how far back the room
might go or if it might be connected with any of the other
compartments. Cautiously, hands stretched out in front of
him, he shuffled further back into the darkness, feeling the
air for any sign of a wall. There was nothing but the blackness. Turning around, he trotted back to the lighted doorway. Petty had to be near. The gunman would quickly
realize the priest had to be hiding inside the bunkers and
he would begin a methodical search, probably by starting
at one end of the four emplacements and then working his
way to the others. What Mark did not know was where
he would start and when he would arrive at the place
where he was hiding. Mark wondered if Petty was carrying a flashlight. He had not seen one when the man was
on the beach. Realizing he was still standing in the open
doorway, the priest quietly moved back into the dark shadows, carefully peering out. Too late, he realized his own
hands were empty. He should have at least grabbed a piece

of wood or something hard and heavy. The priest was helpless without a weapon of some sort.

Mark was debating rushing back outside to find something to arm himself with when he heard a loud bump, followed by a curse. He ducked back further. Colin Petty had arrived. Softly he stepped to one side and fixed his eyes on one of the corners of the bunker. The noise sounded like it came from that direction.

Colin Petty rounded the corner, moving quickly but limping slightly. Either he had twisted an ankle or banged his leg against something. But he was hardly impaired. His right hand was pointed out in front of him, holding a pistol of some sort. Mark knew nothing about guns, but this one looked formidable, heavy and black, with a long, shiny barrel. His left hand was carrying the radio he had used to talk with the *SinCan*. The killer crossed to the center of the emplacement and Mark quietly shifted closer to the side wall, near the iron door. The man was eyeing all three of the openings and Mark ducked his head back into darkness. Moving slowly, he began easing himself behind the door, trying not to make a sound. He could hear the man outside, crossing to the far opening. The sound of Petty's footsteps stopped and Mark could picture him standing at the other doorway, peering into the room's darkness, the gun leveled in front of him.

The footsteps began again. Petty was now crossing to the center doorway. He stopped. Father Townsend rested both of his hands against the back of the heavy door, ready to push it into Petty's body. He felt the door give slightly and the rusty iron let out a slight groan. Petty heard the creak and stopped. Mark froze in absolute silence. He held his breath. The gunman began approaching. The priest waited, bracing himself behind the door. Petty was making no attempt to walk quietly as he approached the opening. Mark could hear the man's raspy breath over his footsteps, just outside the entrance. Petty stopped once more, probably trying to search the darkness for some sign of Mark. One step. Then another. Townsend's muscles were knotted with the tension. One more step. One more.

When he saw the shadow of the arm holding the gun,

Mark pushed against the door with all his might. The rusty iron shrieked as it swung toward Petty standing just on the other side. The gunman heard the sound before he saw the door's movement, and he tried to step back. The heavy door was swinging towards him as Mark pushed from the other side. But then it stopped as suddenly as it started, locked in mid-swing by years of accumulated rust. Mark gave the door one more heave, trying to force it closed. But the door was frozen tight. From the other side he could hear Petty begin to laugh.

TWENTY-FOUR

"You might as well come on out of there!" Colin Petty ordered the priest. He was still laughing, but the sound had turned bitter and mean.

Father Townsend hesitated, then stepped out from behind the rusted, half-closed door. The daylight was blinding after the darkness and he squinted out at the gunman.

"All the way out." Petty took two steps backward, his gun pointed directly at the Jesuit's chest.

Mark moved slowly forward, his hands hanging useless at his sides.

"Lock your hands behind your head," Petty commanded. The priest did as he was told.

"Where are the others?"

Townsend did not reply. He could see Petty's fingers tighten around the gun. The Jesuit felt himself give an involuntary flinch.

The gunman caught it and smiled. Keeping his eyes and his pistol trained on the Mark, he lifted the radio in his left hand and spoke into it.

"I found one of them."

Li Kuhn Suu's excited voice sounded weak and distant on the radio. "Who?"

"The priest," Petty replied.

220

"What about the others?"

"Not yet," Petty answered curtly.

"Hurry up!"

He lowered the radio and offered his captive an evil grin. His eyes, filled with antagonism, never left Mark's face. And the gun trained on his chest never quavered.

"Now, Father," the killer addressed Mark mockingly, a grimace pasted on his face, "we can do this nice or we can do it mean." He raised the gun and pointed it directly into Townsend's face. "It's up to you, Padre."

Petty would pull the trigger, Mark had no doubts about that. At some point he planned to kill him anyway. Mark's only choice was to decide when to die. Would it be better to let the man shoot him now and get it over with, hoping the nun and girl were hidden where Petty would not find them? If they heard a gunshot would they stay hidden? Or would one or both panic? Or should he try to buy time and put off the inevitable?

"How's it going to be?" Petty was waving his gun impatiently. "You want it here and now?"

Mark had to decide. "I'll show you where they are," he said reluctantly.

He knew he had no chance of escape. The gunman followed behind the priest, keeping far enough back so Mark could not turn and attack, but near enough so that he could not run. As he led the man away from the fort, back toward the clearing, he heard Colin Petty radio back to the *SinCan*. "We're going for them now."

"Hurry!" Kuhn Suu's voice urged.

Mark was trying to come up with a plan.

"What were you two hiding here?" he asked, turning his head back toward the man.

The gunman snarled. "Eyes ahead!" he ordered. Mark turned quickly back. "None of your damn business."

"I think I know the answer anyway."

The gunman only grunted. Mark was walking slowly. His hands were still interlocked behind his head, and he has having some trouble following the rough trail into the woods.

"Li Kuhn Suu told me he was from Myanmar," Father

Townsend continued. ''That used to be the country of Burma.'' He stepped across a fallen branch. ''The newspapers say a lot of heroin still comes out of there.''

Petty's voice sounded close. ''More than you know.''

''So you and Kuhn Suu bring it down from Canada on the *SinCan* and then hide it here on the island.''

There was no reply.

''Then someone else takes it on from here, I suppose.''

Petty stayed silent. They were cresting a slight hill and Mark could hear the man's heavy breathing.

''Was that Robbins? Was he carrying it to Seattle?''

Petty snorted. ''Are you kidding? That snoop?''

The path through the woods turned sharply to the left. Mark remembered following Eddie's back along this part of the trail and wondering at the time why the path took such a sudden turn.

''So Larry Robbins discovered what you guys were doing?''

''This was supposed to be a deserted island,'' Petty told him. ''We never saw no one over here. Then suddenly everyone's mother is climbing all over the place.''

Father Townsend stopped and cocked his head. ''Everyone's mother?''

He felt a sharp jab as Petty poked the gun in his back. ''Keep moving, dammit!''

''I know that Dutch Olsen came over here, but he was only looking for old treasure.''

''How the hell were we supposed to know what everyone's snooping for?'' Petty said harshly. ''First there's no one, then everyone. You, the Indian, those old men. Now you got that damn nun and the girl over here. This place is suddenly like a goddamned Disneyland! We're trying to move thirteen million bucks of merchandise while you folks are playing tourist.''

Father Townsend stopped in his tracks and turned back towards his captor.

''But we didn't know anything about you guys,'' he angrily protested. ''You're killing innocent people.''

Colin Petty's huge round face was red, either with anger or the exertion of the hike. He stepped closer to the priest, raising the gun until it was just below Townsend's chin.

"You turn around again," he said icily, "and I'll kill you." He jabbed the gun into the Jesuit's throat. "You got me? Now turn around and move."

Mark swallowed and turned back to the trail. The gunman waited until he had taken two steps away, then began following. Father Townsend tried moving a little faster. They were in thick underbrush and the pathway was narrow. He could remember the thick brambles of the blackberry vines from his hike through here with Eddie.

Dutch Olsen was killed because his elusive search for smuggler's gold had brought him to Goat Island. Larry Robbins was killed for much the same reason. Only he was looking for Indian artifacts instead of treasure. Robbins probably was making a tidy sum off the stuff he found and sold.

They had killed Eddie Walking Boy because he was on the island, too. Petty and Li Kuhn Suu were taking no risks. Anyone who could possibly have uncovered their hiding place was killed.

"If this island was getting too crowded, why didn't you guys just find another hiding place?" Mark asked. He could hear Petty's ragged breath close behind him, but he knew better than to turn and face him.

"Easier said than done," the killer huffed. "Our investors don't like their inventory out in the open any more than is absolutely necessary."

"Your investors." Mark was guessing, "Those were those guys Eddie and I saw on the boat the other day?"

There was no reply. They were climbing another small hill. Mark's hands were still behind his head, so he moved slowly and carefully to keep his balance.

"How far is this place?" Petty asked, panting hard.

He tried remembering how much further it was to the clearing. They were a lot closer than he wanted them to be.

"Just a little ways," Mark answered.

They crested the rise and Father Townsend hesitated. The pathway ahead was narrow and overgrown and descended at a steep angle. He felt the gun in his back.

"Get moving," Petty growled.

"If I try going down there with my hands up like this I'll fall flat on my face."

The gunman leaned forward and peered over Mark's shoulder at the trail below them.

"You can use one of them," he grudgingly conceded, "but keep the other one up where I can see it. And don't try anything!"

Mark lowered his right hand and grabbed a handful of vines as he lowered himself down the trail. His feet slid on the loose wet dirt and he tightened his grip, moving sideways for better balance. Behind him, Petty started to follow him down. The trail was steeper than it looked at the top. Both men were moving cautiously, trying to stay upright. The priest could hear the gunman slipping down the pathway behind him. Mark realized that Colin Petty was probably finding it just as difficult to stay on his feet while holding his gun in one hand and the radio in his other. And in that instant he found his plan.

"Watch it," he warned, "it's slippery right here!" And he let go of the vines.

His body lurched forward and his legs automatically began scrambling, trying to keep their balance. His pace quickened and he could hear Petty grunting as he tried to keep up. The downward pull forced Mark into a trot and his left arm dropped down in automatic reflex. He tightened, waiting for some reaction from behind him, but Colin Petty was in no position to react. He was losing control of his feet, struggling hard to stay upright. Mark reached out on both sides of him, grabbing at branches to slow his forward motion. He waited until the gunman was rushing right on his heels, then suddenly loosened his grip on the branches in his left hand and at the same time, grabbed tightly to a limb on his right. His actions served as a brake, and his body swung sharply to the right of the trail. Petty grunted in surprise, but continued rushing past him. Realizing his own predicament, he dropped his radio and began grabbing at branches.

Mark released his hold and started tumbling back down,

directly toward the man in front of him. While still a few feet away, he lowered his shoulder and pushed off with his back foot, hurling himself at the burly gunman. There was no time for Petty to react. He tried swinging his gun back around, but the priest's body slammed into him at that moment. The gun flew from his hand and both men left their feet, tumbling down the trail together.

Father Townsend managed to stop first. The other man slid only another seven feet beyond him, but that gave Mark enough time and distance to sit up and look quickly around. He spotted the gun on the trail, about four feet above him and lunged upwards. Colin Petty was moving just as quickly, but his bulk slowed him just enough. Mark grabbed the pistol and, still lying in the dirt, aimed it down the trail at the man below him.

"Stop!" His voice sounded high and strained but Petty did as he was told. He was kneeling in the dirt, one hand outstretched towards the priest and he froze. His own pistol was now pointed directly into his face. He did not know whether the priest would actually pull the trigger or not, but his own natural instincts as a predator led him to believe that Townsend would. He lowered his hand and settled heavily onto the trail, breathing hard.

"Shit!" he exclaimed.

Father Townsend followed his captive into the clearing. He forced Petty to lock his hands behind his head like he had done. That seemed to be what gunmen do with prisoners. He made the drug smuggler stop in the center of the opening and had him sit with his legs crossed. Mark stayed a few feet away from him, keeping the gun aimed at his back. He did not know whether or not he could actually pull the trigger if Petty turned on him. And he did not plan to offer the murderer any opportunities for finding out. Still standing behind him, he began looking around for some sign of Sister Carter and Jesse.

The quiet was suddenly disturbed by a loud squawk. He had recovered the radio before directing Petty towards the clearing and now Li Kuhn Suu's shrill voice came over it, calling for his partner. Mark looked at the array of buttons and dials on the radio, but left it alone. Kuhn

Suu called for Petty twice more, then the radio fell silent.

"Sister Carter! Jesse!" Mark directed his voice back into the trees and away from the water. He did not want his voice to travel back toward the *SinCan*, which was anchored just a couple of hundred yards away. He called again, "Teri! Jesse! It's okay to come out!"

Sister Carter's head poked out from the dark opening of the mine shaft. Her long braids were wet and plastered against the side of her head. The rest of her body emerged and was just as wet. She blinked hard at the man sitting on the ground, then turned her attention to the Jesuit with a gun in his hand.

"What happened?" she wanted to know.

"What happened to you?" replied Father Townsend.

The nun looked down at her wet clothes. "I slipped and fell when I was crawling in," she told him. "But I'm okay. You were right about the water—it only goes a little ways back before you're back on dry ground."

"Where's Jesse? Is she all right?"

Teri Carter nodded and gave the priest a sly smile. She crossed the clearing and disappeared back among the trees, heading toward the tall fir. A couple of minutes later she reemerged, leading a very dirty young girl by the hand.

"I hid her in the hole you showed us," Sister Carter explained, brushing dirt out of the child's hair. Jesse's wide eyes were fixed on Colin Petty.

"Li Kuhn Suu is still out on the boat," Mark told the nun. "He's tried calling a couple of times." He held up the radio to her. "I didn't answer though."

Sister Carter took it from him. "It's a radio, isn't it?"

Mark shrugged. "Yeah, a VHF, I think. But I don't know that much about them. There's an on/off switch on the side, and you press that button to talk. The number indicates what channel you're on." He held the radio out, offering it to the nun. "We had CB radios in the village when I worked in Alaska," he explained, "but we always kept it set on the one channel everybody used."

A digital fifty-eight was electronically displayed in a small screen on the radio's front. Teri Carter spun the dial and the numbers changed rapidly: 59, 60, 61, 62. She switched back to fifty-eight. None of the numbers meant anything to the nun.

"I don't know any more than you do," she admitted to the priest with a shrug of her shoulders. "What should we do?"

Mark glanced back down at Petty. "We're at a stand-off right now," he told her. "Li Kuhn Suu can't get to us because the *SinCan*'s dinghy is on the beach. But we can't get to our boat as long as he's out there. Either we find a way to scare him away or we figure out how to get some help."

Sister Carter, still holding onto the radio, walked around to face Colin Petty, making sure to keep plenty of distance between herself and the man.

"I don't suppose you'd tell us how this works?"

The man swore at her and grinned wickedly. She returned to Father Townsend's side.

"We know that fifty-eight calls the *SinCan*," she told Mark. "So we don't want to call that number. Let's just start calling on all the others until we get somebody."

"But maybe we ought to call the *SinCan*," Mark replied, thinking out loud. "Maybe we ought to let Kuhn Suu know we have his partner."

"What would that prove? You think that might scare him away?"

"If he knows Petty is caught he might try to save himself," the priest reasoned. "Why don't you try it?"

"You do it." Sister Carter handed Mark the radio.

Keeping his eyes on Colin Petty and the gun pointed at the man's back, Mark held the VHF in his left hand and pressed down on the bar. "Li Kuhn Suu?" he spoke into it. "Is this the *SinCan*?"

They both listened for some response.

"Nothing," said Mark.

"Do it again," the nun told him.

"Li Kuhn Suu, can you hear me?" They waited for some response.

"Take your finger off the button." Jesse was standing

beside them. "It don't work if you keep your finger down," she informed them.

"Oh, right. I forgot." Mark did as she instructed.

". . . is this?" the radio immediately squawked back.

"Is this the *SinCan*?" Mark asked again, this time making sure to release the bar after he spoke.

Li Kuhn Suu's voice answered. "Colin? Colin, is that you? What's going on?"

"Li Kuhn Suu, this is Father Townsend. I have Colin in front of me. I also have his gun."

His only response was silence. They waited, listening several moments for some reply from the *SinCan*. Finally Mark called the ship again.

"Kuhn Suu, this is what we're going to do. We're calling the tribal police for help. We're going to tell Mike Jennings where we are and warn him that you are anchored out in front of us. It's only a matter of time before help will get here, so you might as well give up." Mark let go of the button and grinned at Sister Carter and Jesse. "That should do it." They waited, but there was no response.

"I'll go check," said Teri Carter.

"Me too," chimed Jesse.

The two of them headed in the direction of the beach and Mark walked around to face the man sitting in front of him. Petty glowered at the priest out of eyes filled with hate.

"We think the *SinCan*'s going to pull out," Mark told him. "You'll be left behind."

The killer made no reply, but shifted his body uncomfortably.

"Things could go easier for you if you decided to help us," Mark suggested to the man. "You could start by telling me if Li Kuhn Suu has the heroin on that boat with him."

Colin Petty continued glowering at the priest. But the look in his eyes shifted to uncertainty, and his head nodded. Imperceptibly at first, then stronger. "Yeah," he finally admitted, "it's on there."

"How much?"

"All of it. It's in the forward cabin, under the bunks. We were supposed to deliver it in Seattle tonight. It gets distributed from there."

Mark held up the radio. "How do I call out on this thing?"

"Go sixteen," Petty told him with a frown. "That'll get the Coast Guard."

Father Townsend moved back around behind the man just as Sister Carter and Jesse were returning.

"The engines are started," Jesse crowed. "He's going away!"

Mark was turning the numbers to sixteen.

"Calling Coast Guard," he spoke into the radio, giving the girl and the nun a triumphant grin. "Mayday! We have an emergency. Can you hear me, Coast Guard?"

TWENTY-FIVE

Father Townsend held back, staying at the end of the long line of people slowly trudging up the street. Ordinarily, he was positioned in the very front of funeral processions. But at this one he was quite content to follow at the end. His relationship with Eddie Walking Boy had felt ambiguous at best; he was still sorting it out for himself. Mark would have felt awkward having any kind of role in the funeral service. The chance to stay in back and pray silently gave the priest time to think.

His right hip was still bruised and sore from his slide down the path, and Mark was walking with a pronounced limp. A few of the Indians gave him shy glances out of the corner of their eyes, and there were whispers and nods, but no one spoke to him. And like his place in the crowd, this too felt all right.

Nearly two hundred people turned out for Walking Boy's funeral. At the end of the service in the tiny reservation church, the six pall bearers had lifted the casket up on their shoulders and slowly began the trek to the Swinomish cemetery on foot. The mourners followed slowly behind as the cortege made its way up the street. The cemetery was about a quarter of a mile away and everybody walked.

Mark felt there was a quiet decorum in doing it this way. He regretted that his funeral processions at St. Joseph's in Seattle could not have this same type of dignity. Here there was no awkward standing around outside the church while the mortuary attendants scurried about, packing up their equipment and whispering urgent orders to the mourners. There was no hustling away to private cars, their engines racing and lights burning while everyone else sat parked, waiting for the parade to begin. There was no off-duty cop waving you into traffic or worse, holding you up. Here, there was no distancing oneself from the sad matter at hand. Your focus stayed on the light brown casket floating above the heads of the crowd, supported on the shoulders of the six men leading the people to Eddie's final resting place.

Mark glanced up ahead and saw that the front of the procession was already nearing the cemetery gates. He felt small, soft fingers grab onto his right hand and he looked down. Jesse was smiling up at him.

"Mom and Dad said you should come up with them. They're waiting for you."

They made their way forward, toward the crowd bunching up as people spilled through the gates into the cemetery. Once inside, while waiting for the others, they wandered off to visit the graves of friends and family. The small cemetery was soon dotted throughout with small knots of people hovering over tombstones. Mark and Jesse found Greg and Linda standing just outside the cemetery fence, waiting expectantly.

Greg Patsy was a tall, thin Indian, with a long, angular face. His sleek black hair was pulled back into one long braid that fell halfway down his back. He had large hands, badly scarred and deeply calloused. His brown face looked tough and weathered and his black eyes were hooded over by a low brow. Only his mouth gave him away. His smile pegged him as a gentle man. Greg's arm was wrapped around Linda's waist, almost as if he was afraid to let go. The father reached out and took his daughter's hand, smiled, and nodded to Mark. Then the four of them entered the cemetery together.

They followed the people to the empty grave dug into the earth beside two tall fir trees growing in one corner. The casket was already resting on wooden planks stretched across the hole. The people edged closer, sensing the ceremony was about to begin. Elders were given chairs to sit near the front. The man and woman who were directing the service stood next to each other at the head of the casket.

Jesse was standing on her toes, craning to see, but the small girl was lost in a sea of adult backs. She squirmed impatiently and pulled away from her father's grasp. Spying an opening, she started to dart ahead. Quickly her father reached out and grabbed her as Linda hissed, "Jesse!" Greg knelt down beside his daughter.

"You have to stay back here," he ordered. "Kids aren't allowed up there. You stay here with us."

Mark looked around and saw that it was true. Parents hung back, standing well behind the other people, keeping their children away from the open grave. Some wrapped their arms protectively around their offspring, as if the dark hole was threatening to swallow their children.

He heard bells. Small brass handbells were being rung, and from the front, soft voices began singing. A sweet melody rose above the crowd like incense while the bells continued. The sound filled Mark's heart and he felt himself relax, allowing the blessing to heal and soothe, as it was intended. *My heavenly Father I shall see . . .* Father Townsend could hear crying now as tears began to flow. When the singing stopped there were still sobs coming from the people as the two prayer leaders led the people in the Sign of the Cross. They signed three times, invoking the traditional formula: *In the name of the Father, the Son, and the Holy Ghost.* People were invited forward to pray for Eddie, for his family, for the community. There was no rush to finish the graveside service. Father Townsend closed his eyes and listened to the voices as they rose and fell. He made his own prayers: for Eddie; for Greg, Linda, and Jesse; for GrandSam and Nan; for Dutch Olsen and Larry Robbins; for their families and friends. . . . The names kept on coming and Mark felt the sadness of the deaths as their impact spread out like rings of water, en-

compassing more and more people. Suddenly he felt over-
whelmed by the tragedy of the past week and he could
feel his own eyes beginning to tear.

He felt Jesse pulling on his arm and opened his eyes.
She was smiling and pointing upward. Mark turned his
face to the sky and saw what she saw. Two bald eagles,
wings outspread, rode the currents high above the cemetery, circling over their heads as if in benediction. Others
began looking up, pointing.

When the prayers were finally ended, the six Indians
who had carried Eddie from the church unpinned the car-
nations from their jackets. Holding back the pins, each laid
his flower on top of the brown casket. Other men circled
ropes under each end of the coffin as the wooden planks
were pulled out from underneath. Slowly Eddie was lowered into the ground. Two shovelfuls of dirt, taken from
the grave, were held out as family members said a last
farewell. Each person picked up a handful of the soil and
tossed it into the grave. They were followed by the elders.
The women went next, and Linda left her place to move
forward in line. The men followed last, and Greg and
Mark took their turns near the end. Finally, volunteers
began shoveling the remaining dirt into the hole. No one
left the cemetery until the work was finished. The dirt was
mounded and packed, then women gathered the garlands
of flowers and arranged them across the top of the grave.
Eddie Walking Boy was laid to rest.

"I want to thank you again." Greg Patsy solemnly extended his hand to Mark as they made their way out of
the cemetery. The two men exchanged smiles.

"I'm glad things worked out the way they did," Mark
told him.

The Indian let go of the priest's hand. "Can I ask you
a question?"

Mark nodded.

"Why did you?" Greg read his puzzlement. "Why did
you help, I mean? You didn't know me, you didn't know
anything about me."

Mark thought a moment. "To be perfectly honest," he
finally replied, "I never thought I was helping you nec-

essarily. At first I was concerned for Nan . . . my grandmother. Then I met your wife and daughter. I felt I was
helping them.''

''But you must have known Greg was innocent,'' Linda
cut in. She was still holding tight to her husband's arm.

''Not at first,'' Mark admitted. ''When I heard about
the fights Greg had with Olsen, and that he was fishing
right where his body washed up, I thought maybe he'd
done it.'' Linda's mouth started to frown. ''But that didn't
mean you and Jesse didn't need help. When Nan and I
first came to visit, I could see the pain you were in.''

''But your grandmother didn't leave you a lot of choice
either,'' Linda remembered. She was smiling again. ''She
sort of volunteered you.''

Mark dipped his head in acknowledgement, grinning in
response. ''That's Nan.''

''When did you think maybe I didn't do it?'' Greg
wanted to know.

''When Jesse took me to see your boat.'' Mark looked
down at the child. ''There were a couple of things that
didn't seem right. I couldn't imagine why anyone who had
shot someone would be dumb enough to leave the rifle
lying around. Especially when it would be so easy just to
toss it overboard. And then there was the shape of your
boat.''

Greg looked confused. ''What'd the boat's shape have
to do with it?''

''Not the shape, but the condition,'' Mark clarified.
''Everything on your boat was in perfect condition. Clean
and in place. That's what I mean by the shape. There
weren't any other boats down there that looked that
good.''

''So?''

''So why would anyone who takes such good care of
his gear risk doing damage by running over something
like a body? Every boat I've ever been on, the owner is
paranoid about hitting anything, even a little piece of
wood. I couldn't imagine you, a fisherman, risking dam-
aging your boat by running it into a body.'' Mark paused
and shrugged. ''Maybe you would have. But at the time

it didn't make sense to me. Not when I saw how carefully you treated your boat. When people cherish a thing, they usually don't abuse it. Although I didn't know you, I couldn't imagine someone who takes such good care of his boat using it as a weapon.''

Linda was smiling happily at the priest. ''Sometimes I think he loves that old boat more than he does me.''

''That's not true!'' Greg protested. ''I never!''

''When Eddie took me around the point in his boat,'' Mark continued, ''I had a hunch you were probably innocent. Once he explained how the currents worked off Pull and Be Damned, I realized Olsen's body had to have drifted before it washed up. Li Kuhn Suu and Colin Petty ambushed him much closer to Goat Island. An outgoing tide carried Dutch and his boat around the point. By the time the tide changed, the body had only floated as far as Pull and Be Damned. But the boat had gone nearly to Deception Pass.''

''I've fished this water my whole life,'' the Indian told him, ''and I'm not sure I could have ever figured that out.''

''Once you explain it,'' his wife said, ''it makes sense. But just to look at it, I think anyone would have missed that.''

''Someone would have got it eventually,'' Mark said. ''Sometimes I think it's easier to figure something out if you don't know much about it. At least you don't start by making assumptions that end up wrong.''

''What about me?'' Jesse chimed in. ''I helped too.''

Mark smiled down at her then slowly lowered himself to one knee, groaning only slightly as he did.

''You were the biggest help of all,'' he told her.

'' 'Cuz I knew about the cave,'' she announced to her father. ''And I found that dead man.''

''No, Jesse.''

Mark's voice was firm and the girl turned away from her father to face the priest.

''That's not what I meant. That was a big help, yes. But I made a mistake taking you there. It was too dangerous, and I was wrong.'' Mark looked up at Greg and

Linda. "I am sorry for that," he told them.

"But you said I was the biggest help," Jesse protested.

"You were," Mark told her. "But because you believed in your father. And you wouldn't let anyone stop you from believing. Even when I told you I didn't think I could be much help, you made me think again. That was the most important thing, Jesse. You believed in your father and you never stopped believing."

Mark stood back up, brushing the dirt from his knees. He looked at his watch.

"Yikes! I've got to get going."

"You have to stay for the meal," Linda protested. "And the giveaway."

Father Townsend held out his hands. "I really can't. I have to be back in Seattle and I still need to say goodbye to my grandparents. I'm going to have to skip out."

Greg Patsy looked solemnly at the priest. "Leaving before the feed is bad medicine," he said. "Lots of bad things happen to people who do that. No Indian I know would ever take that risk."

"Really?" Mark looked doubtful.

The fisherman scoffed, "No, not really." He laughed. "Are you one of those white guys who believes everything an Indian says?"

"Stop teasing him," Linda scolded her husband. "He said he has to go. Stop trying to make him feel bad." She turned to Father Townsend. "You'll come back soon?"

"I will," Mark promised.

"We'll have a dinner then," she told him. "Maybe salmon. If my lazy husband ever goes back to work."

Now it was the priest's turn to laugh. "It's a deal."

The woman reached out and held him with both arms. "Thank you, Father. Thank you for my family." And then she kissed him.

TWENTY-SIX

Father Townsend limped slowly through the back door. His tumble down the hill with Colin Petty was proving more bothersome than he cared to admit. His grandparents were sitting at the kitchen table, waiting for him. Nan had a large bandage covering her left temple, and one black eye, but her color had returned and her spirits seemed good. She was going to be all right. Since bringing her home the previous afternoon, GrandSam had been waiting on her with all the care and attention he could muster. His wife was growing more and more irritable under his constant fussing. And it seemed to be wearing a little thin for the old man, too.

"How was the funeral?" Nan asked her grandson. "And Greg and Linda?

"They're fine," Mark assured her, carefully easing into a chair between the two of them. Nan was beaming.

"And you finally got to meet Greg. What did you think?"

"I like him." Mark replied. "He seems like a pretty nice guy. And Linda and Jesse are sure happy to have him back."

His grandfather let out a discontented grunt.

"GrandSam," Mark tried coaxing him with a smile,

"he's nice. You'd like him. Both Greg and Linda said they'd come up later to thank Nan in person."

"Oh for heaven's sakes! What for?" Nan was protesting, but she wore a pleased look. "They don't have to do that."

"If it wasn't for you, nothing would have happened," GrandSam grumpily proclaimed to his wife. "You got the ball rolling. They ought to be damn grateful."

Nan rolled her eyes. "All I did was try to give Linda a little comfort and support."

"Huh! All you did was nearly get Father Mark killed," the old man pointed out.

"Sam! What an awful thing to say!" Nan's voice was suddenly loud and angry. "You take that back right now!"

Life at the Townsends' looked like it was returning to normal. The storm clouds between the two of them were beginning to roil once again. Mark quickly decided to interrupt before the lightning could begin to flash.

"You two stop it," he scolded. "Wait until I say goodbye, then you can have your fight."

They both turned back to him, grateful for the excuse to back down.

"Did you see that policeman?" GrandSam wanted to know. "He says it's okay for you to go?"

Mark nodded. "I'll have to come back to testify," he replied, "but they're done with me for now. Jennings said that Colin Petty is telling them everything, but Li Kuhn Suu hasn't said a word."

"I hope they fry his ass!"

"Sam!" Nan raised a finger in caution, then lowered it. "Be nice."

"It's hard to believe something like that could go on right in our midst without anyone knowing about it," Sam Townsend proclaimed. "Drug smugglers and murderers— what the hell's going on? It makes you wonder if anyplace is safe anymore. You expect that sort of thing in Seattle, but this is LaConner."

"You forget that smuggling has been going on around here since the 1800s," Mark reminded him. "First it was opium, then during Prohibition it was liquor. This town is no different from anywhere else, GrandSam.''

''And being so close to Canada makes this sort of an obvious place for smuggling, I guess,'' Nan added.

''Those guys probably never did care about fishing,'' GrandSam sulked. ''That SinCan plant on the reservation was probably just a front.''

''That's what the police think,'' agreed Mark. ''They set it up just so Li Kuhn Suu could have a way to bring in the heroin without attracting too much attention. He told me once that there was hardly enough salmon around here to keep their plant going. I wondered at the time why an international corporation like SinCan was willing to stay in LaConner if they weren't turning a profit.''

''They were making money,'' Nan frowned. ''It just wasn't from salmon. What I can't understand is why those men felt they had to start killing. That's what I think is so tragic.''

Mark felt a sudden overflowing of love for both of his grandparents. Despite their constant bickering, they were two kind and caring people. And now they were left bewildered and frightened by the course of events inflicted on their small community. He knew they were only a minuscule portion of the countless people whose lives were irreparably changed by the drugs and violence in the culture. But they were not just statistics, dammit, they were his grandparents. And neither was ever going to be the same after this. He searched for something he could say that would heal them and make everything all right. But sometimes priests are left as baffled and confused by evil as everyone else.

''I don't know if they had to kill anyone,'' Mark gently told the couple. ''From what Colin Petty has said so far, they were never really positive that anyone actually found their hiding place. They spotted Dutch Olsen leaving Goat Island in his boat in a hurry and Li Kuhn Suu decided they shouldn't take the risk. So they waited until he was out in the channel and then got close enough to shoot him. Petty says that when Dutch fell out of his boat he was still alive and trying to swim away. So Li Kuhn Suu steered the *SinCan* right at him and then made a couple of passes over Dutch.''

GrandSam winced and his eyes began to moisten. ''Bastards!''

''That explains the cuts we saw on his back and why his hand was gone,'' Mark looked at Nan, giving his grandfather time to swipe at his tears in private. ''The twin propellers cut him when the yacht went over him. Then the tide carried his body onto the beach at Pull and Be Damned and his boat continued drifting toward Deception Pass.''

''And because Greg Patsy was fishing off of Pull and Be Damned,'' Nan interrupted, ''he became the likely suspect.''

''That's right. And Kuhn Suu helped set it up. He knew that Patsy and Olsen were enemies, so he had Colin hide the rifle on Greg's fishing boat.''

''But why'd they kill Larry?'' GrandSam wanted to know.

Mark turned his attention back to his grandfather. ''For much the same reason. They already knew he was searching around on the island. They knew that both Dutch and Larry had been over there looking around. So Li Kuhn Suu sent Petty to the museum in Anacortes. That was the mystery man who was researching the same boxes that Dutch and Larry were. Dutch was searching the archives for information about lost treasure left by early smugglers. Larry went there later, hoping to find some clue to old Indian sites. More than likely, he was planning to go back later and loot them for artifacts. Petty couldn't find anything at the museum that explained why they were searching on Goat Island, but it was obvious they were both getting too close for comfort.

''So Li Kuhn Suu decided they had to confront Larry Robbins. Larry admitted to them what he was doing over there, and he even offered to give them the Squa-de-lich he had taken. But by then, of course, it was too late.''

''So they killed him,'' said GrandSam flatly.

His grandson nodded. ''Yes.'' All three of them fell silent, lost in their own thoughts.

Nan stirred. "But then why did you go back there, Mark?"

"That was dumb, I know," he admitted. "But I knew the answers had to be back on the island. It wasn't until Eddie was killed that I realized everyone being attacked had been over on Goat Island. Up until then I thought it had something to do with Dutch's shack.

"But you see, after Petty came here and made it look like Eddie was the attacker, I knew someone else had to be involved. Eddie could have killed me on the island if he'd wanted me dead. When the police said that Eddie's hanging looked like murder instead of suicide I knew the killer was still loose.

"Little Jesse was the one who knew about the cave. And that was one place Eddie and I hadn't looked at. So I didn't think he knew about it or else he probably would have shown it to me."

"You should have just called the police," GrandSam told him.

"What would I have told them? I didn't know if there was anything there or not. But you're right," Mark finally admitted. "I shouldn't have taken Jesse over there. That was a mistake."

"And the sister, too," GrandSam reminded him.

"Well, it's over," Nan sighed, patting her grandson's hand. "And you're safe, that's what matters." Her voice caught. "But I don't suppose you'll ever want to come visit us again after all of this." Tears welled up in her eyes and began spilling down her cheeks.

"What do you mean?" her husband protested loudly. "Why wouldn't he? Hell, if it wasn't for us he'd be stuck in that parish all the time. Isn't that right, Mark?"

"Sure, GrandSam, that's right."

His grandmother was openly crying now, and making no effort to hide it. Father Townsend gathered the frail old woman's body into his own and held her tightly. He could feel her sobs surging out from deep inside her.

"Shhh," he whispered in her ear, "it's okay, Nan. I'm right here. Everything's okay."

She buried her head in his shoulder as she sobbed heavily. He knew it was a release and he let her cry. The deaths, the pain and the terror of the past week poured out of her.

GrandSam looked on helplessly as his wife cried in Father Townsend's arms. Slowly the old man reached out and patted her back. His own mouth began to tremble.

"Don't cry, Mary. Please don't cry anymore."

Nationally Bestselling Author

J·A·JANCE

The J.P. Beaumont Mysteries

Meet Peggy O'Neill
A Campus Cop With a Ph.D. in Murder

"A 'Must Read' for fans of Sue Grafton"
Alfred Hitchcock Mystery Magazine

Exciting Mysteries by M.D. Lake

ONCE UPON A CRIME 77520-4/$5.50 US/$7.50 Can

AMENDS FOR MURDER 75865-2/$4.99 US/$6.99 Can

COLD COMFORT 76032-0/$4.99 US/ $6.99 Can

POISONED IVY 76573-X/$5.50 US/$7.50 Can

A GIFT FOR MURDER 76855-0/$5.50 US/$7.50 Can

MURDER BY MAIL 76856-9/$5.99 US/$7.99 Can

GRAVE CHOICES 77521-2/$4.99 US/$6.99 Can

FLIRTING WITH DEATH
76522-0/$5.99 US/$7.99 Can